KISS ME NOW

PENNY WYLDER

Thanks for Reading!
Sign up for my newsletter and leave
your panties at the door!

Sign up HERE!

MORE MUST READS BY PENNY WYLDER

Read all my books for free in Kindle Unlimited!

CASSIDY

Tomorrow, my whole life is going to change.

I know, I know, money can't buy happiness, etc. But it can go a long way toward getting you comfortable, at least. And that's something I haven't felt in a long time. Definitely not when I was growing up with my mother, living from skimpy paycheck to paycheck, or off of the various men she was hooking up with, whenever she was completely out of work.

Then came Norman, and God knows, that was an even worse situation.

Don't think about him right now, I remind myself forcefully as I climb out of the taxi. Tonight is supposed to be my big night of freedom. A night to celebrate everything I've achieved—all on my own. The last thing I need to be reminiscing about is *that* asshole, and everything he put me through.

I shrug off my coat as I reach the front of the club line. My friend Becky's already standing there chatting with the bouncer, and to judge by the sparkle in both of their eyes, I have a feeling that we're going to be let straight inside. And that Becky will spend most of the night wanting to come straight back out for a smoke again, so she can keep this flirt on.

"Hey," I greet her with a kiss on the cheek as I reach her.

"Cassidy! This is Marco." Becky gestures from me to the bouncer and back, then squeezes my arm. "This is my friend I was telling you about. She's going to be the next Coco Chanel, I swear." Becky gestures at my face. "See? Doesn't she look flawless?"

Marco smiles politely. "Beck says you created your own makeup line. That's awesome."

Beck. I side-eye her with a raised eyebrow, and Becky laughs at my expression.

"Marco and I were just chatting while we waited for you," she says, but it's in a tone I recognize well. We haven't known one another since our college days for nothing. "Come on, tonight is your night." She loops her arm through mine. "Let's celebrate."

"See you soon, Marco," I tell him, because I'm absolutely sure I will. Becky elbows me for it, but I can tell she's watching Marco's reaction, and enjoying the way he grins and watches us as we duck past him and into the club.

"What? He was cute!" Becky protests as we stride inside. I just snicker, and she sighs, long-suffering. "Sooo ... how excited are you for tomorrow?"

"I'd say more nervous than excited," I reply. At the bar, I lean across to order us beers. Becky leans across to correct me: two shots and two beers, instead.

I tap my shot of whiskey to hers, pretty sure already that this is going to be a mistake. But what the hell. My meeting tomorrow isn't until early afternoon, so I'll have enough time to recover from the inevitable hangover first.

"So tell me more," Becky insists when I pull her onto the

dance floor, beers in hand after we've both downed our shots.

"The company's called Anderson Investments," I reply over the thud of the bass. "They specialize in small businesses, especially women-owned ones. Apparently the investors are a husband and wife duo, and the wife insists on investing in empowering other women who are just starting out, like she once was."

"That's really cool!" Becky calls back. "So you think they're going to invest?"

I shrug. "I hope so?" Secretly, I'm pretty sure I have this one in the bag. I don't want to jinx it, though. God knows I've gotten close before and wound up with my metaphorical heart broken.

Norman flashes through my mind again, and I force him out. This won't be like that. I'm going to get a buy-in from an actual company, a business transaction. It won't be like me trying to beg money from my rich asshole of a boyfriend, who constantly tries to manipulate me, dangling his potential investment over my head like a carrot to make me put up with whatever he wants to do in our romantic lives.

"That'll be so incredible." Becky's gushing. "Once you have an investor, you'll be able to ramp up production and really get your products out there."

I smile at the thought. I've been working on building up Cass's Cosmetics for four years now, ever since we graduated college. I've gotten interest from some big buyers, too, including a department store with chains in New York and LA. That kind of exposure could make all the difference for me as an upstart cosmetician. I could actually expand into a real company.

But in order to ramp up production enough to actually fill orders at a store that big, I need investment capital. And in order to get investment capital, I need a wealthy person on my side. Someone who believes in me and my products. Someone who's willing to take on a risk.

Someone *not* like Norman, as I learned.

My heart sinks. I shouldn't be thinking about him. Shouldn't be dwelling on that right now. Tonight of all nights. So I force a broad smile on my face and agree with Becky. "As long as tomorrow's interview goes well," I hedge, but she brushes away my doubts like so much air.

"Please, girl. I've seen you give this presentation so many times I know you could knock it out of the park in your sleep. Now let's have some *fun*." And then, before I can stop her, Becky's back at the bar ordering us another round.

Three more shots and a couple hours of dancing later, to no one's surprise except maybe Becky's, she winds up hanging off Marco's arm as he finishes his shift.

"I'm so sorry to cut tonight short," she's yelling in my ear in the parking lot, but I wave her off.

"It's fine. Honestly, I should get to bed anyway. I don't want to show up hungover tomorrow." I've got plenty of time to sleep this off, but, still. You can never be too careful. "Have fun!" I add, and to judge by the little wink Becky fires me over Marco's shoulder, I know they both will.

If there's a faint pang in my chest at watching them saunter off, Marco's strong arm wrapped around Becky's waist, well... I can ignore that, too.

I head back up the club entrance and order a rideshare home. At this hour, it shouldn't be too long of a wait. But before my phone even connects with a driver, I hear a muffled curse, followed by the clatter of something metal hitting pavement.

Confused, I step away from the door and the bright light of the club entrance. Near the entrance, but around a far corner of the brick building, hidden from the view of most of the clubgoers, there's a row of parked cars. Standing next to one of them, cursing and rubbing his back, is an older man. Between his silver hair and his wire rimmed glasses, he reminds me of my grandfather.

The cursing, however, is not very grandfatherly.

He kicks at a tire, swearing up a storm, and I can't help myself. I step over to him.

"Do you need some help?" I ask.

He turns to squint into the club light. I move closer, and his vision clears. "Oh, aren't you a dear." He shakes his head. "But it's this tire needs changing, so I'm afraid you won't be able to help me."

"My dad taught me how to change a tire, don't worry," I reply, hiding a smirk. I realize I don't look like the handiest person with a power tool right now, dressed as I am in a tight black club dress, with my mini going-out purse over one shoulder and a full face of makeup.

But, as my mama always used to say, I contain multitudes.

"Here, let me give it a shot." I duck down to pick up the end of the jack that he let fall beside him. Then I glance up at his worried expression, trying not to feel too offended by his doubt. He's from another generation, clearly. "If I mess up your car, I'll call the tow truck myself, all right?"

He laughs. "Well, if you're that confident, miss... you've got a deal." He backs up, then, and I get to work.

It's easy enough to jack his car up to the right height, and I'm lucky he has a wrench in his trunk. I get to removing the lug nuts that suspend his tire, and he watches, his eyebrows climbing higher every second.

"Not often these days you find any kids your age able to do this," he comments. "Much less... well."

I shoot him an amused glance over my shoulder. "Much less a girl dressed like this?" I ask, arching one perfectly brushed eyebrow.

He grins. "Apologies for doubting you, miss."

"Cassidy," I reply. "And there's no need to apologize. Just give a girl the benefit of the doubt next time. My dad taught me how to do this before he'd let me apply for my driver's license. Said it was a necessary life skill."

"That's me schooled," the man promises. "Lee, by the way. And thank you. Your father taught you well," he adds, watching me work.

I step around his trunk to reach for the donut, when I feel a hand on my shoulder. Expecting it to be Lee, I glance back. Then I freeze, my eyes going wide.

There's an unfamiliar guy standing behind me. Two, in fact, both a head taller than I am, and dressed in dark clothes. I look around, startled, and realize the second guy is already holding Lee by one arm, his fingers digging into the poor man's bicep hard enough to be visible from here.

"Hey, leave him alone," I say, at the same time that Lee blurts out, "Let the girl be."

Lee and I trade a long glance, while our taller assailant sneers. "Wallet. Phone." He looks me over. "And, well, if you aren't quick about it..."

I shudder, not liking the way his gaze lingers. But I'm also not about to give up without a fight. I'm still holding Lee's wrench, after all, and we're not ten feet from the club door. Never mind that this guy has almost a head on me, or the fact that he's got backup.

"Excuse you?" I demand, advancing. "What the fuck is wrong with you? Messing with a defenseless old man?" As I move, I shift my body weight so the wrench in my fist is concealed behind my torso. Then I settle into a defensive stance, knees bent, ready to move quickly in either direction.

My dad taught me this, too.

The man doesn't move. Over his shoulder, I spot Lee, his eyes going wide. He shakes his head, but I ignore him. "Wallet and phone," the man says. "I won't ask again." He holds out a hand.

That's when I strike. I swing the wrench as hard as I can at his wrist. There's a sickening crack as it hits bone, and the man curses. The guy behind him throws Lee to the ground, about to sprint at me too, but I'm already backing off, screaming for help.

The man I struck is cradling his wrist, but when he looks up at me now, there's no more disdain or lingering desire in his gaze. There's only white hot fury. "You'll pay for that," he swears, advancing on me.

Then, out of nowhere, a blur collides with him.

All I see are fists, and all I can hear are grunts. At first, I wonder if Lee has miraculously sprung up off the ground to perform some jiu-jitsu worthy of a guy half his age. But no. One glance shows me he's still sprawled on the pavement, his forehead crumpled in pain.

As for the two attackers, they're both busy defending themselves from another guy, a blur of a man who stands at least as tall as they do. I catch a glimpse of the newcomer landing a solid hit to one attacker's jaw, then wrenching the other's arm around his back in the same motion, using the man's momentum against him to flip him ass over head onto pavement.

I sidestep the brawl and kneel beside Lee. "Are you all right?" I ask in a low undertone.

He huffs at me. "Please, I've certainly had worse. But you

... You're supposed to just give men like this what they demand. It's dangerous to fight."

"Believe me." I offer Lee a hand, and he lets me help him back to his feet. "I've learned the hard way. Sometimes it's every bit as dangerous to give them an inch, because they'll just take a mile."

Lee huffs again, but to judge by the shrewd look in his eye, he's not about to contradict me.

Another grunt interrupts us, and we turn to find both the attackers laid out on the pavement. Standing over them, blood dusting his knuckles, is quite frankly, the hottest man I've ever seen.

It's not just the fact that he's glistening with sweat from fighting off a pair of assholes who would have robbed me— or worse. Although the small cut on his cheek and bruise forming beneath it do serve to highlight exactly how sharp his cheekbones are, how square his jaw is.

But mostly, it's the fact that he looks like he'd be perfectly at home on the cover of some sporting magazine, advertising the team he plays for, or something. He's muscular, but not overly built. Just... solid.

Solid enough that he laid out two guys almost the same size as him in no time at all.

Beside me, Lee starts to clap. After a split second, I grin and join in. Our rescuer turns, and my breath catches in my throat.

Fuck. Not only does he have those cheekbones, that jawline, that *build*, but he's also got unreal eyes. Green, with a twinkle from the reflection of the streetlight overhead. "Are you all right?" he asks, and I assume he's speaking to us both, but he's staring straight at me.

"We are now," Lee replies, with a glance in my direction.

"Although, I have to admit, Cassidy might have had them cornered, given another minute."

"I noticed." His gaze still hasn't left mine. I can't make myself look away. I don't *want* to. "One tip, though?" He gestures at my arm, and I glance down, surprised to realize that I'm still clenching the wrench in my fist. "Next time, aim for the temple, instead of the hand. If you'd incapacitated him completely, it would've narrowed your odds with the second man."

I let out a faint huff of laughter. "Thanks. I'll keep that in mind next time I'm being mugged." With that, I pass the wrench to Lee, and run my hand through my hair. "Shit. Should we—"

"I called the cops already," the man says. He glances from me to Lee to the car in the lot behind us. "Roadside assistance, as well."

"*That* I had handled," I protest, but Lee is already nudging me toward our rescuer.

"Go, go. The last thing I need is you getting into even more trouble on my behalf," Lee is saying.

By this point, I realize we've attracted something of a crowd. A few camera phones are pointed our way, and someone from the club—another bouncer to replace the one Becky took off with—comes over, saying he has basic medical training. He kneels beside our would-be robbers to check their pulses, nodding to confirm they'll be all right, minus the scrapes and bruises.

All the while, my gaze keeps straying over to our knight in shining armor. Or rather, knight in... a pair of jeans and a polo shirt.

The second or third time I glance over, he catches me looking, and moves closer. "Can I give you a ride home?" he asks. "It'll probably be safer, this area, this time of night."

"Actually." I tilt my head. Size him up. It's still early yet. The club might have to shut down when the cops show up, but he's right, this area, it's chock full of night life. Both the good and bad kinds.

Part of me shouts at myself to remember about tomorrow. I have a big important meeting to nail. But it's in the afternoon. Tonight was meant to be my celebratory night out, to hype myself up for it. Now Becky's vanished, leaving me all alone to deal with all of this.

I deserve a little fun, too. "Can I buy you a drink?" I ask.

My hero grins.

2
____

CASSIDY

We wind up at a dive bar down the road. It's much more my scene than the club was to begin with. Don't get me wrong, I love dancing on occasion, but that place catered to a younger, more tequila-heavy crowd than I normally party with.

In the dimly lit bar, I lean across the counter to catch the bartender's eye. "Whiskey for me," I say, "And...?" I glance over my shoulder.

Is it my imagination, or do his eyes lighten with something close to interest? "The same," he says, and settles onto a stool next to me. "So, Cassidy, was it?"

I nod, watching him as the bartender passes us both well whiskeys.

"Lark." He smiles. "I'd say it's nice to meet you, but, well, considering the circumstances..."

"Oh, no." I slide his drink toward him, then raise my own. "It was very nice to meet you indeed." We tap glasses. "To your perfect timing, Lark."

He laughs. "Perfect timing would've been if I'd gotten there quickly enough to knock that asshole out before he got anywhere near you," he admits, and rubs at his cheekbone.

I peer at his bruise. "We should get some ice—"

"No, no. It'll be fine." He offers a wry smile. "Trust me, I've had worse."

I settle back onto my seat, watching him curiously from the corner of my eye. "Where did you learn to fight like that?" I ask after a moment. Because I saw him move. That was no basic self-defense class. He's been in fights before. Real ones.

"Actually..." He smiles, a genuine one this time. "I grew up with five brothers. So, my training started there. And then, you know, perfected it in college. Between playing on the rugby team and going on one too many nights out to even seedier bars than this one..."

"Oi," the bartender barks, before shaking his head and moving away to the far side of the bar.

We both stifle our laughter, trading amused glances. "Better watch your tongue," I murmur.

Lark's gaze shifts to my mouth and then back up again, so quick I wonder if I imagined it. But then... "Oh, I know. It's always getting me into trouble." His gaze drops again, and this time I *know* I'm not imagining things.

My cheeks flush, but luckily it's dark in this bar. I take a sip of my whiskey, and watch Lark from the corner of my eye as he does the same.

"So where did you learn to change a tire?" Lark asks. "Or, for that matter, to swing a wrench like that." He tilts his head, sizing me up. "Not sure I've ever seen anyone use *that* technique before."

I grin. "What can I say? My dad wanted me to be prepared for any challenges the world could throw at a girl."

"Well." He raises his glass once more. "To fathers who prepare us properly, then."

My grin falters. But I lift my glass anyway, tap it to his. What I don't expect, though, is for him to notice my sudden shift in demeanor, the way I don't quite meet his eye this time.

"What's the matter?" he asks, his voice dropping low.

"Just... my dad." I shrug, blinking back a sudden and unexpected surge of tears. "He passed away a couple years ago."

Lark lifts a hand to rest on my shoulder. Where his palm touches me, warmth spreads, tingling, all through my arm, up my shoulder and across my body. After a moment of hesitation, I reach up to thread my fingers through his, and squeeze just once, lightly.

He doesn't say he's sorry. He doesn't offer empty platitudes. That's what makes me ask.

"What about you?" I keep my eyes on the bar, but I can see him in the reflection of the bottles of liquor lined up there. The way his head drops a little, and his eyes darken.

"My youngest brother," he says, after a long moment of quiet. "He was in a car accident last year. Drunk driver. They say he was killed on impact, never felt anything, but..."

"Shit, Lark." I tighten my grip on his hand.

He shifts beside me, then picks up his whiskey again, takes a longer sip this time. "Losing someone that young... Really makes you appreciate the time you still have. Makes you want to live life right." He glances at me again, and this time, I don't look away. I let my eyes linger, the same way his are.

I lose track of how long we just sit, sizing one another up, before he bends a little closer. There's barely a foot between us now. He's close enough I catch his scent, woodsy and smoke-tinted from the whiskey, with a hint of something else underneath, something that reminds me of salt and the ocean.

"Cassidy," he says, and my name on his lips sends a thrum of electricity through me, all the way to the tips of my fingers.

His hand slides along my body, from my shoulder down to the small of my back, where his fingers spread out, strong and so roughly calloused I can feel them even through my thin clubbing dress.

"Lark?" I manage, and my voice only quivers ever so slightly at the end. I manage to hold his gaze, though, keep my chin raised, and I don't even let him see the way my breath catches or my stomach tightens at his touch.

"I'm going to kiss you now," he says, still in that low, thrumming voice. The one that's impossible to resist.

I tilt my head back, my face toward his, and when he dips down to feather his lips against mine, it feels like static shock, touching a doorknob after shuffling your feet across a carpet.

Then he sinks against me, his free hand drifting up to cup my cheek, pulling me off my stool and toward him. I stumble against him—the whiskey's hitting harder than I expected after those other drinks earlier at the club. He chuckles, his mouth still pressed to mine, and then his lips part, taking mine with. His tongue traces the edges of my lips, and I arch my back, both my arms sliding up to wrap around his neck.

I'm not sure how we settle our tab. I have a vague memory of Lark tapping on the bar, sliding his wallet out of his back pocket. Then the next thing I know, we're stumbling outside, his arms around my waist, holding my body against his.

The cold night air wakes me up a little, shoots fresh pulses of energy through my veins.

We part, and in the distant streetlights, Lark's eyes look greener than ever, pools I could drown in. I realize I'm grinning like an idiot, but I don't stop, because he's looking at me with the same expression.

"Where the hell did you come from, Cassidy?" he murmurs, and I wonder briefly if this man is a mind-reader, because I'd just been thinking the same thing. Then he kisses me again, and I forget all about speaking.

His hands slide lower, from my waist down over the curve of my ass. I slide one leg around the back of his thigh and arch my body up against his, while my hands slide down those strong, thick shoulders and over his chest.

God, I can feel every inch of his muscle through the shirt he's wearing, as starkly as if he were already half-naked.

He tilts his head, kisses his way along my jawline and then catches the lower edge of my earlobe, worrying it between his teeth, just for a second, before his tongue traces the curve after. The sensation makes my breath catch, my body sing with want.

"You are goddamn intoxicating, you know that?" he murmurs against my ear, his breath hot enough to make my head spin all over again. "More potent than the whiskey."

I laugh, but it's faint, breathy. It's hard to catch a full breath with this man's strong arms around me, protective and possessive at once. "Look who's talking," I murmur, and he pulls back just far enough to meet my gaze again, his blazing hot.

"You don't want to get mixed up with me, Cassidy," he says, suddenly sounding far more sober than I feel. My heart skips a beat. But I can't tear my gaze from those deep, soulful eyes. I couldn't make my legs work to walk away from him if I wanted to—and I really, really don't want to.

"Try me," I reply, lifting my chin, meeting his challenge with one of my own.

His lip curves in a half smirk. Deadly and dangerous all at once. "Don't say I didn't warn you," he replies. Then his mouth comes down on mine, harder this time, insistent, and my lip spart beneath his, let him take what he wants.

When we part again, my chest heaves. His hands have reached my thighs now, then my ass. He grips me hard, and I gasp at the feeling. He crushes me against him, and I can feel the hard jut of his cock, straining against his jeans. The way he's standing, towering over me, it digs into my belly, stretching the whole length from my waist to under my chest, and it makes me desperate to see him without any clothing on. To touch that cock with my bare hands.

"Fuck," I breathe, and his eyes flash with amusement.

"Don't tempt me." His gaze drips over my body again, and I shiver, feeling every place that he looks at as if it were his hands roaming over me now, touching every inch of me. "I'd love to keep you all night, Cassidy. Make you scream my name..."

I search his gaze, challenging. "What are we waiting for then?" I ask him. Simple, straightforward. It's blunter than I've ever been with a guy before. But something tells me Lark will appreciate it.

To judge by the way that infuriating half-smirk of his widens, I'm right.

I don't even notice him flag it down, but before long, a taxi is pulling up beside us.

"Last chance," he says, eyebrow arched. "I can take you home. Or, I bring you back to mine, and fuck you so hard you won't be able to walk straight tomorrow." He says the latter in a whisper, leaning in to catch my earlobe between his teeth again, biting down until the faint spark of pain makes me gasp.

"Yours," I breathe.

We slide into the back of taxi—or rather, Lark slides in, and then he pulls me inside and shuts the door behind us both. I'm tempted to straddle him, but he makes me put on my belt instead, and in a guilty flash I remember his brother, the accident.

I'm about to say something, but Lark cuts me off by kissing me again. At the same time, his hand inches up the smooth plane of my thigh, toward the edge of my dress.

Our lips part, and he smirks at me, one eye on the driver. "How quiet can you be?" he murmurs softly.

I bite my lower lip in response.

Then his fingers slide higher. Up, up, up the smooth expanse of my thighs until he reaches the crease where my leg meets my hip bone. He traces it with his forefinger, his eyes on me all the while. I glance at the driver again, nervous, but the man's attention is on the road, at least.

"Ah, ah." Lark lifts an eyebrow. "Look at me."

My gaze jumps back to his, and my breath catches again.

His finger slides beneath my panties.

He spreads his hand to cup my pussy in his palm, the rough, calloused heel of his hand like striking a match over my bare-shaven mound. My hips buck up off the seat and into his palm, eager to grind against him, but he draws back a little, smirking.

"So eager." He leans in to kiss the edge of my jawline. "Let me guess. You're already wet for me, too." His breath is searing hot, his words so low I can barely hear him over the rumble of the cab, the faint tinny sound of the radio playing in the driver's area.

I bite my lower lip, my eyes fluttering shut, as Lark's fingers glide over my mound until he reaches my pussy lips. His thumb grazes my clit, enough to make me jump again. I hadn't realized how turned on I was until now, but I can feel my clit, pulsing and heavy between my thighs, swollen with desire.

Then his fingers slide between my pussy lips, and I inhale sharply through my nose, trying as hard as I can not to make any sounds. Slowly, slow enough to feel like torture, albeit an impossibly enjoyable kind, Lark presses the tip of his forefinger inside me.

I try to shift closer to him, but with his free hand, he pins me against the seat, lifting one eyebrow as if to tease me. He knows what he's doing, the bastard.

He leans in again. "I love watching you squirm." His smile widens, and he adds a second finger inside me, my pussy stretching around his thick fingers, little shockwaves of pleasure firing through my system. "God, you're so fucking wet," he murmurs, almost to himself.

I lean against him, surrendering, letting him take the lead. I forget where we are, so much so that when he starts to stroke me, in and out, his fingers curling slowly inside me, I gasp aloud.

Lark kisses me to muffle the sound, and I can feel him grinning against my mouth. "Shh," he breathes, and I have to bite my lower lip, hard, to keep quiet when he begins to move his fingers faster, thrusting in and out of me.

My heartbeat picks up. I can hear the noise of the road under us and the music the driver's playing, but it's all distant, out of focus. The only thing I can focus on right now; the only thing I can see clearly, is Lark. Those eyes of his fixed on me, like he's hungry too, lapping up my reactions.

I twist against him, my hips rising off the seat to thrust against his hand in tiny, quick motions.

In response, he presses the heel of his hand down, until it connects with my clit. I gasp again, and clamp my lips together, hard, to prevent any other sound from emerging.

It gets harder and harder to stay quiet, though, as he strokes me toward a climax. His fingers glide in and out of my tight pussy easily now, I'm so fucking soaked. And his heel stays right where it is, pressed to my clit, so that with every stroke it sends fireworks through my veins, sets off sparks behind my eyelids.

Right as I near the peak, Lark must sense it, because he bends close again, his face inches from mine. "Come for me, Cassidy," he whispers, and then his lips collide with mine, his tongue parting mine.

I cry out, faint enough that it's muffled by his mouth, by this kiss. And the orgasm hits me full force, my whole body shaking from it. All the while, he continues to stroke me, pushing his fingers into me again and again.

Just when I think I can't take it anymore, that I might hit a second orgasm right here and lose all control over my voice completely, Lark draws his fingers out of my pussy. Then, still watching me, his warm, solid body pressed against mine in the backseat of the darkened cab, he lifts his hand to his face, and slowly licks my juices from his fingers, one by one.

My heart continues to pound, my eyes wide as I watch him. "Fuck," I finally breathe, not sure whether I mean the sight of him doing that, or the orgasm he just gave me, or all of it. Everything.

He grins and kisses my cheek, my jawline. "Just wait until we get home," he murmurs. "I want to taste every inch of you."

Those words are enough to leave me practically vibrating until the taxi parks outside his house. He pays and pulls me out beside him. It's dark, so I don't get a good look, but I get the feeling this is an expensive apartment. Doorman building, one of the top floors, if not the top. I don't know—I don't pay much attention in the elevator, because the moment the doors close behind us, Lark pins me against the wall, his tongue parting my lips, his hands hiking up my skirt.

I gasp and peer around him, worried. "What if—" I start to say, worried someone else might step inside the elevator, or call it to their floor, only to find us naked inside.

But then it slows to a halt, and the doors ping open, and I realize that would have been impossible. Because the doors open straight into Lark's place.

"Whoa." My eyes go wide as I take the place in. *Definitely* expensive as hell. It's a modern style apartment, with floor to ceiling windows all along one side that overlook the city, and an open plan kitchen and living room. It's tastefully decorated, all minimalist and stylish, except for the fireplace, which adds a bit of warmth to the room, complete with a throw rug in front of it.

But it screams bachelor pad, too.

Lark leads me from the elevator by the hand, and as the doors slide shut again behind us, he pins me against them, one finger curling underneath my chin in order to tilt my head back, until my gaze jumps back to his. "That cab ride was about a century too long."

"Couldn't agree more," I reply, a faint smile tugging at the corners of my mouth. Then his mouth crushes against mine, and he hikes up the hem of my dress in one smooth motion, drawing it up and over my head.

It falls somewhere to the side. I barely notice, because

I'm tugging at the buttons on his shirt. My fingers fumble with them for a minute, before I give up and just yank, hard, sending buttons pinging around us.

Lark laughs, where his mouth is crushed to mine. "Eager, are you, kitten?" Then he draws back just far enough to take in my expression, and I swear, his eyes seem to darken with desire. "Me too."

My eyes must be doing the same as his, because fuck. I knew I felt muscles under his tightly buttoned clothes, but seeing him shirtless has taken my breath away. He's cut like no man I've ever slept with before, solid as a rock, with those V-line muscles pointing straight down to where... *Fuck.* The bulge in his jeans is huge. I'm reaching for it, when Lark interrupts me.

He grips my ass hard and lifts me into his arms. Instinctively, I wrap my legs around his waist. I can feel that hard bulge of his cock digging into my belly as he carries me, my hands digging into the hard plains of his shoulders, over to the kitchen counter. He sets me on the edge and unsnaps my bra at the same time, practically throwing it aside.

He pauses for a second, like the sight of me naked it is driving him wild, too. "God, you're perfect," he murmurs, his breath tickling my collarbone. Then he dips lower, kisses and licks his way down between my breasts. My head falls back, my whole body arched toward him, like I'm just a puppet and he's the master. He tilts his head to one side, licks along the underside of my breast, making my toes curl and my whole body tingle with the sensation. Higher and higher, his tongue trails, until he sucks my nipple into his mouth, his lips pursed around it. His tongue toys with my nipple, laps against it until I can feel it getting hard.

With his free hand, he cups my other breast, his thumb

toying with my nipple, alternating between gently rolling it and pinching just hard enough to make me gasp.

He tilts his head back, and eyes me for a second, my breast wet from his hot mouth, his lips swollen from kissing it. "You were so good at being quiet in the cab," he says, grinning. "Now I'll have to see if I can make you scream."

Then his hands dip down, tracing my curves, sending heat waves through me as they go, and his thumbs hook under the edges of my panties.

He raises me up just high enough to pull them off, and pushes them down, spreading my legs wide as he does.

My lips part. He's still wearing his pants, which hardly seems fair. But just as I'm about to point that out, he drops to his knees, and pushes his face between my thighs.

His tongue traces the upper edge of my thighs, along the crease where they meet my hips, and then he trails his tongue, flat like a blade, over the outer lips of my pussy. "You smell as good as you tasted," he says, those eyes jumping up to meet mine.

He keeps his eyes on mine, as he straightens his tongue into a spearhead, and presses it inside me.

I moan, holding his gaze, my toes curling and every muscle in my body goes taut as a bowstring. The sight of this man on his knees between my legs unfurls sensations deep in my belly, a sense of pleasure, of rightness, and searing heat. He's hungry, relentless, his tongue plunging into me again and again, and it doesn't take me long to near a climax again, my whole body still sensitive from earlier, hovering at the brink.

"Fuck, Lark," I manage to breathe, never taking my gaze from his. "Right there, oh, God... Don't stop."

But he does still, for a moment. Withdraw his tongue,

and my whole body twists in frustration. "Ask me nicely," he says, breath hot against my skin.

"Please," I gasp, not even caring how I sound anymore. I'm desperate. "Please, Lark, let me come."

He smirks. And then he plunges his tongue back inside me. Licks and licks, until my head falls back and I lose track of time, space.

I cry aloud this time, not bothering to try to stifle it. My voice echoes in the big, open space, and my toes curl, my thighs tightening around his head.

But he doesn't waste any time. I'm still trembling, my pussy soaked and twitching after the force of the orgasm, when he rises to his feet again and pushes his jeans down.

God. His cock, where it springs free, is a thing of glory. Thick and veined along one side, with a glistening spot of precum at the tip. I reach for him, but he's already pulling something from a side drawer—a condom. He tears open the package, but I take it from him then, eyes on his.

"I want to feel you," I tell him. So I take my time rolling the condom down the length of his thick shaft. Jesus. It takes both of my hands combined to fit around him, he's so thick. *Will he fit?* Part of me wonders. But the rest of me is eager to find out.

He steps closer, his hands sliding up my thighs, gripping tight.

"I want your cock inside me." I lean back against the counter to look up at him.

He reaches up with one hand to brush my hair back over my shoulder, then cups my cheek. I tilt my face into his palm, savoring how warm he feels. He tips down, until his forehead rests against mine, and his cock is poised between my legs, standing hard, just inches from my pussy.

"Please?" I add, my eyes flickering back up to his, remembering how he liked that earlier.

His cock jumps with tension, and his smirk widens. "I just want to remember this, that's all," he says. Then he reaches down to wrap a fist around the base of his cock, and guides his tip to my entrance. "Look at me," he orders, and I couldn't stop myself even if I wanted to. My gaze rises to meet his. "I want to feel every fucking inch of you. Savor every second of this."

Slowly, so slowly it makes my whole body arch up and tremble with anticipation, he begins to press his cock inside me. The head of him slips between my lips and into my pussy, stretching me wide as he goes. He rocks his hips forward, pushes another inch into me, and a moan escapes my lips at the sensation of him filling me.

He keeps moving, keeps rocking back and pressing forward again, until, inch by inch, his cock pushes deep into my pussy. Finally, when he's fully inside me, he pauses again, his eyes on mine, savoring my reaction.

His hands slide around my waist, tight, holding me steady.

"God, you feel good," he murmurs. "So fucking tight."

I clench my pussy muscles around him, and he smirks in response. I do, too. "Fuck me," I breathe.

And he obeys me. He draws out and pushes back into me, faster this time, hard enough to make my ass rock against the countertop. His hands pin me in place, and he starts to build up rhythm, pulling out and thrusting back into me faster with each pass. I rock with him—or at least, I try to, thrusting my hips, but I can only move so far with his big, strong hands pinning me there, holding me right where he wants me.

At the same time, my hands trace over his chest, feeling the plains of his muscles, memorizing the feel of his body.

His scent envelops me, musky and heady all at once, and when his mouth comes down on mine again, I moan into his kiss, because it just feels so fucking good to surrender control, to let him take me however he wants.

He buries his face in my neck, his hands so tight they almost hurt, but the pain only adds to the pleasure. He growls, then, and the sound sends sparks through my body. "Fuck, Cassidy." He bites my neck, his teeth sharp, stinging, but I moan with pleasure at the sting.

"Lark..."

"I need you," he says, and those words send a pulse through me, make my belly tighten and my legs clamp tight around his waist. All the while, he continues to thrust into me, over and over, and the pressure builds, my whole body on fire with want for him.

"I want to hear you come for me," he says again, and then, without warning, he pulls me up and off the counter, holding me in his arms. I cling onto him. At this angle, it drives his cock into me, right along my front wall, dragging over my G-spot as he holds me up in his arms and fucks me, hard and fast, his thick cock driving me wild.

"Come for me, Cassidy," he orders, and there's no disobeying the steely command in his voice.

I'm so close, right at the edge, my whole body shaking, my breath coming in fast pants.

"Do it," he says, louder, and I scream as I come undone.

The orgasm hits me full force, makes my whole body tremble. He keeps right on fucking me. He pushes my ass back against the counter and pounds into me, his balls slapping against my pussy lips with every deep, hard thrust. His cock fills me, makes me feel stuffed, so fucking full. My body arcs back, away from him, and his lips find my breast, suck my nipple into his mouth as he continues to fuck me.

I'm still moaning when the second orgasm comes, hard on the heels of the first, making me writhe across the countertop. He slides his hands under the arch of my back, supporting me, holding me in midair as he nears his own finish.

He finishes with a growl, pulling me against him, crushing my soft curves into his chest as his cock thrusts deep into me. I'm still panting, slick with sweat, when he pulls out of me, bends to kiss me, softer this time, his lips lingering against mine.

When we part, he's smirking again, watching me.

"Fuck," I manage to say.

He laughs. And then he sweeps one arm under my legs and scoops me up into his arms. Thank fuck, because I'm not sure if I could have stood or walked quite yet. My legs feel like jelly, wobbly beneath me. But he carries me like I weigh nothing at all, straight into the only closed off room in this enormous apartment.

His bedroom.

He kicks the door open with one foot, and I catch a glimpse of a big king size bed, immaculately made sheets, and more minimalist decor. Then he sweeps me into the bathroom and deposits me at the edge of the big walk in shower, with the rain shower head and all. He flicks on the water, and it comes straight out warm and all encompassing.

Then he pulls me under it, while I'm laughing, and bends down to kiss me again, hot water coursing over both our naked bodies.

We wind up staying up all damn night. And I have no regrets.

3

———

CASSIDY

At least, not until the next morning.

I wake up to the sound of an alarm clock going off, and I groan at the bright assault of sunlight pouring through the enormous windows. For a moment, I'm disoriented, confused. My tiny little apartment on a dingy block in the ass end of nowhere doesn't get this much sunlight in the living room, let alone my closet of a bedroom. My single narrow window faces a dirty fire escape, shaded overhead by my upstairs neighbor's huge illegal balcony.

Then the previous night flashes through my mind, and I understand all the various aches and pains I'm feeling. Especially my pussy, throbbing and deliciously sore. And still naked.

I sit up, startled to realize I fell asleep nude. Normally I never do that. I never feel comfortable enough to. In the moment is one thing, but letting guys see me in broad daylight the next day is another.

When I roll over, though, Lark's shutting off his alarm clock, also completely naked, and I have to say, it's worth risking him seeing me like this, as long as I get to stare at him in return.

His eyes slide over me, devouring me hungrily, and I flush, a full-body blush that travels all the way from my cheeks to my toes. "What?" I ask, and he reaches across the sheets to drag me toward him.

"Just remembering how much I already want you, all over again," he says. But just as our lips are about to meet— and just as I notice the bulge standing straight up in the sheets between us already, his cock hard and ready for me all over again—there's another sharp buzzing sound.

I jump, startled, expecting it to be the alarm again. But Lark rolls away from me, cursing, and it goes off again, and I realize that must be the door buzzer.

I squint at the alarm clock. 10am. Shit. My meeting isn't until the afternoon, but I'd counted on having a little bit more time in the morning to fully prep myself.

With a groan, I sit up and start to fish around under the bed, before I remember that all of my clothes are in the living room. Lark left the door behind him open a crack, so I edge around the bed and pull it open, padding outside to grab my dress first, from where it's lying near the kitchen counter.

That's when I hear the voice over the intercom. A woman's voice.

"We agreed we'd talk it over first, hon," she's saying, and my stomach sinks all the way down through the floorboards.

Hon.

Oh no. Oh fuck no.

Lark has his back to the bedroom, so he hasn't noticed me yet, standing stark naked in the middle of his apartment. He sighs and presses the button to respond. "Now's really not a good time. I'll meet you at the house, all right?"

The *house*? As in, *their* house? My heart beats so loud it's like thunder in my eardrums. I yank my dress over my head, then snatch up the bra and panties from the floor, my head spinning too badly to concentrate and actually put them on. All I want to do is get the hell out of here.

I duck into the bathroom and shut the door behind me, heart hammering. In the living room, I can hear Lark's conversation continue for a few more sentences, muffled through the door. I don't listen. I can't. I'm too busy smacking the back of my head against the door in frustration.

I'm such an idiot. I should have known that a guy like him wouldn't be who he said he was. But I've got to admit, I didn't think he'd be a full-blown cheater. Maybe just a stupidly hot, impossibly sexy guy on the rebound, but this?

I wait until the voices outside have died down, and then I speed out of the bathroom, grabbing my purse and stuffing the rest of my clothes into it as I beeline for the elevator.

"Oh, Cassidy. Morning," Lark says, from somewhere in the vicinity of the kitchen.

I don't look at him. I can't. If I actually meet his eyes—those sensitive, soulful eyes that I fell so hard for last night—I will lose my shit. Either start to scream or curse him out or just cry. Either way, regardless, I'm not giving him the pleasure.

"I was going to make breakfast," he's saying, but I'm already slamming on the button to call the elevator.

"Sorry," I say, my voice tight. "I've got to run. Overslept."

"Oh... okay." I can hear the disappointment in Lark's voice even with my back turned. He pads across the carpet, heading toward me. "Well, can I get your number, at least? I'd love to see you again."

"I..." *Shit.* He's really going to make me do this, he's

going to make me call him out right now. Just then, the elevator reaches our floor and dings open, sparing me. "I don't think that's such a good idea." I step inside and hit the first floor button as fast as I can.

I don't know what I expect. For him to leap in after and stop me? But when I finally turn around, he's just standing a couple paces from the elevator doors, watching me with a sad, confused look on his face.

"Cassidy," he says. Or he tries to, anyway. The doors shut after half of my name, and then I'm sinking down, down, back into the real world.

* * *

I spend the rest of the morning forgetting last night. *You let your guard down and made a mistake,* I tell myself. *It happens.* But I fixed it. And now I never have to see that cheating asshole again.

That cheating asshole, who knew exactly where and how to touch you in ways no man has ever touched you before. Who knew just how to make you scream and lose all control...

Fuck.

A long, freezing cold shower later, though, followed by a coffee with a double shot of espresso, and I'm finally ready to face the real world once more. And especially ready to nail my presentation with the investors.

This is it. My big shot. My chance to finally get to share my makeup with more people than just my friends, family members, and the friends-of-friends who have become loyal customers. I started my business out of my own garage with little more than the savings I scraped together from my old job waiting tables. It's time to take it to the next level.

Worst comes to worst, I remind myself, *you can always fall back on waitressing.*

But going back to the service industry is, quite frankly, the last thing in the world I want to do. I've spent my whole life dreaming of building my own company, something in the fashion industry I've always loved. When I discovered I had a knack for chemistry, and combined that with making unique color palettes of eyeshadows and lipsticks, all using eco-friendly ingredients that wouldn't bother sensitive skin like mine, I finally felt like I was doing the right thing. Like I'd found my path, the one I'm meant to walk.

But, like any startup, money is standing in my way. More specifically, my complete lack of it.

Which is why I need to bring my A-game to this meeting.

I've dressed to the nines, in the suit I saved up to buy before I finally gave notice at my waitressing gig. I knew I'd need it for occasions like this, and I've kept it pressed and ready. Before I head out, I don my best powerhouse red lipstick, paired with a light, natural eye shade. My nails, thankfully, are still looking good, but I still give myself about five once-overs en route to the fancy high rise office building downtown where I'll be meeting with the potential investors.

The one thing about trying to sell a makeup brand is that you really need to look like perfection yourself, as the first ambassador for your brand.

At the office building, a secretary greets me by name and leads me to a board room. "The partners will be right with you," she assures me as she leaves.

My phone pings when the doors shut behind her, and I risk a peek at it. Becky.

So last night was a success??? She adds about a million

winking and kissing faces afterward. I steal a quick look at what I texted her and stifle a smile. I must have sent it from the bathroom of the bar where we wound up after the incident.

Won't be making it home tonight, I told her, *but in a good way.*

My stomach tenses, reading that now. I remember how excited I felt when I messaged Becky. Like Lark might actually be someone I could see for a while. Not *relationship* material exactly, but... he interested me. Intrigued me. I can't even remember the last time a guy did that.

Even with Norman... I fell for him, after a while. But there wasn't immediate chemistry right off the bat. I had to work to make myself fall for him—which I was happy to do, because he was everything I knew I should want. He was reliable, dependable, hardworking and trustworthy. The whole real deal.

Or so I thought. Until he cheated on me.

Just like that asshole Lark cheated on his wife, I remind myself, thinking of the woman pressing his door buzzer, calling him hon. My stomach churns now, and I imagine what will follow for her. Unfortunately, I'm all too familiar with the process.

He'll lie and say it was nothing; she'll believe him for a while, until she finds a bra somewhere it doesn't belong, or an earring in the bed. A million tiny things he can't explain, until finally she's forced to face the truth. She's with a liar who's been taking advantage of her naivety. Using her, and preparing to cast her aside the second he's finished.

Unexpected tears sting at the backs of my eyes. Not tears over Norman. I already cried out my heart over him—and just as quickly realized he wasn't worth any more pain. My only regret was that I wasted as much time with him as I did.

But these... these are new. These are because I thought I'd finally started to connect again, only to be completely fooled by a total and complete *ass*, an ass who—

"Ms. Marks?" The secretary is back, easing the door open to stick her head through. "The partners are here."

I stand, smoothing my pencil skirt, adjusting the hem of my blazer. Then I smile, smooth and easy, the way I've practiced in my bathroom mirror a thousand times. "Thank you," I tell her.

She ducks away, and another woman appears in the entryway, striding toward me with a confident, easy grin, and one hand extended.

"You must be Ms. Marks," she's saying. "It's so nice to meet you. I'm Sheryl, the lead investor at Anderson."

But I can't respond. I can't even *look* at her, because I'm too busy gawking at who just followed her through the door, trailing along on her heels with bags under his eyes, his hair slightly mussed like a hungover puppy dog.

Lark. Shit.

His eyes go wide when they meet mine. But he recovers at lot faster than I do. "Cassidy." He sticks out a hand too. "Fancy seeing you here."

I pointedly ignore his hand and shake Sheryl's hand instead. My smile has gone all tight and forced around the edges. "So nice to meet you, too," I tell her, trying to kick my brain back into focusing on the task at hand.

Lark doesn't matter. He's irrelevant. Sheryl's the lead here.

As for her, she's glancing from me to Lark and back, her head tilting in polite curiosity. "Oh, do you two know each other?" Sheryl draws out a chair and sits smoothly down.

The more she talks, the more it's dawning on me that I've heard her voice before.

This very morning, in fact. Over the intercom at Lark's apartment. I mirror her, taking a seat, and pausing only to flick a glare in Lark's direction. "Hardly."

"We met last night when her car broke down," Lark replies, which makes me want to kick him under the table for all sorts of reasons. "She needed help with a flat tire."

Sheryl fires me a sympathetic smile. "I'm so sorry you got stuck with him, then. Lark's useless at playing handyman."

I laugh aloud, and Lark's expression sours ever so slightly. "I noticed, believe me. Luckily, I know how to change a tire myself." We both grin at him then, and Lark's eyes linger on mine, a torrent of emotion visible in them.

I don't care. He's the one who put me in this situation. Hooking up with me right under the nose of... well.

I glance between his and Sheryl's hands, both folded neatly on the tabletop. Neither of them is wearing wedding rings, at least. So maybe he's not as huge of an asshole as I thought. But there's clearly still chemistry there, something in the way Sheryl's constantly glancing at him from the corner of her eyes, mirroring his posture, his motions.

Whatever this is, it's messy enough without my getting involved. And I've had enough of messy to last me an entire lifetime, thank you very much.

"So, Cassidy. Why don't we talk products," Sheryl asks, and I bend down to reach for my briefcase, grateful for the excuse to think about something, anything, other than Lark's eyes staring into mine. Or the way his tongue felt last night, lapping its way up my inner thigh, his fingers lingering at my pussy, parting my lower lips, stroking and stroking until I—

"Yes, let's." I place my briefcase on the table and pop it open. "I brought some samples of my most popular collections, although everything you see here comes in at least three other color palettes. Now, these are some of my favorites…"

I walk them through everything, one item at a time. My only saving grace is the fact that I've rehearsed this speech at least a hundred times before. To myself, to my friends, to my bathroom mirror. I've practiced so often, I've had dreams of giving this presentation.

So I make it through, despite the fact that every time I so much as glance at Lark, he's still watching me so overtly, not seeming to notice or care that Sheryl's noticing his stares, too. More than once, under the table, his leg brushes against mine, in a way that's far too slow and lingering to be accidental.

But I force myself to remain steady, to not react. Like I said, I've had enough of messy, and this has mess written all over it.

But my tension only seems to amuse him. At one point, when I ask if they have any questions, Lark leans over to pick up one of the lipsticks, his hand brushing mine ever so slightly on the way past. "As the male investor in the room," he starts, his gaze jumping from Sheryl to me, "I did have one question." Those eyes pull me in. Call to me to sink into them. "What does it taste like?" He grins, and Sheryl elbows him discretely.

My face flushes. But I hold his gaze and raise my jaw. "To be honest," I reply, "I didn't give that much consideration. I make my products for the women who use them; not the men who consume them."

Sheryl laughs out loud at that, and the two of us exchange faint smiles.

"Well, we'll have to put the paperwork together," she says, shuffling through some sample contracts we'd pored over, "but I think it's safe to let you know this, at least." She extends a hand. "We'll be investing. A significant amount."

My stomach does a whole ass backflip. I swear I can feel my heart rising up into my throat as I reach across the table to her and grasp her hand again, tightly. "I don't know how to thank you," I start, but she waves a hand, cutting me off.

"Please. We're happy to do it. At Anderson Investments, we prefer to invest in quality products. Products that we really think will do well in the market. Between our marketing know-how and your vision for your brand, I think we have a real hit on our hands." Her eyes sparkle with genuine excitement.

"Congratulations," Lark adds, reaching past her to offer me a hand as well.

I take it, reluctantly, and almost immediately have to stifle a gasp. His touch sends shockwaves through me, like static electricity, but deadlier. One touch, and it's like we're right back in his bed last night, with him grasping my hands, raising them over my head to pin me down while he stretched along me, his hard, firm body digging into my soft curves, his cock hard as a rock, slipping up between my thighs...

I clear my throat and let go of his hand as if it's too hot to touch. In a way, it is. "Thank you," I reply, not quite meeting his gaze.

"As I said, we'll be in touch," Sheryl calls. Then she beckons Lark with a fingertip, turning to head from the room.

He follows her, although not before he glances over his shoulder at me. Just before he leaves, he tosses something onto the table. "My card," he says. His eyes flash with meaning. He knows I left this morning without giving him my number, or taking his in return. "In case there's any more business you want to discuss."

Then he's gone, closing the office door behind him and Sheryl.

I slump back into my seat, all the wind going out of me.

This is what you wanted, I remind myself. What I worked so hard, for so long, to achieve. But now that I'm finally right on the brink of getting the investment I need, what happens?

I wind up embroiling myself in just the kind of personal drama I want so much to avoid.

Shit. For a long moment, I sit there, staring at the business card on the table. Part of me wonders if I should walk away. If I *could.* But I know the money's too good, the chance too perfect, for me to do something that insane.

So, after a long, pause, I reach across the table and pick up Lark's card.

4
____

CASSIDY

I'm halfway out of the building, only barely recovered from the meeting, my head still swimming with possibilities, when the sound of my name stops me halfway down the street.

"Cassidy."

Of course, Lark is still here. He must have waited for me —there's no sign of Sheryl in sight, but I can't help checking for her. Can't help wondering how she must be feeling about all of this.

"Thank you again for the investment," I tell him with a tight-lipped smile. "Although I suppose I should be thanking your... girlfriend, I guess, based on the lack of rings? Or are you one of those married couples who don't do jewelry."

"What?" Lark blinks, staring at me.

I cross my arms. I've had more than enough of the innocent what-do-you-mean defense to last me a lifetime. "I heard her on your intercom this morning," I reply. "That *was* Sheryl, wasn't it?"

He hesitates. It's the first time I've ever seen Mr. Confident actually do that. When he speaks again, the confusion on his face has cleared, replaced by understanding. "I see. So, when you left in a hurry..."

"It's because I don't do cheating. I don't do going behind people's backs."

"Something I understand and completely respect," Lark speaks up quickly, "but Sheryl and I aren't together, Cassidy. She's my ex-wife."

My eyebrows climb to my forehead. "Your business partner is your—"

"We started Anderson Investments together," he interrupts. "Years ago. You know what they say about mixing business and pleasure?" He gives a rueful laugh, then shakes his head. "Look, Sheryl and I split over a year ago. There's nothing between us anymore, trust me. But we are still joint owners of this company, and we've been making the business relationship work, so..."

My shoulders, which I hadn't realized were tensed up around my ears until now, slowly relax. That's better than I'd been dreading, at least. *So maybe he's not a cheating asshole.*

But he's still in a messy situation. A messy situation that reminds me far too much of the one I finally disentangled myself from. I told myself that after Norman, I'd learn my lesson. Be done with anything not simple and straightforward. I meant it.

I run a hand through my hair, hesitating. Lark takes the opportunity to move closer to me, one hand outstretched, hovering in midair between us like he's thinking about touching my shoulder, pulling me close. But I fire him one look, and he lets his hand fall again, a wounded expression crossing his face. A moment later, his features smooth, so quickly I might have just imagined it. But... I don't think so.

"Cassidy, listen..." His voice drops lower. Softer.

God. Standing this close to him, I can smell him again. The same scent that enveloped me last night, heady and powerful. It makes me want to cave. To move closer, let him take me in those strong arms. Let him carry me back to his apartment like he did last night, toss me onto that big bed of his, and kiss my whole body, until I feel ready to burst.

Just the thought makes my thighs tighten involuntarily, my pussy giving a single tight throb. I'm still sore from his thick cock. Deliciously, delightfully sore. It's an ache I should be savoring today; I should be riding high on that post-sex glow, enjoying life.

Instead, I'm standing on a sidewalk outside one of the most important meetings of my life, being made to feel utterly conflicted again. All because of this man.

"I can't stop thinking about you," he says, his eyes catching mine. There's fire in them. The same fire I allowed to burn me, ignite me last night. "All I wanted to do this morning was drag you straight back into my bed and keep you there as long as you'd let me."

My pulse picks up at those words. *God.* I'm already wet again. How does he know how to do this to me so easily?

But it's a trap. I know that now. I take a step backward, even though doing so takes all the willpower in my body. I start to shake my head, slowly.

"I can't do this." My voice comes out a lot stronger than I feel, at least, a lot more certain. Guess I've got practice at staying strong in the face of temptation now.

There's that brief flicker of hurt again, marring Lark's usual confident, I-get-what-I-want expression. But only for an instant. "Because of Sheryl?" Lark lets out a faint laugh. "I told you, there's nothing there. Trust me, Cassidy."

"Why should I?" I raise my chin, narrow my gaze. "You weren't honest with me from the start."

"So we were supposed to have the exes talk on night one?" Lark lifts an eyebrow, smirking. "All right, your turn then. Who's in your past?"

I grimace. "Don't try to change the subject. I don't *work* with my ex. I never even speak to him anymore; it's different."

"If you did, though, I wouldn't mind." Lark shrugs his shoulders. "I've realized recently how complicated life gets. I don't hold it against people, if they're in confusing situations."

Complicated. Confusing. "That's just it," I say. "Complicated and confusing are the exact things I swore off from now on."

"I see." He tilts his head. Takes a step toward me. I mirror him, moving backward, but not before I catch his scent again. My body reacts to his with an animal instinct. It wants him, regardless of what my head is screaming. "So, what I'm hearing is that you thought about me too, didn't you? Otherwise, you could've just written this off as some harmless fun. A hot one night stand, no strings attached."

"You're putting words in my mouth," I protest, my voice coming out high-pitched, too shrill, because damn him, he's hitting far too close to the mark.

Why *didn't* I just assume this was a one-off thing? Why, even after I thought he had a wife he'd been cheating on, did I continue to daydream about the way he touched me, the feeling of his cock inside me, driving me all the way to the edge?

My throat feels dry. I try to swallow.

"If it was just meaningless sex, you won't mind hooking up again." Lark smirks.

"So it *was* just meaningless to you, then?" I counter.

His eyes flash. "I never said that."

"There you go, then." I cross my arms. My lips are dry too, so I wet them, and his gaze drops, tracking the motion. *Shit.*

I expect him to make another move. I'm not entirely sure I could resist him this time, if he did. But he takes a step backward, lifting his palms in the air, mock surrender. "All right," he says, surprising me. "If you don't want to do this, then I'm not into persuading women they belong in my bed."

A sharp pulse of desire sparks in my belly at those words. But I hold my ground, keep my mouth shut, because if I don't, I'll blurt out something stupid. Something I shouldn't say.

"I'll see you around," Lark says. Then he winks. "Business partner."

I don't stop holding my breath until he disappears around the corner. Even then, the very idea of breathing feels dangerous. *What have I gotten myself into?*

5
───────

CASSIDY

The next couple of weeks are a whirlwind of work. Thank God, because any time that I stop working for long enough to think, *he* drifts into my mind.

Every night as I'm drifting off to sleep—or trying to—I start to picture him next to me in bed. The taste of his mouth. The way his lips felt gliding down my chest, his tongue on my nipple, my belly button, tracing from my navel all the way down to my mound. The feeling of his thick cock buried deep in my pussy; the waves of pleasure that hit me as he fucked me, his strong hands wrapped around my hips, hard everywhere I'm soft.

Fuck. I have it bad. Worse than I ever had it with any guy I've hooked up with before. Even with Norman, I was into him as a person, but he was lackluster in bed. More interested in getting himself off than making sure I was having fun.

At the time, I told myself that was just how all guys were. That it was fine. If, every night after we had sex, I had to roll over and finish myself with my own fingers, well, that was just how life had to be.

Then I met Lark.

Lark, who make me come more times in a single night than I would have thought possible. Lark, who wanted to keep seeing me, who would have stopped at nothing to have me again... Except I made him stop. I drove him off. And why? Because I didn't want anything complicated?

What's simple about me right now? I'm daydreaming about him every night, every time I'm alone in the shower, my hands wandering down my body to stroke my own clit until I'm gasping his name.

But at least work is a distraction.

I've had more than a few phone calls with Sheryl since our meeting. Every time I see the Anderson Investments number pop up on my phone, my heart climbs into my throat and my stomach does a little backflip. But it's always her perky, no-nonsense voice on the other end.

"Now a good time?" she always begins our calls. Just like the one we had earlier today, where she asked for an update on the new line.

She wound up investing a lot, far more than I ever could have hoped for. Well, *they* wound up investing a lot, I guess, although I haven't personally spoken to Lark since our one conversation outside the office building just after the investment meeting.

But she's also very specific about which products she'd like me to develop first. "I think there's a real market for the lengthening mascara you showed us and the eye color palettes—you've got a great eye for colors. And that way we can focus on one specific product set to start off, and expand into other products later."

She always words everything in a super complimentary way. But it's also the first time since I started my own line that I've had a boss of sorts—even if she's not strictly my boss, she's definitely calling the shots now. And while some-times it's reassuring to have another opinion to look for, another voice to rely on for the big decisions, at other times, like today, when I've got a great new idea for a lipstick color that I can't play around with... well, it can be somewhat confining, creatively.

I remind myself it doesn't matter, as long as I'm doing what my investor wants. Once we get this first line of prod-ucts out, I'll have all the time in the world to play around more creatively and figure out what the second line to launch will be.

Before my call for the day with Sheryl finishes up, she adds quickly, "By the way, we'd love to see how the proto-type is coming."

I hesitate for a second. I've been working for the last two weeks on the eyeshadow palette, and I've sent a few photos over the phone. "I can mockup some more pictures," I start, but Sheryl cuts me off.

"A bit hard to judge it over the screen though, isn't it? We'll be there at noon, if that time works for you, just to have a look at the progress. Here at Anderson Investments, we like to stay, well, invested." She laughs at her own joke, and I find myself grinning too, even though my heart rate has just kicked into triple gear.

We? Does that mean Lark will be coming with her too? "Okay," I barely have time to squeak before she ends the call. And then I stare at myself in the mirror across my messy living room. My hair's in a topknot because I haven't washed it in a couple days, my eyes are puffy from another long night of no sleep, my brain helpfully filling the time with fantasies of Lark instead.

Shit.

I rush to the bathroom to get myself ready. A long hot

shower and careful application of my best-foot-forward makeup look later, I'm ready to tackle the apartment itself. Normally I'm a pretty tidy person—I have to be, since my apartment is so tiny that any time it gets out of hand, it's practically unlivable—but whenever I'm deep in the creative well, working hard on a project like the one I've been ensconced in this week, the whole cleaning thing tends to get away from me.

I cart empty takeout boxes to the garbage chute down the hall, sweep and vacuum, stack away all my excess belongings, and even manage to start dusting some of the furniture before the door buzzer rings. The intercom has been broken for years, and my super is next to useless, so I just buzz it open, my heart in my throat.

I brace myself for it to just be Sheryl standing before me, in her prim suit, with her perfect hair done up. That would be disappointing, but it would be the far easier option.

Much simpler than if both of them show up on my doorstep. Lark, looking picture perfect and handsome as ever, those bright eyes of his following my every move. If the three of us are alone in my apartment together, Sheryl won't fail to notice the way her ex keeps looking at me.

At least, assuming Lark hasn't moved on already. I remind myself that we only had one night together. A night I told him would never be repeated. He's probably long since forgotten about me.

In fact, by the time there's a knock at my door, I've convinced myself there's no way he would even come here. He'll be too busy hooking up with his latest fling. Someone far more attractive than me. More interesting and funny and sexy and—

I wrench open my front door, and my thoughts stop spiraling. Even my heart stops for a split second, I swear.

Because he's here. Lark stands in the doorway, wearing jeans, a button down shirt, and a small smile. He looks even better than he does in my memories. The planes of his cheekbones are sharper, the green of his eyes brighter.

His smile far more dangerous than I remember.

"Cassidy. Good to see you."

I move aside, my tongue temporarily tied, and glance past him into the hallway, confused. "Where's your business partner?" I ask, unable to keep a faint note of annoyance from my tone.

"Unfortunately, Sheryl couldn't make it today. She asked me to fill in. Something I was all too happy to do." He tilts his head, and his gaze drops over me, taking me in.

My stomach tightens. I know I just showered and finished putting on a full face of makeup—I know I look good—but it still steals my breath away to watch his pupils dilate, to see him take a sharp breath, the same way I must have when I laid eyes on him.

"You look good, Cassidy." He smiles. "I have to admit, even better than I remember."

He's been thinking about me too. The revelation hangs in the air between us, making me dizzy if I think about it too hard. Does he lie awake at night the same way I've been doing? His hand sliding down until he wraps a fist around the base of his cock, thinking of me as he starts to stroke his hard, pulsing length...

I clear my throat. "You, too. Look good, I mean." *Great start to this business meeting,* my inner voice groans. I straighten my shoulders and gesture toward the living room table, which I've laid out with what I have so far: three full eyeshadow palettes in complimentary colors, as well as individual pots of more daring colors to sell on their own. "The merchandise is over here, if you'd like to take a look."

Lark's smirk only widens at my sudden professional shift in tone. But he steps into the room anyway, letting me close the door behind him, and after a pause, he takes a seat on the couch. The couch almost swallows him whole—it's ancient, and the cushions have lost any supportive abilities they once had.

"Sorry," I murmur, coming around the far side of the couch. I don't have any other chairs in the living room, but I make sure to perch on the farthest cushion from the one where Lark is sitting, just to be careful. "This sofa's seen better days."

He snorts. "I've seen mattresses in alleyways that have seen better days, Cassidy."

"Yeah, well, not all of us can afford to live in luxury penthouse bachelor pads," I grumble, and he smirks at me.

"I didn't say I didn't like it. It's got character."

"Character is code for ugly, and you know it," I reply, rolling my eyes. But I'm grinning now, too.

"Only if you think pretty things have to have no personality." Lark shifts a little closer to me on the couch—not that it's hard. With the way the cushions sag, we're both slowly sliding toward the center of the thing, an inevitable progression. It feels like the universe trying to throw us together once more.

I'm determined to resist it.

I reach out to grab one of the color palettes and practically shove it under his nose. "Here. You can be my first tester."

He laughs, holding it up to the light. "Not my shade, I don't think," he teases. But his face softens as he actually studies the makeup. I watch him take a small amount, spread it across the back of his hand, then turn it this way and that to admire the colors.

After a moment, he surprises me by standing and pacing over to the window.

"Natural light," he says over his shoulder. "It helps to see better."

"I know." I smile, watching him. "I just didn't realize you would." There's something absorbing about his expression when he's concentrating. Like he's stepped out of this world and into the inside of his own head. It makes me want to know what's going on up there. To burrow inside and spy.

"I wouldn't have, a couple weeks ago." Lark returns to the sofa, apparently satisfied now. I can't help but notice that when he takes a seat again, it's far closer to me this time. Close enough that our thighs bump against one another, the warmth of his leg searing through mine, electrifying my entire body.

Fuck.

I'm in trouble.

"You aren't the only one who's been busy the last couple weeks." Lark catches my eye. We're so close that in my overbright apartment lighting, I can see the individual flecks of yellow scattered through his green irises. I can see the way his pupils dilate ever so slightly, as we hold one another's gazes. "As soon as we signed your contract, I started to research makeup design and color theory. Just the basics, of course. I don't have your eye."

He hands the palette back to me, and I take it, our fingertips brushing as I do. His hands feel strong as ever, and the sensation sends fireworks through my veins.

"You're very talented, Cassidy," he says quietly. "Even a novice like me can tell."

"Do you always research every new company investment you take on?" I ask, my own voice coming out soft too. *Or was this one different?* I don't ask that second question. It tiptoes too close to asking what I really want to know.

Have you been thinking of me as much as I've been thinking of you?

"I try to, yes." Lark's eyes jump back and forth between mine, studying me. "It's good practice to understand some of what you're putting your money into. But..." He glances down at where our legs touch on the sofa. Back up at me. "There are some companies I take more interest in than others, I have to admit. Some businesses that seem more... promising, to me."

"I see." I swallow, my throat feeling far too tight. "And does the potential for success of those businesses have anything to do with your... ah... personal biases, by any chance?"

He laughs, a low undercurrent that sends fire through my veins. "I should think so. Everything is personal, Cassidy." He reaches up. There's a stray strand of hair I hadn't noticed, come loose from the ponytail I put my damp hair into earlier. He brushes it back off my shoulder, his fingers lingering against the bare expanse of skin there, because I wore a tank top today, so stupid, I should have worn something more covered up.

A whole sheet over my body, maybe.

Even then, I get the feeling Lark would have been able to reach me through it.

"Especially business," he murmurs, his face barely inches from mine.

My breath is unsteady in my chest. My whole body feels like it's vibrating, eager to lean into his, to surrender to the desire that's been coursing through me, unrelenting and trapped, for weeks.

"I thought you told me you learned not to mix business

with pleasure," I reply, my voice a barely-there breath. But he hears me anyway, the corners of his mouth edging up into a dangerous smile.

"Guess I'm a slow learner," he says. Then he leans in, and God help me, I do the same. His lips collide with mine, searing hot, and his hand reaches up to cup my cheek, his fingers buried in my hair.

I groan into his mouth, and he grins against my lips, pulling back just far enough to rest his forehead against mine, gazing into my eyes.

"I haven't been able to get you out of my damn head for weeks, Cassidy Marks."

The sound of my name in his mouth thrills me. Sends sparks dancing in my veins. "Me neither," I admit. "I should have—I *wanted* to, but—" I fall silent when he kisses me again. This time, I sink against him, let his free arm snake around my waist and pull me closer. At the same time, his lips part against mine, and his tongue tangles with my own, forceful, claiming.

I relinquish control. There's a sense of relief in it, in finally letting myself fall, when I've been struggling to hold myself back for so long.

My hands slide up over Lark's chest—God, I forgot how fucking muscular he is—and loop around his neck, tightening.

In response, he shifts in his seat, and in one smooth motion, drags me across the couch until I'm straddling his lap. This time he's the one who groans, his lips vibrating against mine with the sound. As my legs sink into the soft cushions to either side of his lap, I can feel a solid press against my inner thigh.

He's already rock fucking hard.

My belly tightens at the knowledge that I have the same

effect on him as he does on me. It seems impossible to me, and yet here he is, unable to keep his hands off me. Unable to forget about me, the same way I couldn't forget about him.

Somewhere in our entanglement, I feel something brush my shin, and glance over. Unable to help it, I laugh.

My damn eyeshadow palette. Lark was holding it. Now it's face down on the couch, the colors smeared in a rainbow riot across the dingy gray cushions.

Lark notices where I'm looking and he laughs, too. "My fault," he admits.

"You're paying to clean this," I inform him, right before I cup his face between my hands and lean in to kiss him again.

"I'll do one better," he replies when we break apart again. At the same time, he slides his hands up the back of my shirt, tugging it up and over my head, then tossing it aside. He pulls me against him again, his face level with my chest, and starts to kiss and lick his way around the edges of my breasts, still tightly confined in my bra. "I'll replace the whole damn couch, I promise."

With my head tipped back, my eyes fluttering shut at the sensation of his tongue on my skin, I almost don't hear what he said. The moment the words register, though, I jerk back upright, my eyes flashing. "I don't need your charity."

He'd been in the process of unhooking my bra. Now it hangs between us, my nipples bare and hardened, but he's not touching them. He's peering up at me, expression unreadable. "It's not charity if I destroyed the thing. I'm merely replacing what I owe you."

"I don't want to be spoiled," I reply, chin raised.

But that only makes him grin, slowly. "Don't you?" One hand slides up to cup my breast. His thumb traces over my nipple, which was already hard in the cool air of my apartment. Now it could probably cut a diamond. "That's a shame," he says, bending close. He runs his tongue over my other nipple, making me gasp and arch up—which he takes advantage of, his free hand gripping my hip and pulling me down against his cock, the hard length of his shaft falling right between my legs, pressing against my swollen clit. "Because I had so many plans for how exactly I'd spoil you today, Ms. Marks..." He speaks with his mouth close to my chest, his breath heating the damp spot he left against my nipple. Then he sucks it between his lips again, gently closing his teeth around my nipple, and I gasp, my head falling back, my protests forgotten.

I'm pushing my hips down, grinding against his cock, desperation building. The couch argument can wait. I want him now—no. I *need* him. "Fuck me already, damn it, Lark," I say, my voice practically a growl.

In response, he grins, and reaches down to undo the buttons on the presentable work pants I wore today—foolishly thinking this would just be another business meeting. Not planning for this.

Somehow I never plan for Lark.

By the time he finally gets both of our pants out of the way; when we're perched on the couch naked, me still straddling his hips, I'm so wet I'm surprised it's not dripping down my inner thigh already. His cock is swollen, red with want, and he takes his damn time rolling a condom over himself before he positions the throbbing tip at the entrance of my pussy.

"I've dreamt of this for weeks," he tells me, his eyes blazing where they catch mine. "I've been missing that sweet, tight pussy of yours so goddamn badly..."

"Lark, please..."

I try to sit right on him, but he holds my hips in both hands, smirking all the while.

"Not so fast," he tells me. "I want to savor this."

When he finally guides me down onto his cock, it takes every ounce of self-control I have not to cry aloud with pleasure. I manage to keep it to a low, throaty moan, as the sensation of his cock sliding into my pussy, slowly spreading my lips, making me ache to contain him, fills me up.

I move slow, sinking onto him. Every time I think I can't possibly take him any deeper, I move a centimeter closer, feel him stretching me to my limits.

"God, you're perfect," he groans, and the tightness in his voice almost undoes me as much as the feeling of him inside me.

When he starts to move again, tiny motions at first, bucking me up off him and pulling me back down again, I have to cling to his bare chest for support, because I'm already halfway to an orgasm already, the sensations filling my body like nothing I've ever experienced.

He takes it slow. Torturously slow. But by the time we both come together, my whole body jerking against his, it feels like we've melded into one body, one mind.

That's the moment I know I'm in trouble.

6

CASSIDY

I wake up the next morning to a loud buzzing at my door. I roll over with a groan, unsure why every muscle in my body is screaming for mercy—until I remember the couch.

And after the couch, the shower.

And after the shower, this very bed, which dammit, I'll need to wash the sheets now. But not yet. For now, I roll back over with a groan and pull a pillow over my head. Lark left sometime this morning—I vaguely remember him kissing my cheek and promising to keep his promise soon, whatever that means. I wasn't awake enough to process it.

Just like I'm not awake enough now for whatever that commotion is outside.

But the horrible raucous buzzing continues, and I finally sit upright in bed, realizing. Oh shit. Doorbell.

"Coming!" I shout, which is inane, because nobody can hear me at the front entrance from all the way up here. Groggily, I pull on the nearest clothing—a pair of sweats and a baggy sleep shirt. Then I pad into my living room and hit the buzzer. My hair is a mess. I take one look in the mirror and grimace, pulling it up into a ponytail and heading into the bathroom to splash the worst of the sleep from my face.

I don't expect the knock on my door, a few minutes later. I had figured the buzzer was just the mailman or someone locked out of another unit in the building.

Confused, I pad back to the entrance and ease open the door a crack, my stomach a riot of butterflies. Because, sure, I might be expecting Lark.

Instead, I find a man in a delivery uniform outside, holding out a form. "Ms. Marks?" he asks.

"Uh, yes, that's me." I rub at my eyes, frowning. "But I didn't order any—"

"Right here, boys," the man calls over his shoulder, and the next thing I know, a series of delivery men are shouldering open my door and hauling a brand new couch through it.

I watch, my jaw dropping, as they work. *Lark.* I thought I told him not to do this.

The main delivery man notices my expression, and grins. "Mr. Anderson warned us you might be, ah, surprised by the delivery. Don't take it too personally. He has a tendency to do this sort of thing."

I fold my arms and watch the man's assistants expertly disassemble my sagging, stained couch, and reassemble a replacement in its place. "To do what, barge into other people's lives and force gifts on them?" I reply.

"Pretty much." The man laughs.

But, I have to admit, looking at the new couch they're unwrapping, Lark chose well. It's in a similar style to the one I owned, with big, puffy cushions and a simple fabric pattern—dark gray this time instead of light, which I have to admit does pair better with my shaggy carpet and steel coffee table.

Still. He could have at least consulted me first.

"You should see his apartment," the delivery man continues. Before I can say *I have*, he adds, "Or the house he used to share with his wife, for that matter. Everyone who visits compliments Sheryl on her eye, but he's the one who really put the place together. All for her sake, of course."

His wife. Not his ex-wife. My stomach does an unpleasant backflip, all my earlier worries flooding straight back. "So I take it you've worked for Anderson Investments for a while?" I ask, trying to keep my tone casual, light. As if the answer doesn't interest me more than I could possibly explain.

"Been with them ever since they got their start," the man declares proudly. "One of those power couples. You could tell from the get-go they were both driven, smart, wanted to make a name for themselves."

"I see," I reply, and I can't quite hide the quiver in my tone. Thankfully, the man doesn't seem to notice.

"Shame about their troubles of late." He shakes his head. "Can't help but think it's because Lark's a stubborn one. He didn't see what was right in front of him all the while."

My throat has gone tight. I clear it, forcing myself to smile and nod. To act normal. "Isn't that always the way?" I say.

The man laughs. Across the room, his men have finished assembling my handsome new couch—which looks like it probably cost more than every other piece of furniture in my apartment put together. They're carrying out the disassembled pieces of my old one now, when their overseer pauses, glancing at the rainbow, makeup-stained cushion.

"You got kids?" he asks, squinting at it, and then around my place, as if wondering where I've stashed a toddler.

I flash back to last night. To Lark pulling me onto his lap, the makeup spilling around us. "No," I say. "But you could say someone immature did that."

The man laughs again, and then offers me his hand. "Well, it was a pleasure to meet you. I'm sure if you're an Anderson employee, we'll meet again soon."

I shake, a small frown creasing my forehead. "Oh, no," I start to say. "I'm not a—"

But he's already following his men out the door with a single backward salute at me. I wait until they're in the hallway, and then shut the door behind them, locking it, and leaning backward against it. My head hits the wood with a faint thud.

I raise it, and let it fall back again with a harder smack this time.

What a mess.

And if I thought the day started out awkwardly, it's only about to get more so. Less than an hour after the delivery men leave, I get two texts in a row. One from Lark.

I still cannot stop thinking about you. Tell me how you like the new addition to your apartment. Or better yet, how about I come over to test it out tonight?

And another from Sheryl.

So sorry I wasn't able to come to the demo yesterday. What about a makeup (wink) meeting today? Lunch downtown at 1pm? My treat.

Followed by an address, a restaurant I've never been to, mostly because the only thing I'd be able to afford there is a single appetizer plate.

Shit.

* * *

It's hard not to think about the fact, as I watch Sheryl unfold her napkin and set it primly in her lap across the table from me, that just last night I was in bed with her husband. Her ex-husband?

Either way. Guilt churns in my stomach. The dish she ordered me, some kind of rare steak from Japan I've never heard of, smells incredible. But it's difficult for me to even hold my fork and knife long enough to cut it, let alone raise it to my lips.

Sitting between us on the table is my makeup palette. The same palette that destroyed my former couch, albeit now it's been cleaned and refilled properly. Looking at it now, I picture it in Lark's hands, as he turned it admiringly this way and that in the sunlight streaming through my windows. Then I think about the way it slid from his grasp onto the couch beside us, when he pulled me over to straddle him, his hard cock digging into my thigh.

"It's beautiful," Sheryl says, dragging my attention back to the present. "Do you mind?" She reaches for it but waits for me to nod before she takes a few swatches and tests them along the inside of her wrist, admiring the color in the dim restaurant lighting.

She doesn't cross to the window for a better look. I try not to hold it against her.

While she examines the merchandise, I force a piece of steak into my mouth. It melts on my tongue, buttery and supple. It's possibly the most delicious steak I've ever eaten.

It's hard to swallow. I have to wash it down with a gulp of sparkling water—Sheryl refused still when the waiter asked, practically offended by the notion.

"What did Lark say?" she asks, after a long pause. The lump in my throat doubles in size, having nothing to do with the steak.

"Pretty much the same thing." I manage to keep a tremor from my voice. Good.

"He has a better eye than me for these sorts of things," Sheryl admits, setting the palette down to take a bite of her own meal. "I'm more of a flavors-and-scents type. He's the visual one." She points with her fork. "Is something wrong? If they've overcooked it, I can send it back."

"No, no. It's delicious." I raise my fork and knife again with effort. "I'm just... savoring."

"A girl after my own heart." Sheryl smiles at me, conspiratorially.

I grin back, trying not to let the guilt overwhelm me. Lark told me things were over between them. And I believe him. But the look in her eyes whenever she brings him up... Not to mention how *often* she brings him up...

I think about the delivery man again, from earlier today. *Shame about their troubles.* And here I am, adding to those troubles. Maybe at first I was innocent, unaware of Lark's complicated situation. But now?

"Do I have anything in my teeth?" Sheryl asks, an eyebrow lifted, and I realize I've been staring.

"Sorry, no." I drop my gaze. Search for an excuse. "I was just trying to figure out what shade of lipstick you're wearing."

She grins. "I appreciate how your mind is always on your work. Makes me feel confident to be your first investor." She cuts off another piece, and I mimic her, the savory steak tasting like a solid block on my tongue. "I'm not sure of the name actually. Or even the brand. To be honest, I rarely wear makeup. Some old trifle Lark bought me years ago."

I take another, longer gulp of water. Clear my throat. "So you two are...?" I let the question linger, unfinished.

Sheryl's smile turns rueful. "*Were*," she corrects, and I have to admit that the single word nearly makes me slide off my chair, weak with relief. At least that part is true, then. "We *were* married, for four years."

"And you still manage to be business partners?" I can't keep the note of surprise from my tone.

But it doesn't seem to bother her. She leans back in her chair with a sigh. "Lark and I never did do anything the conventional way." Her expression has turned inward, fond. "When we got married, we opened Anderson Investments the same year. Everyone told us it was mad, but we insisted. In for a penny, in for a pound, I always thought. Suppose some of those people are probably thinking *told you so* right about now, but..." She shakes her head, her mouth drooping at the corners. "I don't mind. At least the business still keeps us somewhat connected now. Friends, if not anything more."

"So, if you're friends... you'd be okay with it if he moved on?" The words are out of my mouth before I can think better. Before I can shove another piece of steak past my lips to make me hold my tongue.

Sheryl's gaze jumps to mine, suddenly sharp. When she smiles again, it's sharper than last time, pointed. "Are you interested in him?" she asks, point-blank, in a way that throws me completely.

"Of course not," I blurt. Because what am I going to do? Admit right here at the lunch table that I'm still sore from her husband's cock inside me last night?

God, what am I doing? I swore I would never be that woman, the type to break up someone else's marriage. Granted, theirs may already have ended, but it's clear Sheryl still holds fond feelings for Lark. She looks so wistful talking about their past... and so sad talking about the way it ended.

I lean forward, palms flat on the table. "There's nothing

between me and him, Sheryl," I say, looking her dead in the eyes. "I promise you."

And in that moment, I mean every word. Because I decide right then and there, I'm not pursuing him any further.

7

CASSIDY

It turns out having a real investor with actual cashflow makes things move forward with exponential speed in the business world. Next thing I know, within days, we've already got a couple of media interviews on the docket, plus a featured ad in two major fashion magazines.

I don't know how Lark and Sheryl did it. Lark assures me—through texts, since I've put off seeing him face-to-face again, claiming to be busy, because I haven't worked out yet how exactly to explain my sudden change of conscience— that it was all Sheryl's doing. But I'm not entirely sure I believe him, based on how infrequently Sheryl replies to my emails to check in on various details.

Either way, regardless of who I have to thank for it, Thursday morning dawns with me dressing for a photo-shoot with a famous photographer, representing one of the top beauty magazines in the country. On set, I'll be responsible for providing all the professional makeup artists with the supplies—*my* supplies, my makeup, on the faces of models I've seen featured in all the magazines I grew up dreaming of being featured in. But it's not lost on me that I'll be on display too. There's even going to be a small headshot of me, taken for the back details of the magazine, where I'll be featured in a New Creators to Watch section.

I realize they'll probably redo everything I do the minute I get to set, but I spend hours getting ready anyway, primping and styling myself to perfection before I finally set out.

Lark meets me in the parking lot of the studio, also dressed to the nines. The sight of him in a formal suit and tie takes my breath away the second I step out of my car. It takes all my self-control not to stride across the lot and fling myself into his arms right here.

Instead, I dive into my trunk to avoid him, then reemerge with my arms full of bags. Bags of all the makeup I put together for this event.

Lark holds out a hand, offering to take one, but I shy away from him. "I can handle carrying a few palettes," I inform him, chin raised.

"Never said you couldn't." He tucks his hands into his suit pockets and falls into step beside me. "So. Busy week, hmm? You haven't had a minute to spare for me."

"And why should I?" I reply, my tone light, my face turned slightly away so that I don't have to watch his expression when those words register. "It's not like we owe one another anything."

This time, I can't help myself. I peek over, and my heart catches at the hurt expression on his face. "Cassidy…" But whatever he's about to say is drowned out when the studio manager opens a door up ahead and catches sight of me.

"You must be Ms. Marks!" He drifts down the stairs, dazzling in a pinstripe suit and eyeshadow I'd kill to have designed myself. "Marcel. It's such a thrill to meet you— Lark has been gushing about your talent ever since our last dinner, and I knew I had to invite you to set." He kisses both of my cheeks, then wraps Lark in a tight hug.

Over his shoulder, Lark flashes me a pained smile.

All Sheryl's doing, my ass. Still, I keep my own smile painted on, as Marcel practically drags me into the studio, chatting excitedly the whole way about how much Lark gushed about my products and how excited he is to use them on set today.

I'm starting to wonder if Lark has taken a special interest in my products just because of me, or if he's always the one to run things in this company. I'm not sure which answer I'd prefer. I hope he's not just pretending to love my products because he wants me to keep sleeping with him.

But somehow I doubt that. I watched him go over my palette that first time, and there was genuine admiration on his face. Plus, Lark doesn't strike me as the kind of guy who lies about what he feels. Even if it would be more convenient to do that.

For example, today. As Marcel leads me around set, introducing me to the different makeup artists and standing by as I explain my color ideas to them—each of the artists seems nicer than the last, and more encouraging of my work. But the whole time, every time I glance over, I find Lark watching me intently, his gaze laser focused.

And any time we move to the next counter to talk to another artist, his hand brushes my thigh, my waist, the edge of my bicep. He's constantly finding excuses to touch me lightly, teasing, the small smile on his face whenever he does, telling me he knows exactly what he's doing.

Every time, I force myself to turn away. To stay focused. To continue with my pitches as though Lark isn't standing just a foot or two away, those bright eyes of his boring into mine, the scent of his cologne mingled with his aftershave trailing after me like a memory I can't shake. The memory of him spread-eagling me across my bed and bending down to kiss his way between my thighs, his tongue leaving a searing hot trail in its wake, until he reached home, lapping at my pussy like it was the sweetest thing he'd ever tasted.

Oh, God. I force the image from my head.

By the time I finish handing out all my supplies and presenting to everyone on set, it's time for the models to arrive. Finally, I get a bit of a breather, although—"You absolutely have to stay to watch!" Marcel gushes. "This is the most exciting part, getting to see your work used firsthand." He drags a chair for me and another for Lark over to the edge of the stage, from which we have a view of all the different stations where models have been seated to have their makeup done, and in the other direction, the camera backdrop where they'll be getting their photos taken.

It means, too, that everyone in this studio has a perfect view of the two of us, as well.

Which is why I tense up after, the moment we sit down, Lark slides a hand onto my knee. "You're angry with me," he says, his voice a low thrum. He leans close, just a bare inch from my shoulder, and I can barely think through the sudden pounding of my heart.

My eyes jump around the room. Marcel is in the corner talking to a man he introduced us to earlier, the photographer, although I can't remember his name. I'm so bad with names.

"Cassidy." Apparently heedless of the fact that we're in public, right here in the middle of this studio, Lark reaches up to tuck a fingertip under my chin. That's all it takes. He tilts my face toward his, his touch gentle as a makeup brush on a cheekbone. "What's wrong?"

This close, I can see those flecks throughout his whorled

green eyes again. I watch his individual black lashes, the slight part in his lips. He's looking at me with such sincerity, such open honesty, that I can hardly bear it. I flinch backward, away from him. "We're in public," I say, gesturing around.

Lark doesn't follow my gesture. His gaze remains focused straight on me. "So?"

"So, don't you care if people notice you flirting with your new investment opportunity?" I reply, unable to keep a note of bitterness from my voice.

"I don't care what they think. I care what *you* think. And clearly I've done something to upset you, based on how you're acting today, although I cannot for the life of me figure out what."

I set my jaw hard, and tear my gaze from his to stare blindly across the floor. I should be enjoying this moment, watching the fruits of my labor come to fruition or what have you. Marcel would kick me if he knew I barely even processed the artists hard at work with my supplies all around the studio. But all I can think about is the man beside me.

A man I owe an explanation, at the very least.

I clear my throat after a pause. "The other day. After you sent the men to deliver my sofa..."

"Is that it?" Lark's eyebrows climbed his forehead. "I'm sorry; I really thought getting rid of that old thing would be helpful—"

"No, it's not that." I wave him quiet. Meet his gaze again. "Sheryl asked me to lunch. And talking to her, hearing her side of things, I just..." I shake my head. "I can't do this, Lark. I won't be the person who stands in the way of a second chance at happiness with your wife. Even if she is your ex."

For a moment, we only stare at one another, his eyebrows climbing his forehead. And then, to my surprise, red heat flushes through Lark's face. "You're joking, right." He says it so flatly that it takes me a moment to register he's actually waiting for a response.

"It's just... it seems complicated. I don't know if you two are really finished—"

"I told you that we are." He slides off his chair and crosses to stand in front of mine, a hand on either arm, his face hovering an inch from mine. "I don't give a fuck what Sheryl thinks I should do, or how I should be living my life. I'm the one who lived through our breakup. You have no idea what she was—" He breaks off, scowls. "How she..." He shakes his head. "It's *my* decision now. I get to choose how I live *my* life, and what my future is going to be. I choose my own happy endings from now on."

The heat in his voice, and the passion in his face, both surprise me. Throw me. He seems angry, almost, but more than that. *Desperate.*

He breaks away from me and spins around, one hand running through his hair in a tight fist. "God. That..." He clamps his lips shut tight, and a frustrated growl escapes. "You don't know what happened, Cassidy," he says now, back still to me. "And if I have it my way, you won't. The past is the past, and I've buried it."

When he turns back around, all the fury has gone from his expression. There's only the passion I've always seen on his face when he looks at me, the sheer desire. He moves closer once more, and I forget where we are. I forget we're sitting in the middle of a crowded studio, with camera crews and models and stagehands all surrounding us. I look at Lark, and he's all I can see. It's tunnel vision.

I have a feeling it's the same for him.

He tips forward until our mouths are a breath apart, until we're sharing the same air. "I want *you* to be my future," he says, softly. "The future I choose. The *woman* I choose. If you believe nothing else I said, believe that."

My heart leaps into my throat. My lips part, and his eyes drop for a split second.

"Cassidy..."

"Kiss me goddamn it, Lark," I breathe.

His lips collide with mine, and I sink into him. Slide my arms up to wrap around his neck as he draws me up and off my chair, pulling me to him.

I don't notice our audience until we break apart, breathless, and Marcel starts to clap, a sly little smirk playing at the corner of his mouth.

"Now I see why you were *so* effusive about this one, my friend." Marcel winks at Lark, who grins, one arm draped casually around my shoulder.

I lean into him for support, my heart still racing, and try to drag myself back into work mode, back onto the set. All I can think about, though, is the man beside me. The fact that I can feel his heartbeat racing in tune with my own, everywhere our bodies touch.

8

CASSIDY

After a long day at set, all I want to do is go home and collapse into bed. But we barely make it five steps past the studio door before Lark pins me against the brick wall of the parking lot and kisses me again, searing, invigorating.

"That was torture," he murmurs, lips inches from mine. "Being so close to you all day, unable to touch you..."

I drape my arms over his shoulders, and I kiss him slowly. Languorously. Taking my time, now that I know we have all the time in the world. "You can touch me now," I breathe when we break apart, and fire flashes in his gaze.

"Trust me, I've been thinking about this all afternoon." A studio door opens nearby, and I glance over his shoulder. One of the models descends the staircase, still wearing my makeup on her eyes.

I'm not sure I'll ever get used to that. Or get used to having my own photo taken. I posed for that last, and I was so nervous, but Lark held my gaze the whole time, flashed me thumbs up and smiled whenever I hesitated or started to get shy.

By the end, the photographer told me I was a natural.

But I don't think so. I think I just had the support I needed to power through.

Lark follows my gaze to the girl, who's followed out of the building by a few more members of the camera crew, hauling out equipment. "Come on." He grabs my hand and practically pulls me through the parking lot behind him, laughing.

"Where are we going?" I demand, but he doesn't answer. Not until we reach a BMW on the far side of the lot, the windows tinted. He unlocks it, and I pause, eyebrows lifted. "I should have known you'd have a bougie car," I say.

"She's not bougie, she's vintage," Lark protests. Then, to my confusion, he opens the back door.

"What are—" I start to ask. I don't have time to finish. He grabs my waist and lifts me bodily, his mouth colliding with mine, his tongue parting my lips to wrestle with my own.

I'm so lost in the kiss, I almost don't notice what he's doing until he spins us around and lays me down in the backseat. Then he climbs in after and shuts the door.

I stifle a laugh, watching him. "Are we back in high school?" I tease.

"I can't wait until we get home." He reaches down to push the hem of my skirt up around my waist. I gasp as his fingers brush my upper thighs, hot and rough. "My cock is so fucking hard I'm going to lose it unless I have you."

He punctuates those words with rough kisses on my stomach, pushing my shirt up and out of the way too. Then his lips press to my inner thighs, one after the other. Down to the backs of my knees, the edges of my calves. His tongue knows all the right spots to find to make me arch up against him, twist against the seat.

For all his talk about needing me, he sure takes his time teasing me, toying with me. His fingertips trace the edges of my panties, then he presses a thumb against my clit through them, trailing down to my pussy lips, smirking.

"I love how wet you get for me, Cassidy."

My breath catches, and I reach down to try to pull him closer, on top of me. He's lying along my leg, and I can feel the hard press of his cock against my thigh. But he won't give me what I want, not yet.

"First I want you ready for me," he says. And then his face is between my thighs, pushing, nudging them apart. His stubble grazes the soft skin there, rough and deliciously scratchy. He catches my panties in his teeth and drags them down, making my breath catch.

I run my hands through his hair, then bury them in it, in fists, as he starts to lick across my mound. His tongue flicks the edges of my clit, and I gasp, arching up off the seat. He cups his hands underneath me, squeezes my ass hard enough to make me groan with want.

And all the while, his tongue continues its slow exploration, tracing each lip of my pussy before he delves between them, lapping and sucking at me. Just when I think I'm going to lose my mind from desire, he finally arches up and pushes his own jeans down.

I reach to catch his boxers, pulling them off myself, and marveling at his length when his cock springs free. I always forget how thick he is.

"Feel that?" he murmurs, as I fold both hands around his base and stroke along his length, my thumbs tracing the thick vein that stands out along his shaft. "That's how fucking hard I am for you, Cassidy. I can't stop thinking about you, constantly..."

"I know the feeling," I confess, and our eyes lock. He bends until our noses brush, our eyes inches apart. I feel him gently take my wrists, both of my wrists wrapped in one of his large hands. And he raises them up over my head and pins me back against the seat, before his lips feather across my cheekbone, my jawline. Down the edge of my neck.

At the same time, with his free hand, he spreads my legs. I raise them up, wrap them around his torso, and feel my hips lift off the seat, striving toward him.

He pauses just long enough to slide on a condom, and then I feel him at the entrance of my pussy, poised right there. I'm already soaking wet, but still he waits, his teeth grazing my neck, making me gasp.

"I want to fuck you now," he says, his voice a barely repressed growl.

"Please," I gasp. That's all he needs. He pushes inside me in one smooth thrust, and I groan, arching up off the seat against him, savoring the feeling of his cock filling my tight pussy.

"Every time." He leans back to look at me, paused there, his cock filling me up. "Every time, I forget how fucking good you feel, Cassidy." He pulls back out of me, just a little, making me gasp in protest. But a second later he thrusts back into me, his hips perfectly angled so the slight curve at the tip of his cock drags against my inner wall, right over my G-spot. "God, your pussy is a fucking marvel." He pulls out, thrusts back in again, and I make a little mewling sound, which makes him smirk, bending close again.

"I love those little sounds you make," he tells me, his lips on my throat, my neck.

I let my head fall back, my back arching up. "I love how you get them out of me," I tell him, which makes him smile against my neck, before he starts to thrust harder, faster. To really fuck me, the way only Lark ever has.

My hands are still pinned over my head, but I move my hips in time with his, thrusting against him, my clit brushing up against his pelvic bone with every deep thrust. Before long, I'm nearing the edge, breathing hard, and he's grinning at me, knowing exactly what effect he has on me, almost better than I know it myself.

"That's it, Cassidy," he says, his voice a low thrum of command. "Come for me."

I'm so near the edge he doesn't need to tell me twice. I let out a cry, and he continues to thrust into me, fucking me so that the orgasm spikes through my veins, and the pleasure keeps coming, starts to build again as he pounds into me.

I lose track of time, of space. By the time Lark releases my hands to grab my hips, near his own edge, I'm close to coming again myself. I reach up to wrap my arms around him, my legs tightening around his torso. I dig my nails into the fine muscles of his back, and he pulls me up off the seat with the force of his thrusts.

"I want to feel you come," I pant against his shoulder. "In me."

It doesn't take much more asking than that. Lark growls and reaches down to grip my ass hard with one hand, his other tight around my hip. He thrusts into me again, again, and his gaze flicks to mine. He lets out a groan that turns into my name as he finishes, deep in me, still thrusting his hips, and I arch up against him, tightening my pussy around him, trying to milk every last drop.

When he finally sags against me, both of us slick with sweat, a pleasant, relaxed sensation spreads through my whole body, tingling and numbing at once. He leans up to kiss me again, and I can taste my own sweat on his lips. Then he leans back, smiling.

"Let's go home," he says, simple as that.

* * *

We wind up wrapped in sheets in his bed, an enormous pizza between us, and the cheesiest horror movie I have ever been subjected to playing on TV.

"They are *not* about to go toward that sound!" I protest, waving at the screen.

Beside me, Lark laughs and tucks me harder against his side. "It wouldn't be a proper horror movie if humans didn't act like they'd had their brains surgically removed," he points out.

I elbow him playfully, and he leans over to tickle me in retribution, which makes me squirm away, although not before I grab another slice of pizza. "You're the worst," I tell him, then take an enormous bite. It makes a faint string of cheese melt down my chin, and Lark arches an eyebrow, watching me, amused.

"*I'm* the worst? You're the one getting grease on my sheets."

I flush, and glance down, worried he's right, but he only laughs.

"Kidding. Anyway, if we do stain them, more reason to get the maid service in tomorrow." He shrugs and leans back on the bed, stretching out, unconcerned.

After a moment more of hesitation, still a little paranoid I've spilled pizza sauce on his sheets, even though he clearly doesn't mind paying to get them cleaned, I follow his lead and nestle back up beside him, just in time for the last remaining virgin on screen to be eaten by a monster.

I groan. "See? I told her not to follow that noise! Why do the women always die first? Women definitely would be the smarter ones in an actual apocalypse."

Lark snorts. "But then how else would we motivate our leading male to go save the day? Clearly the ladies are just there as props for his growth." Heavy sarcasm drips from his tone.

I smirk at him. "Someone's a closet feminist."

"There's nothing closet about it." He wraps an arm around my waist and drags me even closer to him, until I'm practically in his lap, pizza and all. I protest, but he ignores me and kisses my neck, my shoulder. "Women are the better half of the species, I've long since accepted this. And I treat them as such." With another wicked grin, he reaches around me to press his lips to mine.

I sink back against him, a pleasant warmth flooding my belly, all the way out to my limbs.

I've never done something like this with a guy. Just hung out in bed and watched cheesy movies. There's something about Lark that not only excites me, but also makes me feel like I can relax around him. Truly be myself. I've never felt this way with another guy—certainly not with Norman, or any of the other people I dated briefly here and there.

I can't help but wonder... maybe this time, things really will be different. In a good way.

9

———

CASSIDY

The next day, Lark refuses to let me work. "You just spent weeks breaking your back to meet all those deadlines," he tells me, in between nipping and licking his way down my body that morning.

It's my new favorite way to wake up, I have to admit.

"Today, you're taking some time off," he insists. "Not just for yourself. For me too." He winks. Then he pushes his face between my thighs, and that pretty much settles it.

After a long, slow, languorous wake-up—which involves several failed attempts to actually make it out of bed—we finally get dressed and head out of the apartment. Lark won't tell me where he's taking me, but there are some clues. For one, the big cooler of drinks he packs, along with a blanket. For another, the towels I spot rolled up in his trunk, beside which he tucks everything.

We live near the shore, but I never actually go to the beach much. I mean to, especially in summer, but it's always such a production to do it—and I'm always so busy with work—that I rarely get around to it.

Which is why it surprises me when Lark drives us

further up the coast than I've ventured before, past all the familiar and touristy beaches that I'm used to visiting.

"I'm taking you to my favorite spot," is all he'll tell me, whenever I ask.

The further we drive from the city, the fresher the air outside feels. I roll it down, and we both sing along, out of tune, to the songs playing on the radio. Every time I steal a glance over at him, I catch him doing the same to me, and we both laugh, hearts lighter than I think they've ever been. At least I know mine is.

When he rests his hand on the gear shift—because of course his fancy BMW is manual, and he goes on at length about how much better they are to drive and handle—I let my hand rest over his, and he turns his palm up, laces his fingers through mine.

His thumb strokes the back of my hand, and just that simple motion is enough to set off a fresh cascade of butterflies in my stomach.

By the time we turn off the road, I'm teasing him. "We're lost aren't we?"

"Have a little faith," he fires back, before he pulls my hand up to his mouth and turns it upright, spreading my fingers to kiss my open palm. That touch. I feel heat all the way down into my belly, and hot between my thighs. I shift against the seat, trying not to let the flush creep up my neck to my face. And probably failing completely, to judge by the little smirk he aims in my direction.

Then I notice the road we're winding down, and my lips part in surprise. The road winds down the edge of the cliffs at this part of the shoreline, growing narrower with every zig and zag. My stomach drops at the sight of the drop. But even more than that, at the bottom...

"Where is this?" I ask, my eyebrows climbing my forehead. I've lived here—or at least, within a short drive of here—my entire life, and I've never been to this part of the coast. The beach at the bottom is small, but beautiful. It's cupped between two sheer cliff faces, a little slice of white sand that looks like the Caribbean. The water, I know, will be colder, but still, from here it's a gorgeous, deep blue.

"I found it when I was a teenager," he explains, as we reach the last loop of road. There's not even a parking lot, really. Just a small gravel turnaround, with no marked signs. He parks at the very end of the road and turns to meet my gaze. "The summer after my dad died, I used to come here all the time to think."

"Oh, I didn't... I'm so sorry, Lark." I squeeze his hand.

He just smiles. "It was a long time ago. I still miss him, but..." He squeezes back. "Whenever I would come here, and lie on the sand just watching the waves..." He glances away from me again, out over the water. "I used to feel connected to him again, you know? To something bigger than myself."

I follow his gaze, out over the sea. The waves are big—this beach would be a surfer's dream. But I'm glad we have it all to ourselves. It feels like we've escaped to a private world, just the two of us, and here, we can be anyone we want to be. Here, whatever this is growing between us doesn't need to be complicated or messy. We can just... be.

"I can see that," I murmur, and Lark flashes me a smile.

"Come on." He steps out and crosses to open my door before I can even reach for it. I laugh when he does—I'm not used to guys treating me like this, opening doors for me. But he insists. He also insists on carrying everything, despite me offering to help with the umbrella at least, multiple times.

I trail him down to the shoreline, and together we lay

out the blanket, and he digs the umbrella into the sand while I open the cooler. "Champagne?" I laugh. "Is that a beach drink?"

"It is when you have something to celebrate," he replies, after he's finished aligning the umbrella to give us the best shade. He drops down beside me, and pops the cork to pour us both glasses. He even brought proper champagne flutes, albeit the plastic kind, I assume so we don't break glass here on the beach.

When he's finished, he holds out my glass, and raises his own.

"What are we celebrating?" I ask, my eyes sparkling with amusement.

"Easy." He taps his glass against mine. "Us finding each other. You're easily the best thing to happen to me in years, Cassidy. I want you to know that."

My heart skips. I conceal my pleased flush with a long sip of champagne. It's delicious, the bubbles tickling my nose on the way down. Then I dig my toes into the sand and glance out over the water. The waves are big today, wild and cascading. But the sound those big waves make is relaxing, more than anything. A crash and shush, over and over, that would lull me to sleep in a heartbeat if I let it.

"Did you used to come here with Sheryl?" I ask, because I'm an idiot, and apparently I can't just let myself enjoy good moments.

Lark glances over at me, his eyes unreadable in the reflected sunlight off the water. "No," he says, after a quiet pause. "I've never brought anyone else here. I wanted to keep it to myself; it's always been my private place to think."

Holding his gaze, my heartbeat quickens. "Why bring me, then?"

He sets his champagne aside. Then he reaches out to

take mine, and tucks it into the sand, before he leans in to cup my chin, drawing my face toward his, until we're mere inches apart, his breath a tickle over my lips. "Because I want you to know me. And because I want to know you, too, Cassidy. All of you. I don't want any secrets between us anymore."

"Neither do I." My eyes jump back and forth between us. "What you see with me is what you get."

"And you're mine," he breathes. It's not a question. A statement, one that sends a thrill through me.

"Yes," I murmur, because it feels like I should answer him anyway. We're so close. Another centimeter and our lips would touch. I tilt my face up, but he doesn't kiss me. Not yet.

"Just as I'm yours. I promise, Cassidy." Only then does he kiss me, slow and sensuous. Before, our kisses had been searing fire, electricity. This one is more like lava, a slow burn that spreads throughout my entire body. I wind my hands through his hair, and for a moment, we're the only two people in the world, here in our private bubble. Here where nothing can touch us.

It feels like the moment lasts forever, the whole day stretching out before us, and beyond that, the weeks, the months. We have all the time in the world, I think in that moment.

What a fool I was.

10

CASSIDY

I stand outside the therapist's office, pacing back and forth, trying to build up my courage. I didn't tell Lark I was coming here today, or any of my friends. Hell, I barely even admitted to myself what I was planning to do, until I showed up in the parking lot this morning with the appointment penciled into my planner.

Lark and I have been going out for a couple of weeks now. We haven't given it a label or anything. I don't want to rush this. I want to savor every minute. But ever since that day at the beach, we've spent nearly every night together, either at my apartment or more often at his—his bed is just bigger. It's more practical.

But more than once, I catch my old self peering through. It doesn't matter how many times Lark tells me he cares about me, or how often he says he's never met a woman like me. That voice in the back of my head, the one that was already prevalent since long before I met Norman, but which only got worse over the duration of our relationship, returns to hiss in my ear.

He doesn't really love you. He can't. There's no way a man like him will ever be interested in a girl like you for long.

It's all bullshit. I *know* it's bullshit. But at my weakest moments, alone in my apartment after Lark leaves in the mornings, or when I'm out on a run near his apartment and eying all the other perfect mothers dressed in designer clothing with their tight, fit, skinny bodies, I can't help but hear that voice again.

So, I finally decided to do something about it. Or at least, ask someone what I can do. I don't really know how all this works. The receptionist on the phone was super polite and nice, but I've never talked to a therapist before. I have no idea what she's going to say.

Maybe she'll confirm my worst fears. Tell me I really am unlovable, or that I'm just doing the same thing with Lark that I've done in previous relationships—throwing myself into a messy situation because I can't handle dating someone who's nice and normal and available.

It's not that messy, I argue to myself.

Right, argues the nasty voice straight back. *You're just working with him and his ex-wife both, all while secretly sleeping with him. After you promised her there was nothing between you two.*

I haven't talked to Sheryl much since our lunch outing the one time. Lark seems to have taken over handling my company—or rather, he seems to have always been the most involved one, and these days Sheryl's given up on keeping up. I have the occasional phone call with her, but it's cursory, just check-ins and making sure I know what's up next on the docket.

After the big photoshoot at the magazine, which turned out to be a big hit, orders have been flooding in from all over the world. The next goal will be for me to ramp up production to keep up with those orders. Sheryl and Lark gave me funding and full discretion over what manufacturing company I want to partner with as I ramp up, and I've spent all my work time over the last week interviewing different factories. I know I want to work with a green company, one that pays their employees a fair wage and will only use organic products in my makeup, ones that haven't been tested on animals.

That, it turns out, narrows my field of potential manufacturers by a lot.

But earlier this week, Lark and I met with a company based nearby, which met all of those criteria. Right away, I fell in love with the way they do business. It didn't hurt that the woman who led us on the tour was friendly, smart, and answered all of my questions without batting an eyelash.

By the end of the day, Lark and I stepped aside to talk about the decision in hushed whispers, and I was bright-eyed with enthusiasm. "It's got to be her," I insisted.

"You know best," he told me, with a wink. "But, if you asked my opinion, I'd agree." Then he called Sheryl for me, to talk her into the idea.

I was grateful for his unyielding support. I'm grateful for Sheryl's, too, although during my few phone conversations with her, I always come away feeling nauseous with guilt.

She doesn't know about Lark and me yet. Lark keeps asking me when we can tell her. He doesn't want to sneak around anymore. He wants to be able to declare his affection for me out in the open.

But I can't stop thinking about the lunch I had with Sheryl. The promise I made her. *There's nothing between me and him.* It was a lie then, and it's become a worse one now.

So, before we break the news, I wanted to get myself right. See this therapist, talk through my own past issues.

Maybe then I'll be up to facing the truth, to going official with Lark before the whole world.

With one more deep breath, I start up the steps into the office. There are at least half a dozen floors, and the map inside the entrance is confusing as hell. I wind up wandering in circles down the end of one hallway, completely lost. The floor map says I'm looking for room 312, but this is room 305, and the corridor dead-ends here. Behind me are rooms 300-305, and beyond that just the elevator bank.

With a suppressed groan, I get ready to double back, when one of the doors nearby creaks open half an inch. There's a woman standing in the doorway with her back to me, talking.

"I think we really made some great progress today," she's saying, in that voice I've come to recognize as the TV therapists' voice. Calm and soothing.

The door that's partially open reads *Marital Counseling* in black block letters, along with the name of a therapist beneath it, a Dr. Ann Latrobe.

"Just work on the exercises I've assigned to you, and I'll see you both back here next week," she continues, still audible as I cross past the door and continue up the hallway, most of my attention focused on the door numbers, searching for my own entrance.

Someone within the room, a man, murmurs quietly, followed by another woman, and then the door fully opens, the doctor's bright voice growing louder in the hallway behind me.

"Always a pleasure, Mr. and Mrs. Anderson," she's saying.

My heart skids in my chest. Leaps into my throat.

But I tell myself I'm being ridiculous. It's a common

name, after all. There are probably dozens of Andersons in this city alone.

Except then I hear the reply. In a low, devastatingly familiar voice. "We'll see you next week, same time."

No. My feet have stopped moving. I realize I should keep walking, get out of sight. But I can't force myself to step forward, can't force my legs to function. I've forgotten all about the room I'm looking for, or in fact why I'm even here myself. All I can think about is that voice.

And the other, soft feminine voice that joins in a moment later. "That went well, I thought. Don't you?"

I can't hear the mumbled reply through the rushing sound in my ears. But I do register the footsteps starting up the tile floors in my direction, at the far end of the hallway. Finally, belatedly, I spur myself into motion, moving faster than I could explain, if anyone were to stop me at this point.

I don't care. The last thing I want to do is be caught here like this. Spying. Overhearing something I'm clearly not meant to overhear.

I make it to the elevator bank without incident, and hurry toward the opposite wing on the far side of the hall. *Rooms 306-315,* like a total idiot I failed to notice that on my first trip through this hall. Which is why I wound up over-hearing something I wasn't meant to hear, seeing something I shouldn't have seen.

There's a reflective mirror opposite the elevator bank. Just before I duck around the far corner, I catch a single glimpse in it.

Behind me, at the far end of the hallway, I glimpse Sheryl and Lark walking side-by-side. Mr. and Mrs. Anderson, fresh out of marriage counseling. And, apparently, very much not divorced.

I can still hear him at the windswept beach he took me

to, the beach where he claimed he'd never brought anyone else. *I don't want any secrets between us anymore*, he said, his voice a low thrum, so real I can almost feel his breath against my neck, warm at the edge of my ear.

How *could* he? How could he say that, how could he make that promise? When all along, he knew he was harboring the biggest secret of all?

My stomach flips again, and I have to pause to lean back against the hard paneled wall of the therapists' office, feeling sick to my stomach. Tears sting at the backs of my eyes. That nasty little voice returns triply loud, far worse than ever before.

You see? it hisses in my ear. *I told you this was too good to be true. Of course a man like Lark could never fall for a girl like you. Nobody wants you.*

I press my hand over my mouth to stifle the sound, all too aware of the distant ping of the elevator, the low chatter of Lark and Sheryl's voices as they climb into it. I manage to hold it together until the voices disappear. Until I'm alone in the empty hallway, the minutes ticking away, my therapy appointment entirely forgotten.

Only then do I let the tears fall down my face, and the cries shake my shoulders.

Because right there and then, I realize what I need to do. Lark and I are over.

11

___

CASSIDY

"I can't get enough of you, Cassidy Marks. You know that?" The fire in Lark's words is secondary only in heat to the sensation of his hot mouth, moving along the edge of my jaw. He catches the tip of my ear in his mouth, gently bites down until I gasp at the faint sting. Then he grins and keeps moving, his lips gliding down my neck, teeth grazing the delicate skin ever so lightly.

I arch up against him, but it's no use. He has my hands pinned over my head, both wrists held in one single large hand of his. His body, lying atop mine, is so strong and steel-sturdy, every press of his perfectly chiseled abs digging into my soft curves. I can only twist a little beneath him, enjoying the complete loss of control, the way he's in charge now, and oh, he knows exactly what to do.

He peels my shirt off with his free hand and uses it to tangle my hands to the headboard. I don't mind, except for that it means I can't trace my fingers along the edges of his muscles.

But it's fine, because a second later, he drags his own

shirt over his head and tosses it aside, his muscles gleaming in the moonlight that shines through my bedroom window.

"I've dreamt of you every damn night for so long," he says, his voice low, thrumming with desire. "I've dreamt of all the places I want to touch you..." His hands brush my curves ever so slightly, making me tremble. "The places I want to kiss..."

His lips brush the hollow of my throat, the sharp juts of my collarbone. He flattens his tongue against my breastbone and traces it down, down, between my breasts. He cups them each in one hand, his palm rough against the smooth, supple skin. I can tell my nipples are already rock hard, but they only get stiffer when he rolls his tongue over to one breast and sucks my whole areola between his lips.

I moan, my back arching up off my sheets, which I can tell are already damp from sweat.

He laughs faintly, his breath a hot white gust against my chest, as he shifts to the other breast, his tongue swirling around it. "I love watching you react," he tells me, smirking up at me.

From here, in the moonlight, those his deep green eyes snag on mine, impossible to look away from. He's got the kind of gaze a girl could drown in. "Well," I breathe, still trying to catch my breath, to make my lungs function normally. "You definitely know how to make me squirm."

He grins at that, his teeth flashing in the dim light. "Oh, I plan to do a lot more than that tonight." His palm traces over my stomach, flattened against my curves. Down, down, until he reaches the fabric of my thin panties. When did he take off my pants? I don't even remember. The whole world has gone hazy at the edges, and I have eyes only for this man.

For all the dirty things he does to me at night.

"I want to hear you screaming my name by the end of this," he says, voice low and thrumming with urgent energy.

Then he hooks a thumb under the edge of my panties, nudges them down my thighs, and I gasp as the cool evening air hits my bare pussy. God, I can already tell I'm wet. But the situation only grows more urgent as Lark bends to kiss my navel, his tongue flicking into the narrow hole there, his 5 o'clock shadow grazing my smooth stomach, making me tickle and squirm.

He kisses his way lower, until his beard grazes the top of my mound. I gasp, and he grins up at me, unrepentant. "Yes," he says, his voice a command. "More of that." Then he flicks his tongue over my clit, expertly, because God knows he's always been able to find it more easily than any other man I've ever slept with.

I arch up off the bed, and he takes advantage of the motion, sliding both hands underneath me to grip my ass tightly in his fists.

He licks my inner thigh, from just above my knee, all the way up to the crease where my leg meets my hip. Then, before I can twist and press my hip closer to his face, he pulls back, licking up the other leg the same way. Slow. Torturously so.

"Dammit, Lark," I murmur, my head drifting back toward the pillow.

"Did you expect me not to tease you into oblivion tonight?" He clicks his tongue, smirking. "You know me better than that by now, Cassidy."

When he dips again, he spreads both my legs with firm, strong hands. Then he traces his tongue along the outer lips of my pussy, slow, savoring.

"I always forget how incredible you taste," he murmurs, just before he parts my pussy lips with two rough fingertips, and presses his tongue between, lapping at me, tracing the tip of his tongue around and around my entrance.

My groan turns into a moan, and I twist against the sheets, my hips bucking toward his face.

He lets me, and I wrap both thighs around his face, pressing myself up against him, so I can feel the brush of his beard against my inner thighs, rough, almost tickling, in comparison to that fucking tongue of his.

The tongue that he's pressing deep into my folds now, lapping back and forth along the length of my slit.

"Louder," he orders, but he doesn't need to tell me twice. He pushes the tip of his tongue inside me, and I moan loud enough that I'm surprised my downstairs neighbors don't pound on the floorboards. Then he swirls that tongue inside me, and I buck and twist, before I settle into a rocking motion, arching up off the bed and against his face as he pushes his tongue further into me, until his lips are pressed against my pussy lips, his tongue deep inside me, curled and stroking along my inner walls.

He hits my G-spot, and my breath hitches. I'm saying something, begging him to keep going, but I can hardly even process my own voice through the fog of pleasure in my brain.

Just when I'm at the edge though, right on the brink of orgasm, he pulls his tongue out of me. I groan in protest. "Lark," I start, but he's already over me, naked too, and when did he lose *his* pants? Normally I love that part. Watching him slowly strip, until his cock is bare before me, thick and throbbing and ready for me.

Just like he is now.

He positions himself at my entrance with a sly look. "I need to fuck you now, Cassidy. I cannot wait another fucking second," he says. He pushes into me, a slow, smooth motion that makes my moans turn into faint little cries of pleasure.

The way he stretches me, fills me... I've never felt like this before. As if I'm so completely full, all the way up.

He lies down along me, and I know I'm sticky with sweat, but so is he, the mingled scent of our bodies and our sex filling the room as he grips my hips, his lips colliding with mine, his tongue parting my lips so that I taste my own juices on his mouth.

When he draws back, it's only to lock gazes with me, his intent and intense as ever. "I've missed this," he breathes, which throws me for a second, because haven't we been doing it all night?

But then he's pulling out, thrusting back into me, and I lose track of our conversation of words.

At some point he must have untied my hands, because I have use of them again. I wrap them around his strong torso, my legs around his hips, and I pull him down against me, thrusting my hips up against his to drive his cock deeper with every thrust.

He starts to move faster, harder. Losing all control. I love this part, watching him lose it.

"God." He runs a hand through my hair, then grabs a fistful and pulls my head to the side, bending to bite at my neck gently, before he kisses it, alternately biting, kissing, until I know he's going to leave a mark. He pulls back just far enough to laugh faintly, his breath ghosting over the heated skin he just bruised. "I wanted to make sure you'd remember this," he says.

As if I could forget.

But he's moving faster, harder again, and I buck against him, thrusting in time with him, until the whole bed is slamming into the wall, over and over, and the orgasm rushes toward me again, my clit already throbbing from his earlier ministrations. His cock seems to hit just the right angle every time, my G-spot thrilling with sensation. I let out a strangled cry, as the orgasm sweeps through my body, a rush of pleasure all the way from my scalp down to my toes.

It seems to go on and on. I can feel myself tightening around him, convulsive, feel the deep ache of his cock as he continues to fuck me, close to his own finish. His breath speeds up, his heart races against mine, and—

Buzz.

I inhale sharply, my eyes snapping open.

I'm alone in my bed, the sheets tangled around my naked body, soaked in sweat. At least some of the dream was right. I groan and sit up, rubbing at my temple where it throbs.

Oh, right. Hangover. Because I spent last night with Becky drinking wine in my living room. Because I'd been refusing to hang out with her for weeks, because at first I was busy all the time with work, and then, for the last week...

I roll over and bury my face in the pillow, as reality hits me. The same way it's been doing every morning for the last seven days. Every time I wake up, all I want to do is plunge back into sleep. At least when I'm sleeping, I don't have to face reality. I don't have to deal with the fact that Lark—*my* Lark, the first man I've connected with in years, the first man I've *ever* had chemistry like this with...

Is a married man. He's taken. And whatever messy split or makeup he's in the middle of, I cannot get involved.

No matter how much it makes my heart hurt to walk away. I did it because it was the right thing to do.

Another buzz sounds through the apartment, and I

groan again, louder. Dammit. Who's here? I roll out of bed and fish around under my bed for a night shirt. I must have taken it off myself in the throes of my stupid sex dream.

I've been having them more and more. Every night since I called things off with Lark. I'd been too chickenshit to do it in person, especially since he nearly caught me in the hallway of the therapists' offices. I'd gone to visit a therapist in order to take better care of myself, to figure out my own relationship issues, and why I have such low self-esteem.

Instead, ironically, I found a fresh reminder of exactly why, when I stumbled across Lark and his supposedly ex-wife Sheryl leaving couples' counseling, answering to Mr. and Mrs. Anderson.

That same night, I texted him. *I can't do this anymore.*

Since then, he's called and texted dozens of times. I hit ignore every time, deleted the texts unread. Better not to even slightly tempt myself.

Eventually, I know, I'll have to see him again for work. Anderson Investments, which Lark and Sheryl co-own, remains my little makeup startup company's biggest—and only—investor. But thankfully, for the last week, it's been Sheryl who's sent me emails asking for updates; Sheryl who's written to let me know about upcoming events and orders that I'll need to work on; Sheryl who's become my main point of contact.

I don't know if that's because she told Lark she wanted to take over, or because Lark asked her to after taking the hint that I don't want to see him. Either way, at least it's giving me time to get over him. To get over the stupid fantasies I'd started to have, the dreams that maybe this time, this relationship, might be different...

Another buzz at the front door. "I'm coming," I grumble, and pad out into the living room to hit the button that will open the downstairs door. The speaker is broken, so I have no idea who I just let in. Not until the doorbell rings, and my headache starts to throb again, double-time.

"Good morning!" exclaims Becky, looking far too bright-eyed and bushy-tailed for a girl who spent last night drinking even more than I did, while I moped on my couch.

My new, beautiful designer couch, which Lark bought for me a few weeks ago, after the first night we spent together. He spilled makeup all over my old, ragged one.

When Becky complimented me on the new sofa last night, I almost burst into tears all over again.

Now, she shoves something at me. Pastries, I realize belatedly, taking in the scent of sugar and yeast coming from the box. "Figured you could use a pick-me-up before your big thing today."

"My what?" I ask through the buzz in my ears, the throb between my temples. All I can think about is how embarrassed I am about the mess I was last night. Well. About that, and about the sex dream that woke me this morning.

God, even in my dreams that asshole knows how to make me come harder than anyone in my entire—

"Don't you have the big TV thingie today?" Becky asks, a moue of concern on her face. "You mentioned it last night. Before our impromptu cursing of He Who Shall Not Be Named and everything he did to you."

It's coming back to me, slowly. Becky insisting that since it was a full moon, we should stick our heads off of my fire escape and howl at the moon, demanding it curse Lark Anderson with bad sex for a decade, in retribution for him hurting me.

My face flushes bright red. God, I hope none of the neighbors heard the details.

Then I process the rest of her sentence. TV interview. On

the Right Now Show. With Jackie Shells, international supermodel, who thanks to some convincing from Sheryl— and a heap of samples of the makeup from me—has just recently agreed to become the face of my makeup brand.

Sorry. *Our* makeup brand.

And that's in... I check the clock over my stove top, heart pounding. Less than two hours. "Shit." I practically race toward the bedroom.

Becky watches me go with a smirk. "Relax," she calls over the sounds of me tearing through my closet for the outfit I have all planned out, but which I'd forgotten to actually lay out last night. Because I hadn't been planning on getting roaring drunk. I hadn't planned on being so distracted all this week that I forgot about the most important interview I'll probably ever have in my entire life.

"The Right Now studio's only a twenty minute drive from here," Becky calls into the bedroom. "I'll drive you. I'm just parked downstairs."

"I was going to get there early and run through prep questions," I exclaim. "I was going to talk to Sheryl for like an hour beforehand. Fuck!" I realize the skirt I wanted to wear is crumpled up in the laundry hamper.

Becky knocks at the door jam. "Can I help?"

I let out a sigh and hold up the pressed blouse I think will look good with my skin tone on television, in mute supplication.

"Need to match this?" she asks, and I nod, knowing that I look even more pitiful right now than I did last night. Becky takes the blouse from my hands. "Go eat your croissant, ok? There's coffee too, it's on the counter. I'll handle this."

Mutely, I follow her advice and make a beeline into the living room. The sun's already peering through my curtains. I overslept by a long shot. But Becky's right. The studio is nearby. And they'll want to do all my makeup themselves anyway, so at least I don't have to worry about that part of the morning routine.

I open the box of pastries and dig into the chocolate croissant, pausing only for desperate gulps of coffee. By the time I finish both, the worst of the hangover has worn off, chased away by the miracle of caffeine and sugar mingled sprinkled with adrenaline.

I've just about convinced myself that I can handle this after all—I can nail this interview, seal my place as one of the big up-and-coming names to watch in the makeup world, and impress Jackie Shells to boot—when my phone pings with a new message. It's from Sheryl. No doubt asking me what time I'm getting to the studio, since if I know her, she's already there obsessively early, walking her way through prep.

It is from Sheryl. But it's not the message I'm expecting. Not by a long shot.

Sorry to do this at the last moment, she writes, *but something's come up. Urgent board meeting for another corporation that I can't miss. Don't worry, though. You'll have plenty of support at the interview. I'll be sending Lark in my place.*

She follows this with a thumbs up and a smiling emoji. As if that's supposed to calm the sudden explosion of nerves in my gut.

Great. So on top of everything else—on top of all the pressure I'm already under... I have to deal with walking onto the live TV set today and seeing the man who just broke my heart.

12

CASSIDY

Becky drops me off outside the studio with a long hug, a smacking kiss on the cheek, and a resounding, "Go knock 'em dead, tiger."

"Pretty sure you're supposed to say break a leg for stuff like this," I reply, clambering out of her car to slam the door behind me.

"I thought that was for stage actors," she protests, and I shrug, laughing a little as I wave her away from the curb. Then I turn to face the music solo.

My stomach is a riot of nerves. Worse than it's maybe ever been in my life, and I used to head up the debate team and speak in public all the time in college. Normally I'm confident, poised—especially when I'm talking about a subject I know so well. And what could I know more about than my own product line, the makeup I've been dreaming about bringing to the world for years, and which I'm finally succeeding at making?

But I've never had to talk about it in front of this big an audience. And never with a recent ex standing in the same studio, watching me do it. All while *his* recent ex—or maybe not-entirely-ex—hovers in the wings waiting for a full report about how I performed afterward.

My stomach knots have become a full-on tangled mess. I can feel the caffeine I downed earlier—an extra double shot of espresso because I was still feeling the hangover—ratcheting through my system, amping up the nerves to something close to panic.

You can do this.

I square my shoulders. I haven't come this far, or worked this hard on my brand, just to let one badly mistaken fling throw my entire career off track. This should be one of the proudest days of my life. I'm going to *make* it be that.

With Herculean effort, I repress all these messy emotions, stuffing them into that mental box labeled: to deal with later. Then I storm up the front steps of the studio and toward the doors. Even despite my late wakeup, I'm here fifteen minutes earlier than the time they requested I arrive by. That's me all over—punctual to the extreme.

I pull open the front doors and introduce myself to the guard sitting near the entrance. He checks my name off a list, prints me a badge and waves me through. And on the other side of the sliding doors, a familiar face greets me, all smiles.

"I knew I'd be seeing you again soon," exclaims Marcel, the same studio owner who showed me around back when we were photographing my makeup samples for our first press release. It feels like both a million years ago and just days ago.

I'm so grateful for someone familiar—someone who's not Lark, anyway—being here that I practically leap into his offered hug, squeezing him tight. "What are you doing here?"

"Lark mentioned your big gig, so I managed to sneak

into this studio as a guest for the day." He winks. "Didn't want to miss your first televised interview, since I knew you at the start. Makes for too good a story!"

I laugh and squeeze his shoulder. "Well, I'm glad you're here."

He tilts his head, sizing me up. I wilt under his gaze, pretty sure that he's immediately dissecting the bags under my eyes and the tension in my face. He leans in closer again. "And, I must admit, I have ulterior motives, too. Lark's been worried about you, you know."

My cheeks flush, and I glance away. "I'm sure." My tone comes out drier than I expect.

Marcel sighs. "Look, honey, whatever happened between you two, that's between you two." He catches my chin and tilts my face to the light, eying me critically. "But *I* am here to make sure that you knock it out of the park, for your sake and for your investors' sakes. Plus, we cannot have you on camera looking like a zombie, or nobody's going to trust a single product you're offering," he points out.

I grimace, but I can't exactly contradict him. "It's... been a rough week."

"Tell me about it." He drops my chin, thankfully, and takes my hand instead, leading me across the studio toward a back hallway with doors on each side. I catch a brief glimpse of the stage beyond it, surrounded by more cameras than I've ever seen in one location before—film cameras, still shot cameras, every type of lighting equipment you could imagine.

All aimed at the middle of the stage, where there are just three plush chairs set all in a row. One of which I'll be occupying in a little less than an hour's time.

There go those nerves again, churning away.

"Do not spiral on me," Marcel commands, and I yank my gaze from the distant seats to focus.

"Right. Sorry. I'm fine now."

He arches a brow at me, clearly not buying it for a second. But he does lead me into a narrow dressing room—an entire room of my own, not like the photography shoot we did at Marcel's studio where everyone just did their makeup at little tables right beside the backdrop.

Inside, I spot familiar objects. My makeup sets, all lined up and ready to go.

"Where's the makeup artist?" I ask, scanning the room.

Marcel guides me into a chair and practically forces me back. "Uh uh. I told the manager I'm taking charge of this one personally."

I grin at him. "You used to do makeup?"

"Before I bought my studio and moved over to the production side of this industry, hell yes. That's where I got my start."

I watch him sort through the palettes and select just the right hue of foundation for me on the first try. I don't need to check the label to know he's picked out the one I always use, and it makes me smile. "Guess that's why you were so into my stuff when we first met."

He laughs. "Is that an ego I'm hearing?" He winks, and I flush all over again.

"That's not what I meant," I protest, but he waves me quiet.

"No, no. It's good to know what your talents are. And you, my dear, have a gift for this. Now, eyes shut."

I close my eyes and relax a little as he dusts the powder over my face, then works on my eyes next. There's something relaxing about letting someone else take charge. I'm so used to doing everything myself. It's nice to feel pampered for once.

I'm almost—*almost*—able to relax. Until I hear it. *His* voice, from the hallway.

"—looking for Cassidy Marks's room?"

My pulse picks up, and every muscle in my body, which had bordered on finally unclenching a second ago, tightens back up.

Marcel must notice, because he leans back, the brush leaving my skin, and I open my eyes to find him watching me with an all too knowing expression. "Uh oh. I recognize *that* look. You're in even more trouble than I thought."

"I don't know what you mean," I say, but my voice catches and gives me away. I grimace.

"Please. We all saw the two of you at my studio. You couldn't keep your hands off one another." Marcel gives me a long, lingering once-over. "You're in deep, girl." Then he arches an eyebrow and adds the words that send me tumbling straight through a fresh new maze of confusion. "But don't worry. So is Lark, believe me."

Just then, a rap sounds on the other side of the door. "Cass?" His voice sounds tense. On the edge of broken. It tears at me.

It's too soon. I'm not ready to see him, barely even ready to go on camera, let alone deal with the emotions I've been repressing for a solid week. It feels like all the blood in my body rushes to my head at once, and I cling to the sides of my chair, feeling dizzy.

Marcel takes one look at my expression and has pity. "No boys allowed!" he calls at the door.

On the other side, Lark laughs. "You're a boy," he points out.

"No *straight* boys allowed," Marcel amends, and then, in

case Lark missed the point, "Go away. I'll bring her out when she's ready. And don't worry, we'll be on time. Go have a coffee or something."

There's a long pause from the other side of the door. My heart pounds in my ears, my temples. Part of me wishes Lark will ignore Marcel. Storm through that door anyway and demand a minute alone with me.

But another part, the sensible part, I tell myself, is relieved when he lets out a defeated sigh. "Fine, but you'd better bring her out early for the screen tests. I'll meet you in twenty."

My eyes jump to the clock above the doorway. It suddenly feels a lot more intimidating now. A countdown to the minute when I'll have to come face to face with all the feelings I've tried so hard to run away from.

"Eyes shut again," Marcel orders. "We're on a tighter schedule than I thought."

I close my eyes and let him work, but there's no relaxing this time. All I can think about is Lark's voice calling my name. *Cass.* There was a hollow note to it, and I can't help wondering if he's missed me anywhere near as much as I've missed him.

"If it makes you feel any better," Marcel says as he moves on to my lips next, making me open them into a round circle and then purse them alternately while he works, "that boy has been an absolute wreck all week too."

"Really?" I peer up at Marcel, who flashes me a smirk.

"Not that he'd talk about it, of course. He's got walls higher than Fort Knox. But I've known him long enough to tell when he's upset, and I haven't seen him this bad since, well..." Marcel glances at the closed door. "Since him and Sheryl's first big falling out."

"What happened between them?" I ask. I know I

shouldn't, but a part of me wants to know. Maybe if I do, that will make it easier to let go of my stupid fixation on Lark. To walk away from this mess once and for all.

"Not my story to tell," Marcel replies with a sigh. "But you ask me, they weren't well suited to begin with."

"And now…?"

"Now?" Marcel takes a step back, and gives me an approving once-over, before he twirls my chair. "Now, it's time for Lark to leave his past behind, and win over his future." In the reflection, he winks. "That being you, in my opinion."

My eyebrows shoot up. My perfectly outlined eyebrows, that is. Between that and my long lashes, and a peachy pink color on my lips, I look like a completely different woman. I turn my face this way and that, admiring Marcel's work. Every makeup artist has a slightly different style, a different flare to their designs. Normally I like to do my own makeup, because I know what I want to enhance.

But sometimes, letting someone else do it is like catching a whole new side of yourself. A side of you that other people see, which you maybe hadn't even noticed yourself.

"You're a wizard," I murmur.

Over my shoulder, Marcel laughs. "Please. I had a lovely canvas." Then he swats my shoulder. "Let's get going before your Prince Charming has my head for making you late."

My stomach tightens again at the reminder. But fortified by Marcel's handiwork, a fresh face of makeup, and with his words buoying me—*it's time for Lark to win over his future*—I feel a little bit readier than I did before.

Outside the dressing room, the studio has exploded into a whirlwind of activity. Camera crews, set design, and assistants hurry back and forth in every direction, heels and steel-toed boots alike clacking across the wooden flooring. Someone set up a buffet table near the main stage, laden with pastries and fruit, along with several carafes of coffee. Just the sight of food makes my stomach do an unpleasant backflip.

But then I catch sight of who's standing beside it, and that backflip turns into something more like a washing machine tumble cycle. My whole body switches to high gear, churning.

Marcel doesn't wait for me to recover. He leads me by the elbow to the corner of the snack table where Lark is waiting, and then he announces, "I've got to go talk to the stage manager," and vanishes.

Lark looks good. Better than I remember, even, which is saying something. Because I've had a lot of very detailed fantasies about him in the days since we parted.

He's dressed in a suit, his tie done up, and his hair freshly swept to one side, beard shaved close. But when I look closely, I catch signs of distress. Faint reddish lines in the whites of his eyes, and a hint of a shadow beneath them, like he hasn't been sleeping well.

I blink, realizing I'm staring, but that's okay. Because he's doing the same thing. Gazing at me like I'm some kind of apparition, or a puzzle he can't quite work out.

"Hey," I say, after an awkwardly long pause.

"Cassidy…" But whatever he's about to say is cut off when a woman appears at his shoulder.

"We're about ready for her, if you're done prepping," she says. Then she's gone, as quickly as she appeared, and I notice her drifting toward Marcel. Stage manager, I guess.

I expect Lark to just listen to her and lead me up on stage to the chair where I'm about to give a live television interview—and damn him, that should be the most exciting thing for me right now, I should be thrilled about it, excited about it, losing my mind with nerves about it.

Instead, all I can think about is that he smells the same. A deep, almost smoky scent, cologne mingled with a salty note that's all him.

He steps closer, raises a hand as if to brush my shoulder, and sparks ignite throughout my body, before he even so much as touches me. He lets his hand fall again, and disappointment dampens that rush of sparks. "Can we talk?" Lark asks quietly. "After the interview. Please?"

Maybe it's the quiet desperation in his eyes. Maybe it's just the fact that I've been wanting the same thing. At the very least, a chance to hear the truth. To say my piece, too, and to let him know that I'm not the kind of girl who plays second fiddle to anybody.

Or the kind of person who breaks up marriages, either.

"Okay," I murmur. Just one word, but it brightens his whole countenance. His eyes light up, and the corners of his mouth lift in the first thing approaching a smile that I've seen from him yet.

It almost makes me feel guilty. Almost.

Then a few more stagehands appear to wave me toward my chair, and I lift my hand in a weak little farewell, and let them sweep me off to the interview.

All the while, as I go, I can feel Lark's gaze burning into my back. And somehow, I get the feeling that whenever I turn my head during this interview, I'll catch sight of him watching me the entire time.

I would have thought that would make me even more nervous, but as I settle myself in a little pouf on stage and wait for one of the world's most famous models to join me... it actually feels reassuring. At least I know there's one person in this studio watching who's here for me, and not the other famous people I'm sharing the stage with. And regardless of whatever happened between us outside of this room, I know that in here, at least, when it comes to my business?

Lark has my back. Always.

On stage, I settle into the middle big pouf of a chair. Supermodel Jackie Shell will be on one side of me, and the host will be on my other side. The lights are brighter than I expected, and they feel warm on my cheeks—or maybe that's just my own blood rushing to my face in anticipation.

Because this is real. I'm really doing this. With a deep breath, I put on a broad smile, and prepare to face the cameras.

13

CASSIDY

My interview might have started out nerve-wracking, but by the end, I'm vibrating with a whole different emotion: excitement. Because by the end, I know I'm nailing it. Jackie and the host are both ridiculously fun to chat with, and they even insist on having me do (or rather, re-do) some of their makeup live on camera while I explain what ingredients I use (all-natural and free from preservatives that often irritate sensitive skin), and why (cruelty-free products that haven't been tested on animals because I feel like that's a practice that we need to retire in the beauty industry).

By the end of our interview, both Jackie and our host are swearing up and down that they'll be customers of mine for life— "and I swear, she's not paying me to say that," Jackie adds at the end, laughing along with me.

The thrill of being on television and not just holding my own but actually *having fun* while doing it, is a high I don't know that I'll be able to top anytime soon.

But almost as soon as I step off the stage, I start to spiral all over again. Because one glance to the side of the stage, and there he is. Lark. Waiting to talk to me as promised.

My soaring spirits do a quick dip toward crashing and burning. Then they hoist up again as Lark gives me a sheepish grin and a half-wave with one hand, because damn it, he's still as drop-dead sexy as ever, and all I want to do is run straight into his arms and forget about the past week.

I especially want to forget about what I overheard in the hallway of my new therapist's office last weekend. The event that triggered this whole separation.

Unfortunately, I can't. *Always a pleasure, Mr. and Mrs. Anderson. Their* marriage counselor. And then Sheryl's reply. *That went well, I thought.*

If she's right, if it did go well... if they have a shot at reuniting... I won't be the person who comes between them. I refuse. No matter how devastating Lark looks in his well-pressed suit right now.

No more avoiding this, I guess. At least I still have the buzz of adrenaline from the interview coursing through me. Not to mention Marcel's voice whispering in the back of my mind, telling me that Lark seemed devastated all week too. That he's as stuck on me as I am on him.

It doesn't make this situation any less of a complicated mess. But it makes me feel a bit better, at least, for how cut up I've been over it.

At least I'm not the only one. Not overreacting. Not making up this emotion all in my head.

As I approach Lark, I try to remember what my therapist suggested to me in our second session last week, as the self-doubting voices rear up in the back of my mind all over again. She told me not to identify with those voices, with the anxieties that tell me I'm not good enough for anyone. Those are just things I've been conditioned to think, as a sort of self-defense mechanism, after all that I've been through in past relationships.

But while it's easy to tell myself that, it's a lot harder to believe it as I'm approaching the one guy who I thought was different. The guy who somehow managed to wound me even more than the rest.

When I reach his side, I notice that none of the stagehands are fluttering around anymore, or even the catering people I'd noticed carefully removing the buffet earlier. He positioned himself in a far corner, out of sight of almost anyone but me. Like he doesn't want to be interrupted.

It only worsens my nerves because I don't know if I trust myself alone with him, if I trust that I can say what I need to say.

But when I reach his side, he doesn't let me say a thing at all. He cuts in first.

"You look incredible today," he says. "Not that you don't always, but... wow."

My cheeks flush, and I'm grateful for the camera-level of foundation Marcel gave me because it hides the blush. "Thanks. You look all right yourself." *All right?* Mentally I kick myself.

But Lark just grins, the same devilish grin that I fell for hard. "I was starting to worry you'd been avoiding me," he says. It's meant to be a joke, but I can see the flash of hurt in his eyes.

"Lark..." I start, but he cuts me off.

"Look, Cassidy, I don't know what's upsetting you, but I want to help. There has to be some way I can help." His brows contract. "Tell me what you want me to do, and I'll do it."

But I can't. Because what I want is to tell him to leave his wife once and for all. But that's selfish of me, terrible. And a part of me is still angry with him. He told me they'd split up, and now I know they're still married, trying to work things out.

"There's nothing you can do," I tell him, crossing my arms. "It's not about us." Not exactly. "It's just... this whole situation. I can't."

"Why not?" He takes a step toward me, and it's almost more than I can bear. The look in his eyes, the heat radiating from him. He's so close I can practically taste him again. I know exactly what those lips would taste like if I let myself sink into a kiss. I know how that body would feel, rock hard and solid as he pulled me against him.

"It's too complicated."

His brow furrows. "Because of Sheryl?" he asks, totally thrown, as if he hadn't already guessed my concern.

Which only makes my anger flare back anew. "Yes, because of Sheryl. Because I work with you, and I work with your—" I catch myself barely in time. Manage to insert the extra word. "Your *ex*-wife. It's too messy."

"I told you, she's my past," Lark says, echoing what Marcel told me earlier. Yet I can't shake the image of him hand-in-hand with Sheryl at the therapist's office, seeing a counselor. Trying to work on his marriage.

She didn't look like your past last week, I think, but I don't say it, because we're in public, and we just finished filming a live TV segment, and who knows how many eyes are already on us right now, curiously watching the new up and coming makeup creator arguing with her business investor.

Lark takes my wrist, and I freeze in place, trying my best to ignore the spark in my veins at his touch. "Cassidy." His eyes bore into mine. "I can't get you out of my head. I can't stop thinking about you, *dreaming* about you."

My pulse skips a beat at that. Unbidden, an image rises to mind. Lark, naked in his big king size bed. One hand fisted around his thick, veined cock, as he strokes himself, thinking about me.

Fuck. I'm starting to get wet just imagining it, and feeling his hand wrapped around my wrist. Gentle, now. But there was a time he used that hand to pin my wrist over my head while he fucked me senseless, and god damn, I cannot get him out of my head, ever, can I?

"I know you've been feeling the same way," he says, lower, taking another step closer to me, until we're mere inches apart. Close enough our chests would touch if I so much as inched forward. "We don't have to suffer like this. We can figure it out together, if you'll let me."

It would be so easy. So easy to sink into him now. Melt and forget everything else. Forget my anger, my upset. To just ignore the whole messy situation and let myself have the one man I've ever craved this badly.

But I still have my principles. Whatever else I've become; however far and hard I've fallen for him... it can't trump my beliefs. And my beliefs tell me that whatever I'm doing now is wrong.

"I'm sorry," I breathe. And then, gently as possible, I twist my arm free from his grasp, striding away across the studio floor.

"Cassidy, wait." His footsteps chase after me. "It's late. At least let me walk you to your car."

One glance through the studio's lone window—I assume they limit them because they need to control all the lighting sources inside the building—tells me he's right. It is a lot later than I thought. The sky is already darkening toward a fiery orange sunset overhead.

"This neighborhood isn't the safest at night," he continues, drawing closer the longer I stand there eying the skylight.

I hadn't realize how much time passed while we were filming and between all the prep work and the interview itself, the multiple takes we had to do, and then all the tear down work.

Doesn't matter. "I'm perfectly capable of taking care of myself. Good night, Lark." With that, I push through the studio doors out into the lobby.

This time, he lets me go.

There's a security guard on duty still, which makes me feel just a little bit better about shooting down Lark's offer. I sign out, and then tap on my phone, calling a ride share car. The pickup point is on the far side of the parking lot. I glance outside. There are only two streetlamps in this lot, one right next to the building, and another on the far side of the lot. That's got to be where the ride shares pick up.

With an annoyed sigh, I push through the doors and out onto the street. The air smells faintly damp, as if there might be a storm brewing somewhere in the distance. I shrug on my sweater and pray the rain holds off until my car arrives, at the very least.

Three minutes until arrival.

I half-walk, half-jog across the lot, all too aware of the way the light behind me flickers when I cross beneath its orange glow. Overhead, the fiery sunset colors have faded from the sky, leaving behind a dark cobalt blue that darkens, the longer time stretches on.

By the time I reach the far lamppost, the car is still sitting right where it was on the map when I ordered it, and the time stamp still says three minutes. So irritating when they do that.

I tuck my phone into my back pocket and wrap my arms around myself. Then, conscious of how defensive I look, I unfold them again and lean against the lamp post casually, eyes on the road. A few cars trickle past. Some of the drivers or passengers shoot me weird, confused looks. I guess they don't get a lot of pedestrians in this area of town.

Then a truck slows, and my pulse jumps. It's not the license plate number I'm looking for, so it can't be my ride.

Sure enough, the side window rolls down, and a man with tattoos up both arms leers out at me. "Hey babe," he calls. "Give you a ride somewhere?"

"No thank you," I reply through as tight a smile as I can manage.

His friendly—if you could call it that—expression immediately melts. "Fucking bitch." He narrows his eyes. "What, too good for me, is that it?"

The last nerve of my fraying patience snaps. "Yes, that is exactly it. Now fuck off," I shout, my voice rising.

Not smart. I know it's not smart. It'll only provoke him. Sure enough, he puts the truck into park and glares at me furiously now. "What the fuck did you just say to me?"

And then, from over my shoulder, a familiar baritone. "You heard the lady. She told you to fuck off." Lark's hand comes to rest on my shoulder, gentle and reassuring at the same time.

I square my shoulders and resist the urge to sink back against him. My heart is still hammering in my chest because I've met a million assholes like this truck driver and I don't know what will happen if he escalates. Will Lark have to fight him?

But the asshole just turns and spits out his window, then slowly drives off, scowling at us in his rearview and muttering curses the entire time.

"I told you not to follow me," I complain the moment the asshole driver is out of sight.

"And I ignored you, obviously," Lark replies, stepping

around me so we're face to face, my back still pressed up against the lamp post. "Sometimes you're too stubborn for your own good, Cass."

"Coming from you, that really says a lot," I reply. I can't help it. The corner of my mouth tugs up into a smirk.

Lark's does too. Then his hand drifts up, hovers between us. I don't pull away this time, even though I know I should. His hand cups my cheek, and his fingertip brushes the corner of my smile, lightly. A barely-there touch that does more to ignite the fire in my veins than any other guy could with a lot more ammunition. "What are we doing?" Lark asks quietly, and I know what he's asking.

Why are we separate right now? I can feel the tug in the core of me, drawing me toward him, a gravity I've been fighting to ignore all week.

One I can't bring myself to anymore.

"I don't know," I admit, my breath so quiet the words are almost a whisper.

He bends toward me. So close I watch his pupils dilate where they're fixed on mine. I forget all my earlier resolve. There's only so much willpower I can use up in a day before all my resistance drains from me. Lark is as addictive as a drug, and damn it, I need another hit.

His hand slides from my cheek along my jawline, until he's cupping the back of my neck. He draws me toward him, and my eyes fall shut.

His lips collide with mine, harder than I expected. I don't mind because I'm too busy wrapping my arms around his neck, dragging him toward me. His tongue parts my lips, the kiss deepening, until it feels like he's claiming my mouth for himself, marking his territory.

I want him to.

I raise one leg to wrap around his waist, and in response,

he pins me against the lamppost. I gasp at the feeling between my thighs, the hard press of his cock through his jeans, where it grazes my upper thigh. Just bare inches from my clit. I arch my hips up and angle myself toward him, and he laughs a little, his lips still pressed to mine.

"God, I've missed you," he murmurs.

"Shut up and kiss me," I hiss back, which only makes him laugh more. He turns to obey my command, kissing his way along my jawline until he reaches the edge of my neck. Then he bites down, sharp and unexpected, not enough to hurt, just enough to make me gasp.

Then he keeps kissing, down to my shoulder, across my collarbone to dip his tongue into the hollow at my throat. At the same time, his hands wrap around my waist, tightening, and—

"Shit," I gasp. The car I called is parked out on the road. It honks, just once. I'm about to peel away, when Lark's grip tightens.

"I'm parked right over there." He nods toward his car. "At least let me drive you home."

There's a long beat where I hesitate. I know what this will lead to. Behind us, my ride honks again, a little longer this time, the driver through the windshield visibly annoyed.

But Lark's hands are still tight around my waist, his hard cock still digging into my thigh, and I'm only a human, in the end. "Take me, then," I tell him, and I don't mean straight home.

In response, Lark wraps both arms under my thighs, and in one smooth motion, lifts me up against him. Reflexively, I wrap my legs around his waist, my hands digging into his shoulders, as he carries me across the lot toward his car. Over his shoulder I watch my ride share rolling his eyes and giving up, restarting his engine to drive away. My phone buzzes with the cancellation notification, but I hardly even notice.

Because we've reached Lark's car, and he's pinned me against the door, kissing me again, his hands at the fly of my jeans when he sets me back on stable ground.

My heart beats faster. We're still in the middle of the parking lot. But it's dark out, and with my ride gone, there are hardly any cars on the road which we're hidden from by Lark's car anyway.

He grins at me, his eyes twin green flames in the dark. "I can't get you out of my damn head, you know that, Cassidy?"

My belly tightens at his words. Not least because I do know what he means. Far too well. "I dream about you..." I admit, my voice quiet. "Every night."

"What do I do to you in those dreams?" he asks, his voice dropping lower. Almost husky now. He kisses my neck again, my throat, my jawline.

I tilt my head back, savoring the sensation of his hot mouth on my skin. "Everything," I say, and I can feel the vibration of his mouth as he laughs. "You... kiss me," I start.

In response, he leans up to press those searing lips to mine. "Go on," he adds when we pull apart again, and it takes me a second to catch my breath.

"You peel off my clothes," I murmur.

His hands return to the clasp of my jeans, and he finishes undoing them, pushing them down, so I'm standing in my panties in the parking lot, backed up against his car.

"You let me take yours off," I add, and then I reach out to do the same to him, pushing his jeans off. He steps out of them, in his boxers, and then, before I can do anything, he pushes those down too.

Fuck. I forgot how big he is, how thick he is when he's hot for me. Which is, frankly, every time he's close to me.

It drives me wild, how hard I make him.

"Then what do I do, Cassidy?" He steps closer, and I reach out with both hands to wrap them around the base of his shaft. I stroke along his length, savoring the velvety smoothness of his skin, the contrast between that and how hard his shaft feels beneath.

"Then..." I swallow hard. Raise my gaze to his again. "You fuck me."

He takes one last step, and his cock is pressed right up against my belly now, hard shaft pressing against my soft skin. "How do I fuck you in these dirty dreams you have?" he whispers, leaning down to lick the shell of my ear, making me tremble. It's chilly outside now that night is falling. But his body is so damn hot against mine, searing.

"Hard," I reply.

He pushes my panties off with one thumb, easy as ripping apart wrapping paper. Then he spreads my thighs and stands between them, bending to position himself until the head of his cock is at my entrance. He parts my pussy lips with two fingers, one stroking between them, along my slit, until he grins at me. "Someone's wet for me," he says, before he bends to rest his forehead against mine.

"Always," I admit, my gaze focused on his.

He keeps his eyes on me as he pushes inside me, slow enough that I can feel every centimeter of his cock as he fills me. A groan escapes my lips. I forgot how good this felt. I've been dreaming of him, yes, but dreams can't possibly compare to the real thing, to the thick, full sensation of his cock straining against the walls of my pussy.

He keeps moving, grinning at me now. "I love those noises you make," he murmurs, before he tips his head sideways to kiss my cheek, my jawline, the side of my neck. He nips at my skin lightly and I inhale sharply, making him laugh again, low and sure. "Just like that," he says, and I huff out a breath in protest.

"Not my fault," I tell him. "How can I not make noise when you're—" I break off on another gasp, as he pulls back suddenly and thrusts into me again, faster this time, deeper. "Fuck," I murmur, losing track of my argument.

He's still watching me, smiling that sly smile that says he knows exactly what I'm feeling, and how to make me feel it more. Damn him. He still knows every inch of my body better than I know myself.

He knows exactly how to get me where he wants me.

He pulls back and thrusts into me again, hard enough that car rocks a bit behind me. I tighten my thighs around his waist, hooking my ankles behind him, and at the same time, I wrap my arms around his torso, my fingers catching on the ridges of his back muscles.

"God your pussy is so fucking tight," he murmurs, those hot eyes on mine. He pulls out again, thrusts back inside me, and I can feel the graze of his shaft along my G-spot, already sensitive as hell because damn him, my clit is already swollen with desire.

How can I help it, when I've been fantasizing about him all week? Longing for him, even when I know he's the one person I shouldn't be longing for.

"Lark," I breathe, and I don't know where I'm going with this, whether I'm going to beg him to stop or to keep going. But it doesn't matter, because he reaches up to press a finger to my lips. Then he slides his fingertip inside, and I wrap my lips around it, sucking hard on it, eyes fixed on his.

I can see the moment his pupils dilate, feel the pulse of his cock jumping inside me as he tenses at the sensation.

"Fuck," he growls, low and throaty in a way I recognize, that tells me I've pushed him over some kind of edge now. He draws his fingertip from my mouth and runs both hands down my sides until they reach my hips. There, he grips tightly, fingers digging indents into the soft skin at my hips. He pulls me up and away from the car, and I arch my hips toward his, let him put me right where he wants me.

He fucks me hard, then. Draws out and thrusts back into me again and again, pinning me right where he wants me. All I can do is hold on through the sensation, my hips bucking in time with his, faint gasps of pleasure escaping me with every thrust.

"Fuck, Lark, fuck me," I groan, not even sure what I'm saying anymore, I've lost control of my vocal box. "I want to come for you, fuck."

"Good, because you're going to have to," he replies, and damn him, his voice sounds so steady even now, like he's barely even winded as he drives into me, making my whole body tighten against his, every nerve ending in my body singing out, screaming for release. "That's it, Cass." He's grinning, watching me, fire in his gaze, and I know what he's feeling. He loves watching me come undone.

I know because it's exactly why I haven't taken my eyes from him since we got to his car.

"Come for me," he says, and at the same time he angles his hips up, drives into me hard and fast, hard enough and fast enough to push me right up to the edge.

"Fuck," I shout, or maybe I just think it. I'm not sure. The whole world goes white around the edges, and my vision narrows until all I can see is Lark's face, his expression as he watches me break apart.

The orgasm hits hard enough to steal my breath away, to sing all the way down to my fingertips and toes. But Lark doesn't pause, doesn't hesitate at all. He just keeps going, and just when I think I can't feel any more, he reaches down between us with one hand, still thrusting into me, and grazes his thumb across my clit.

I cry out, loud enough that anyone passing within a two block radius knows exactly what's happening here. But I'm past caring about that. Past thinking about anything except the sensations firing through my body, flooding me with pleasure.

Lark finishes a moment later, with a groan that echoes mine, and I watch his eyes flutter shut, his face suddenly open and so, so vulnerable as pleasure hits him, too.

He slumps against me when he's done, and I keep my legs wrapped around him, fold my arms around his body too. He feels so good like this, pressed fully against me, every inch of our bodies touching.

A distant, far away part of my brain is screaming at me to remember why I'm avoiding him, to pull away, push him back out of my life. But that voice is distant now, and the rest of me is all too happy to ignore it as I let him hold me in his arms, draw me closer to his body.

For now, I think, gazing up into his eyes, I can forget practicality. Forget what I should do, and instead, focus on what I really want.

On *who* I really want.

14

CASSIDY

Images blur behind my closed eyelids. A car door slamming. An apartment door slamming open, with me pinned against it, my legs around a solid, steady torso. Lark's mouth on mine, on my throat, my collarbone, my chest.

The kitchen counter, where we sent pots and pans flying in our haste for him to set me on top of it and push between my thighs again.

Then the living room couch where we stumbled afterward, still entangled, my lips on him now, tracing my way down the smooth, hard planes of his torso until I reached the fine V that led to between his legs. Kissing every inch of his cock before I so much as licked his length, enjoying the way his shaft clenched and shuddered at my touch, and the way he inhaled his breath between his teeth, sharp and desperate.

I sucked him into my mouth, licked and pulled until he came apart shouting my name.

Then the shower, his bed. Him again, between my thighs, for so long and hard I ached by the end of it, but a pleasant, bone deep kind of ache that I never want to lose.

And now... my eyes detect the pinkish glow of dawn approaching. I'm vaguely aware that wherever I am is warm and comfortable. A lot warmer and more comfortable than my apartment be at this hour of the morning, with its shitty heating system and my thin blanket.

Then, belatedly, I register the sensation of lips on my skin. At my hipbone now, followed by a tongue tracing a searing line across my belly to delve into my navel. It flicks on its way back out, making me shiver and burrow deeper into the blankets around me, the pillow so soft it engulfs half my face when I twist against it.

The lips move lower. Kiss a fine line from my navel down to the shaved clean mound. Then the tongue returns to trace a searing, white hot line along the curve where my legs meet my hips, tracing the crevice.

I moan a little and shift, so I'm lying flat on my back, prone and open. My legs are already parted, but I feel warm hands cup my calves and press them wider apart. I feel the weight of the bed shift beneath my hips, then warm hands slide beneath me to grip my ass. Cupping, more like, almost gently. But so, so warm.

And the tongue again, tracing each of the lips of my pussy in turn, taking it slow. So slow that by the time the tongue presses between the folds of those lips, I'm groaning, my hips arching up off the bed of their own accord. The hands on my ass tighten, pull me farther upward, and then a whole mouth presses against my pussy, wide open and hot, hot, hot.

The tongue traces the full length of my slit, back to front, hesitating just before reaching the throbbing, aching point of my clit. It runs back along my length again, and returns to swirl around my pussy entrance, licking, teasing.

"Please," I moan through gritted teeth, not even sure if I'm awake right now or dreaming still. Not caring either way.

The tongue presses inside me so, so slowly. I twist against it, try to press upward, thrust my hips against that hot mouth. But the hands shift from my ass up to my hips, pinning me down. In control.

This isn't my game; it's his, and I sink back to the mattress, obedient. Enjoying the feeling of relinquishing control over my body, if only for a little while.

His tongue pushes all the way inside my pussy. Then it does a slow twirl inside me, licking, tasting, testing. When the tip of his tongue grazes over my G-spot, I gasp and buck. Then there's a soft chuckle, hot breath against my wet pussy, and his tongue curls up, the tip digging into that sensitive spot.

It flicks back and forth, back and forth. Slow and strong. So damn sure.

I moan again, longer and louder this time. His tongue keeps moving, right over that spot, circling, pressing, digging. My hands move on their own, slide down over the comforter to clench fistfuls of the blanket. My back arches, my hips dug into the mattress still, and I'm sweating, panting for breath, as the pressure builds behind my navel, my hipbones.

At the last possible second, his tongue slides out of me, and I cry aloud in protest, deprived of the cliff I'd been so close to. But then his tongue flattens to a blade, laps over my clit, a strong, steady stroke that has me panting again right away, my whole body arched and trembling.

He licks me over and over and over until I'm right up at the edge again moments later, and I come with a cry so loud I'm surprised the neighbors don't pound on the walls to complain.

But then I come back to myself, still trembling, as a warm, smooth body climbs up mine to draw me into his arms, and I remember—I'm not at my apartment, with its dingy, paper-thin walls and my threadbare sheets.

I open my eyes to find Lark gazing down at me, his arms around my waist to cradle me against his naked chest.

Actually, his naked everything. I can feel the hard press of his cock pressed up against my stomach, and it sends a fresh pulse of desire through me, my nerves already on fire from his tongue.

"That's definitely one way to wake up in the morning," I murmur, tilting my face toward his to let him kiss me gently.

When we part, he's grinning, and I can taste myself on his mouth. It doesn't do anything to help calm my racing pulse or the spiking heat in my veins. "Happy to oblige." He tucks my head beneath his chin and sighs, his breath stirring my hair. "If I had it my way, you'd wake up like that every morning, Cassidy."

I tense. Wrapped up like I am against him, of course he notices.

"Stop overthinking," he murmurs. His lips brush my temple, the edge of my cheek.

I want to listen to him. I want to do just that, to forget about my own concerns and let this moment last a little bit longer.

And, yeah, I want him to fuck me again. I'm still sore from last night, but the ache between my legs is sweet, a muscle-deep sensation that leaves me wanting more. I swear if I clench, I can still feel the outline of his cock inside me. Not to mention his actual cock pressed against my stomach, hard and wanting.

But... "This was a mistake," I breathe. The words slip out before I can stop them.

Lark pulls back, his eyes unreadable when they catch mine. "What, exactly?"

"Me. Being here. Us." I shake my head, squeezing my eyes shut so I don't have to watch the hurt that blossoms on his face. "I shouldn't have come. Last night was…" *Incredible.* "Not a good idea."

"Why do you feel like you have to keep pushing me away?" he says. His hand traces the edge of my jawline. Tucks under my chin and tweaks until I open my eyes. He's staring at me still with that inscrutable look, like he's seeing straight through all the walls I keep attempting to throw up and into something vital at my core. "Let me in, Cass. That's all I'm asking."

"You want *me* to let *you* in?" My voice cracks. "What about you, Lark?"

He draws back, his forehead furrowed. "What do you mean?"

"I mean, if you want me to open up, maybe you need to do the same." I slide away from him, across the bed. My whole body aches at the separation. But my mind knows it's the right move. "What really happened with you and Sheryl?" I ask.

And I can see it in his face. The moment his gaze goes from open and curious, to slamming shut. It's like a wall has come down between us.

And he calls *me* closed off.

"That's not relevant to us," Lark replies.

"It's relevant to me. I want to know the whole story before anything else happens here." I gesture in the air between us.

His expression darkens. "You don't know what you're asking me to do."

"I'm asking you to be honest. Is that so hard?"

In response, he pushes the covers back and rolls out of the bed. I try not to watch him go, but it's a struggle. The man seriously has a perfect ass. Not to mention abs, thighs, *cock*... I squeeze my eyes shut while he starts tugging on clothing, just to keep myself focused. "I've told you, time and again, that Sheryl and I are done. I don't know why you refuse to believe me, but there's nothing there anymore. It's in the past. And I don't linger in the past, okay? I live in the now, Cass. That's what I'm focusing on. Here and now."

"There's living in the past, and then there's being willing to talk about it," I protest, levering myself up onto one elbow. "All I'm asking is for the story, not for you to relive it."

"Yeah, well, for me it's the same thing, all right? I can't talk about it."

"Can't or won't?" I fire back, pushing myself up to standing too. He's half-dressed now, so I do the same, snatching at my clothes, flung all over the room last night in our haste.

"Either," Lark replies angrily.

"Fine." I finish yanking on my jeans and grab my top from a lamp it somehow wound up slung over. "If you can't open up, then neither will I." With that, I tug the shirt over my head.

When I emerge on the other side, Lark's standing in the middle of the room, still only half-dressed, his own shirt dangling from one fist. "Cassidy..." He runs one hand through his hair, and I try not to get distracted at the way his muscles ripple when he does. "Can you just... give me time? To get there, at least? I'm not ready yet, but I hope soon that maybe—"

He breaks off. Probably because I'm already shaking my head and taking slow steps backward toward the door. "Lark, I just... I can't. Okay? I'm working on myself too right now." Because he's right, I do have that wall up. Even if I get the feeling he's not the guy I can let the wall down around—because I'm pretty sure he would wreck me if I did... I know I need to eventually.

"I need to concentrate on me just now," I say. "I'm sorry."

I expect him to call out. To chase me again, the way he's been doing this whole time. But when I turn around and start toward his apartment door, he lets me go for once. Still, I can't help stealing one last backward glance when I reach the elevator, just before the doors close behind me.

Lark's still standing right where I left him in the middle of his bedroom, shirt in one hand. Motionless, as if he's just been stunned out of motion.

My heart wrenches. But then the elevator doors shut, blocking him from view, and I sink back out of the clouds, down to the street level again.

15

CASSIDY

I lie on my back and count the lightbulbs that stretch along the ceiling of this office. I already know there are twenty inset lights, each one dim, but together they provide enough glow to write by. At least, so I assume, based on the scribbling sound coming from the chair adjacent to my couch.

"Tell me more about Norman," my therapist says, her voice low and unassuming.

My throat tightens anyway. "Do I have to?" I murmur, still squinting at those lights.

"You don't *have* to do anything, Cassidy," she replies, although not before I hear her scribbling another quick note. "But if your goal, as you just told me, is to learn how to open up to possible relationships in the future, and you believe that this is what's blocking you, then I think it would be helpful to practice talking about it with someone neutral, don't you?"

I sigh. Mostly because what she's saying makes a lot of sense. Unfortunately. "It... we dated for two years. He was the one who pursued me, hard. I wasn't sure, but..." I shake my head. "He had this way of convincing me to do things. Things I didn't always want to."

"Are we talking sexually?" my therapist replies, her voice still careful and even.

"Sometimes." I shift against the couch. The lights, which earlier seemed so dim, now seem way too bright. "Not as much that though." I lever myself upright to look at her. "Just, everything was all about what he wanted. All the time. He wanted me to dress up, so I dressed up. He wanted to go to a show, so we went to the show. He wanted to go out to dinner, so we went... He never asked what I wanted. And the few times I tried to ask, he'd flip out at me." I bite my lower lip, remembering. "He used to tell me that..."

When my voice falters, my therapist leans forward, crossing her arms on her lap. "It's all right, Cassidy," she says. I don't realize I'm crying until she passes me a tissue.

After she does, I just sit there holding it for a minute, confused. Like I've come unmoored for a minute. "He told me that since he made all our money, it was his decision." I breathe in slowly through my nose, and out through my mouth, the way I've been practicing over the last couple of weeks, coming here. "And if I argued or anything, he'd accuse me of trying to use him for his money, being a gold-digger. But I wasn't, I swear I didn't even *care*, sometimes I used to wish we'd lose all the money just so he'd act *normal*."

"You understand that that is manipulative behavior, don't you, Cassidy?" my therapist murmurs.

I bob my head. "But I just felt..." I tug at the tissue so hard it comes apart between my fingers. So I ball it into my fist instead. "I felt like I'd never find anyone better, so." I clear my throat, scowling. "He knew it, too. He played on my fears. He used to tell me I was ugly, annoying, shrill. He said no other guy would put up with my bullshit, and I believed him."

"It sounds to me like you're describing negging," my therapist replies. "That's a tactic used by manipulative people, to do exactly what you're saying. To keep your self-esteem low enough that you'd stay with him. But it's important to unearth those beliefs and confront them now, so you can unlearn them."

I find myself nodding, my throat still tight, my eyes stinging with unshed tears.

My therapist sighs and shifts in her seat. "I'm afraid that's all the time we have for today, Cassidy. But I'm very proud of all the progress you're making. This isn't easy. Doing this work. I hope you know that and can feel proud of yourself for confronting all this, too."

"Sure," I breathe, my voice barely there. I'm barely even listening anymore. I'm lost in memories. Of nights out with Norman, how he'd parade me around on his arm, talking over me, introducing me to his friends but never allowing me to speak or have an opinion of my own.

I was just a trophy for him. A trophy he called ugly and overweight and shrill, in order to keep me trapped. It took so long for me to free myself from him. And to be honest, I forgot how bad it was, after. I was just so relieved to be on my own again, I didn't stop to think about how badly I'd been manipulated, how much he'd lied to me.

I should be over this, I keep thinking, and I am. I'm over *him,* anyway. But the behaviors I learned—the way I hide myself, the way I defer to everyone else in the room... that's taking longer to forget.

Across from me, my therapist is smiling, reaching out to offer a hand. I force myself to stand up and shake it, plastering on a smile.

"Thanks," I tell her. And I try to believe what she's telling me. I try to believe that eventually, this will get easier.

At the very least, I refuse to wind up like Lark. I'm going to learn how to talk about my past. How to open up with the right guy. The right guy, who won't be him.

Who won't touch me the way he does. Who won't keep me up all night, tossing and turning, unable to get images of him out of my head. The feeling of his body pressing me into a mattress, the sensation of his tongue running down the curve of my neck, his hands tracing the arches of my hips...

Fuck.

I force him out of my mind, as usual, and say goodbye to my therapist, before I edge out into the hallway. The lights out here are even brighter, and I squint against them, feeling the same way I usually do after a session—emotionally drained, but a little bit lighter, too.

I try to hold onto that last part as I stride through the hallways of the building and wait for the elevator down to the ground floor. But as I'm stepping out of the building into the parking lot, taking a deep breath of the muggy, pre-storm air, the sky overhead dark despite the fact that it's only the middle of the day—my calm is immediately shattered.

A familiar figure is striding toward the building just as I'm exiting. My stomach clenches, any sense of relaxation or unburdening I felt inside the therapist's office flying out the window.

"Cassidy!" Sheryl's eyes light up the moment she spots me, and she changes direction to hurry toward me.

That only makes my guilt churn worse in my gut. "Hey, Sheryl," I reply, and hope she doesn't notice the tightness in my voice.

"Long time, no see. I've been meaning to call to tell you, you did a great job on that TV interview last week." She grins, bright and open and apparently oblivious to the fact that immediately after that interview, I did exactly what I promised myself—and what I promised *her*—I wouldn't do. I hooked up with her ex-husband.

Or current husband?

I don't even know, and that only makes it worse. I grimace. "Um, yeah. Thanks."

"I didn't realize you go here too." Sheryl jerks a thumb toward the building, and my whole face turns bright red. That, at least, she notices. She waves a hand. "Oh, I didn't mean..." She steps closer and glances around the parking lot. "You know there's nothing to be ashamed of, Cassidy. Going to therapy is great, a really important step. Everyone should have a therapist, honestly. It just helps to have someone to unload on about it all, you know?" She smiles again, and I can't help but smile back, despite my riot of nerves.

"It is really helpful, yeah," I agree.

"I know, it's done wonders for me and Lark," she says, and there goes the feeling of guilt again, worse than ever. "I swear, I don't even know where I'd be without my counselor to talk to."

Her counselor? Or theirs? I can't exactly ask for clarification right now, so I just keep smiling like an idiot.

"Anyway." Sheryl reaches out to catch my shoulder and gives it a tight squeeze. The whole time, her smile remains friendly, almost maternal. "Like I said, you did a fantastic job in that interview. I've been talking to Lark about how we should get you on more shows like that. The numbers really jumped sky-high afterward, you know. We had so many people searching for the brand, and so many orders pouring in too."

I know. I've kept close track of the numbers myself. It's been the only thing distracting me from the mess I've turned my romantic life into. At least I still have work to fall back on, and work that's blooming like it never has before. "I'd love that," I tell her, meaning it, and her smile widens even more.

"Great." She glances past me at the building, and surreptitiously checks her watch—a watch encrusted with diamonds, that looked like silver to me at first, but which I now guess must be platinum. "I've got to run right now, but I'll have Lark get in touch with you about what media outlets you think would be ideal to have our publicist pitch you to, all right?"

"Oh, I—" I start to say that I'd rather talk to her about it than Lark, but she cuts me off.

"Perfect!" Then, before I can stop her, she grabs my shoulder once more and squeezes tightly, before she breezes past me toward the building. "Have a great one, Cass," she calls over her shoulder.

Long after the door swing shut behind her, swallowing her up, I continue to stand there frozen in the middle of the parking lot, unable to quell the guilt surging in my gut, trickling through my body like slow poison. *Lark told you they're over,* I remind myself. But it doesn't help.

After everything I've been doing to work on my own past here at therapy, I can't help but relate to the situation Sheryl must be in. She is clearly struggling to improve herself too, despite an ex who she hasn't gotten over yet. An ex who refuses to even talk about what they went through.

It's a little too familiar for comfort.

16

CASSIDY

The next few days are a blur of work. I get to bury myself in my favorite activity—experimenting in the studio on new color palettes, new formulas to use to add to the growing line of beauty supplies we've already launched. Thanks to all the orders and income flooding in, we have more than enough capital to start to reinvest in more products and additional spinoffs of our first line.

Whenever I talk to Becky, she's quick to warn me about expanding too soon, stretching myself too thin, trying to accomplish everything at once. She's also constantly trying to convince me to come out with her again, go for another club night. "How will you get over this guy until you get under the next?" is her usual motto.

While I see her point, I just can't bring myself to do it. Any time I think about it, something always stops me. I tell myself it's just work.

But really, it's memories of his hands tracing the lines of my curves, his lips on mine, the white hot look in his eyes whenever he drinks me in, like I'm the only one for him.

So the whole clubbing to get over him thing is out.

Which leaves working as the only thing that keeps my mind off of Lark. I throw myself into it with abandon, all too happy to be able to force him to the back of my mind, if only for a little while in the heat of the workday, while I'm buried in projects.

After work, I have to contend with a deluge of messages from him, because Sheryl, true to her word, assigned Lark the job of narrowing down which of the many media outlets we'd like to pitch ourselves to next, where another appearance from me to talk about our makeup would have the biggest impact on sales and word-of-mouth outreach.

I really think you'd do an amazing job presenting on this show, he'll text, and I'll ignore his message an hour before I reply with something curt like *If you think so.* I'm not unprofessional enough to ignore him completely, but I don't want him reading anything more than a professional business interaction into my replies.

I don't want him to know how much I'm still thinking about him. Dreaming about him, every night, my traitorous body working up images of him wrapping those thick, strong arms around me. Holding me close.

It doesn't miss my attention, either, how hard he's working for my career, in spite of the fact that I've basically told him to screw off as many ways as I can count. I have to admit, as much as I believe he's a bad idea for me personally, he's there for me when it comes to work.

I can't count the number of sellers who have popped up with bulk orders, mentioning that Lark hand-sold the products to them in passing. Or the number of requests I've gotten for smaller, blog-style interviews or features with Insta influencers, all because Lark took the time to write them personal messages, gushing about how hard I work, how much I believe in my products, and how long I've dreamt of getting these out into the world.

Every time one of those Insta influencers forwards a screenshot of Lark's message to me, or says they've got to get their hands on the product "if it's anywhere near as good as Lark claims," my heartbeat picks up a little, and the nauseous tension that's been in my stomach all week eases just a bit.

He's the perfect business partner, I'll grant him that.

Then I remind myself that that's probably what Sheryl thought, too, when they first decided to start their investment company together, and I kick myself mentally for even going there.

But my anxious thought spiral gets harder than ever to avoid one night when I'm doing some much-needed cleaning up around my apartment. After all the work and the hecticness of the past month, things have gotten a bit out of control on the home front.

I decide to take a whole Saturday off and dedicate it solely to tidying up, getting my home back into working order. I'm digging around under my bed, fishing out tossed-aside pieces of clothing that I didn't even realize got kicked under there, when my fingers graze against an unfamiliar piece of fabric.

I draw it out from beneath the bed, and my breath hitches. It's a silk tie, expensive-looking, a little wrinkled from lying under my bed all this time. But I recognize it instantly.

It's the one Lark was wearing, the second time we hooked up. Holding it in my hands brings the memories flooding back. The way we'd sat side by side on my old, ratty couch, so careful not to touch. Me, because I was afraid he'd set me on fire. Him, because he was clearly trying to respect my boundaries, despite the flirty smile he wore whenever he caught me stealing glances at him.

I recall the slow slide, as my stupid ancient couch cushions gave way, like the universe trying to force us toward one another. I remember my thigh brushing his, then my leg, from knee all the way to hip. I remember how I tried to ignore the heat burning through me from the inside out.

How I reached for the makeup palette he was holding, only to fumble it, have it spill next to us on the sofa as he drew me into his lap, his hands warm and strong around my waist, and already familiar, even though it was only the second time we'd ever let ourselves touch.

The way his lips tasted that day, his scent enveloping me...

And the way I felt the next day when the replacement sofa arrived. My stomach both sinking and sailing at once, because no guy had ever done something like that for me. He took care of me, even before he knew me at all. Even before he knew how hard I'd push him away.

Without realizing it, I tighten my grip on the tie, savoring the smooth silken feeling between my fingers, tears stinging at the backs of my eyes.

Then I remember something from therapy. In our last session, we talked about how things ended with Norman. I didn't break up with him, something I'll forever be embarrassed by. I just wasn't strong enough. Even though I wanted to, anytime I tried, he'd lure me back in with promises that he'd change, he'd be better this time.

That, or he'd flat out stop me from leaving by barring the door, trapping me in with him.

But one day, he told me he'd met someone else. She was younger than me, prettier. I didn't care. I was so relieved.

Now, I regret not warning her. Or at the very least, being the one to walk out the door on my own two feet.

My therapist tells me it's not my fault. That this is a normal reaction to what I went through.

But afterward, I hoarded pieces of my relationship with him. It was like, even though I knew things had been terrible with Norman, I wasn't ready to let go, because letting go meant I was alone again. And that terrified me.

She told me it was important to stop clinging to the past. To learn how to move on and let go—of people, of possessions, of memories... And of objects, too.

I look down at the tie clenched in my fist.

She's right. I need to work on letting go. On being able to release things that aren't serving me anymore.

Like this tie. *Like the man who wore it.*

I look for my phone, buried under a pile of cleaning material, since I'm still only halfway through the apartment. As I should have expected, there's a new unread message from Lark already waiting. *Photoshoot tomorrow,* he says, *with your favorite photographer, so I know you'll enjoy it. Say you'll come?*

I stare at the message, a knot of confusion in my stomach. *Actually,* I type out, looking from my phone to the tie and back again. *Are you free tonight? I was hoping to talk.*

Of course. I'm just at mine, working on some proposals. Come by anytime.

The speed with which he replies, and the eagerness in his answer, sends off guilty alarm bells throughout me. He might think this means I'm having second thoughts about what I told him last time.

But I need to do this. I need to let go in order to move on. So I tell him I'll be over in an hour, purposefully not even giving myself enough time to do my makeup properly or go all out. I just throw on a cute top (I'm not a saint), dust on some mascara and go.

Lark's building looks as shiny and new as ever when I park outside. I climb the steps up to the glass front door with my heart in my throat. Tucked safely inside my purse is the tie that I ironed and rolled up in a neat little ball to return. My plan is to say my piece, hand it over, and head home hopefully feeling lighter and more ready to let go and move forward with my life.

It's what my therapist would want me to do. Or so I tell myself, anyway.

The doorman at the desk lets me in with a smile and a nod, and pushes the button on the elevator to let me up to Lark's floor. I try to smile back at him, and spend the whole elevator ride checking in the mirrors against the back wall to make sure that my hair isn't a complete disaster. My smile looks wooden, tense.

Probably because I feel like a ball of nervous energy.

But when I step off the elevator, all of that melts away at the sight of Lark. He's leaning against his kitchen counter with a book open, reading it with a little crease on his forehead, like he's concentrating hard. It's not until I knock gently, stepping through the doors to allow the elevator to close behind me, that he jumps and sets the book face-down on the counter.

When he does, I catch a glimpse of the title. *Marketing Beauty Brands.* A small smile touches my face. "Work research?" I ask.

He smiles back. "I want to make sure I'm doing everything I can for you, that's all."

Something flutters in my stomach. I force myself to ignore it. "Do you do this much homework for all your investments?" I side-eye him.

He lifts one shoulder in an easy shrug. "The ones I truly believe in, yeah."

There's that flutter again. *Oh.* I clear my throat and force myself to remember why I'm here. "Listen, I—"

"I just wanted to let you know, Cassidy, before you say anything else. I've gotten the message."

I stop talking, blinking in confusion. For a split second, I try to remember if I drank enough any one night this week to have left a drunk voice message for him or something and then forgotten about it.

But he catches my expression and shakes his head, still smiling. "I mean, I understand that you want to take time for yourself. I won't pursue you anymore. I can take no for an answer, you know. Once you repeat it often enough." His eyes twinkle as he says it, but behind them, I'm sure I can detect a note of sadness in his voice. "From here on out, it's all business with me, okay?" he continues. "I don't want you to worry, or to think I won't put my all into helping you just because our relationship didn't work out the way I'd hoped.

My heart sinks, even though this should be exactly what I want to hear right now. He's not going to pursue me anymore. That means I don't have to fend off his advances, or constantly worry that I'm going to be weak and give into them.

It's a good thing, I tell myself.

So why does it feel so bad? Looking at him now, all I want is for him to take it back. To tell me he's not going to move on, that he can't live without me. But those kinds of admissions only happen in movies, and anyway, would I *want* him to say that? Isn't the healthiest type of relationships the one where both people are in it voluntarily, not because they're afraid of what will happen if they're alone?

I remind myself of Norman. Of how hard I fought to free

myself from that mess. Just like I need to move on from this one.

So I clear my throat. Move toward him, just a step, to show that I'm cool with this. That I trust him to be the same. "Thank you. For saying that."

He leans against his counter again, one hip cocked, watching me over the rim of his reading glasses. And dear God, if I thought the man was attractive before, put a pair of glasses on him and a book in his hand, and I'm in danger. "Well?" he asks, and I almost blurt out an apology for checking him out. He tilts his head, looking bemused. "You said you wanted to talk to me. What's going on?"

"Nothing. I just, um..." I rub at my temple. Try to remember the speech I've been rehearsing ever since I made the decision to come over here. As I'm thinking, I can't help it. I drift a little closer. Just so he can hear me better, I tell myself. "Something similar, actually," I finally say, giving up and deciding to just wing it. "I've been seeing a therapist, working on myself—"

"That's great, Cassidy." He looks genuinely happy for me. And he sets his book aside, turning to face me, so our bodies are just inches apart in the cool air of his apartment.

I nod. I try to ignore those inches between us. "Anyway, I'm working on, uh, moving on and letting go of the past. So I just wanted to say... Yeah. I'm good with business only. Onward and upward from here, right?"

Except there's a pit in my stomach. A pit that's only growing wider and sharper, the longer we gaze at one another. *Our relationship didn't work out the way I'd hoped,* he said. Am I being crazy right now? Walking away from the best thing that's ever happened to me, from a guy who genuinely wants to be with me, because I'm concerned about *his* past? If he doesn't judge me for mine, shouldn't I offer him the same benefit of the doubt?

But then I remind myself of what I saw. Lark and Sheryl at couple's counseling. And of what I've heard from Sheryl herself. All her hopeful looks and bright smiles when she talked about Lark. I *cannot* get between them. Not if there's a chance their marriage could still be saved.

If it were me in Sheryl's shoes, I'd want me to walk away right now. So that's what I need to do. Even if I'm pretty sure I'm breaking both of our hearts as I do.

"I'm glad we're on the same page," Lark is saying, and he's not smiling anymore. Neither am I. I guess we've both given up on trying to hide it for the time being. He's gazing into my eyes like he wants to memorize everything he sees there, every single inch of me.

I know what he's feeling, because I'm doing the exact same thing. Gazing at him like my last glimpse of land before I submerge at sea, with no hope of rescue in sight.

I swallow hard, aware of the sudden lump tightening my throat. "Yeah. Me too."

He takes a slow, careful step forward.

Every nerve ending in my body stands on end. His scent, so close now, envelops me, makes me dizzy with want. "Can I ask you for one last favor?" Lark asks, his voice lower now. So quiet that if I wasn't holding my breath, I might have missed it.

"Anything," I breathe, before I can think better of it.

"One goodbye kiss," he murmurs.

If I thought my nerves were on fire before, it's nothing to now. I feel like a live wire, electric from head to toe. And the man hasn't even *touched* me yet.

"You can say no," he quickly adds. "I just—"

"Yes," I interrupt, before he talks himself out of it. "Just one," I clarify, more for myself than for him.

Then he's moving. Closing that final tantalizing gap between us. His arm snakes around my waist, so familiar, and he pulls me taut against him, crushing me against those washboard abs and tight muscles the way I've always loved. His mouth collides with mine, and his kiss is searing hot, hotter than in any of my dreams or memories, because this is the real thing, this is Lark in my arms again.

My hand drifts up to his cheek. He's cupping mine too, his thumb grazing the corner of my lips even as we continue to kiss, tilting our heads and letting our lips entwine as he deepens the kiss. The tips of his fingertips brush my temples, my hairline, the edge of my cheek.

I want this moment to last forever.

If I close my eyes, I can almost convince myself—for the span of a few heartbeats that somehow feel like minutes— that it will.

Then he pulls back, steps away from me, and the cold air of his apartment rushes between us cruelly once more. There are only a few inches between us again, but it's a gulley now, a huge valley I cannot allow myself to cross ever again.

My lips are still tingling, hot to the touch. My hand drifts up, my fingertips grazing them without thinking.

Lark watches me, his eyes shadowed. Unreadable. Still filled with the same pain that fills my own. Then, with a Herculean effort, I shut my eyes. Stare at the floor instead.

When I look up again, Lark pats his book, still face down on the counter. "Well." He clears his throat, and am I imagining things, or does his voice sound tighter when he speaks again? I know mine is practically squeezed shut right now, like there's a fist around it. "If there's nothing else you wanted to discuss, I'd probably better finish reading this. And *you* had better get some rest," he adds, before forcing a bright, fake-seeming smile. "After all, you've got your big photoshoot tomorrow."

"Oh, right. Of course." I glance from him to the book and back, then start to back away toward the elevator. My pulse feels insane, erratic. My palms are tinged with sweat, my nerves singed from contact. Somehow, though, I manage to keep my voice relatively steady. "Um. Then I guess I'll see you at work tomorrow."

"I'll see you there." He waves, and I hit the button to descend down to the ground floor and out of this mess. Then his voice stops me. "Oh, Cassidy?"

I half-turn, just as the elevator doors open. But I don't get on. Not yet. I glance back at Lark, who's smiling a real, genuine smile this time, one that stretches across his whole face.

He lights up, whenever he smiles like that. It reminds me all over again why I felt so attached to him so quickly. "If you're nervous," he says, "don't be. You're going to knock it out of the park tomorrow. After all, you're becoming a regular pro at this."

I laugh a little. "Yeah, right."

"I mean it. You'll see. Before long it'll be your face on all the promo material, right up there beside the models." He winks.

Now I laugh even harder. But Lark doesn't relent.

"I'll bet you," he calls.

"Goodnight, Lark," I tell him. But at least I'm smiling this time, as the doors shut behind me. And when I step out of his building once more, waving to the doorman who—I wonder if I'm imagining this or not? —does seem surprised to see me leaving again so soon... I wonder if maybe my therapist was right. If there could be something to this whole letting go thing.

But the moment the cold air outside hits me, I have to squeeze my eyes shut. Whatever calm I'd hoped to feel has been burned away by the feeling of Lark's lips imprinted on mine, the taste of his mouth.

In spite of myself, all I want to do is go right back in there and do it all over again.

17

CASSIDY

The next morning, I wake up, surprisingly dream-free for once. But the moment my eyes open, I'm already picturing the look on Lark's face when he told me he'd stop pursuing me. How much it seemed to pain him.

How much it hurt me, too.

Not to mention *that fucking kiss.* Our last one ever. And he certainly kissed me like a dying man, like he'd never be able to touch me again.

Because he won't be able to, I remind myself. That was the deal. One last kiss, and we're done.

This is for the best, I tell myself, again. It's getting harder and harder to remember that. Then I roll out of bed and pace into my shower to get ready for the big photoshoot today.

It's not until I'm heading out the door, rooting through my purse to swap my wallet over to a sleeker, more professional bag, that I find the small ball of silk rolled up at the bottom. *Shit.* All that and I didn't even remember to give his tie back after all.

I hold it for a moment, studying the fabric, my fingers

tracing over it. I wonder if maybe this was my subconscious trying to tell me something. Telling me that I'm not as ready to let go just yet as I think I am—as I *should* be.

Then I push the tie to the bottom of my bag and square my shoulders, forcing myself to forget about it. I've got bigger things to worry about today. Namely, acing this shoot.

I do one last check to make sure I have all the supplies I'll need, and then I head out the door. The studio's easy to find—I recognize it as the same space we used the first time. Marcel's studio. A slow smile spreads across my face as I pull into the parking lot. Now I understand why Lark told me I'd be working with my favorite photographer.

Inside, Marcel's in a flurry of activity as per usual. I watch him flit between camera equipment, the makeup stands and the artists standing at the ready, and the line of models waiting to get done up. Before he catches sight of me, though, I notice him stop by one stand in particular, and trade a long, slow kiss with a handsome guy whose cheekbones nearly rival Marcel's own.

I'm grinning by the time Marcel makes it to my side for a tight hug. "Someone's enjoying himself," I point out, grinning. I watch Marcel's guy line up for the makeup stand, and realize he's one of the models when he strips off his shirt to reveal some seriously cut abs.

"I couldn't let you have all the fun, could I?" He nudges my side, winking. Then I follow his gaze across the room to Lark, standing in deep conversation with the set manager next to the coffee cart.

My heart does a weird little flip—rising and sinking again all in one motion. The same way it always seems to around Lark, a regular roller coaster of emotions. I want to know if he's still thinking about our kiss too. If it meant as much to him as it did to me. But I can't exactly bring it up, after what we agreed.

"Oh, uh…" I tear my gaze from Lark. "Lark and I decided we're better off as friends."

Marcel's eyebrows shoot skyward. "You *both* decided this?" he asks, with another long look in Lark's direction, as if he knows something I don't.

"Um, yeah." I clear my throat. After another piercing look, I throw up my hands, relenting. "Okay, fine, I told him no, and he agreed to stop pursuing me. Asking me out. Whatever you want to call it."

"I knew it." Marcel's eyes narrow. "That boy is more hooked on you than I've ever seen him on anybody. No way he would've suggested a friends-only thing."

"Can we change the subject, please?" I fold my arms, tilting my head back and resisting a groan. I already went through all of this with Lark, and it was hard enough. Hearing Marcel, one of Lark's friends, talk about how into me Lark was, isn't helping.

We made our bed. Or rather, we made our two, separate beds. Time to lie in them. Alone.

"Sure, honey. You ready for today? I was thinking we do same as our first shoot, but a bit more drama on the product. We've showcased your demurer looks so far, the barely-there makeup styles. It'd be fun to get a little extra today."

My cheeks flush. "Uh… how extra, exactly?" I do make some bright colors too—I've always liked them myself, for big nights out. But I didn't picture super over-the-top makeup being my brand, per se.

He laughs at my expression. "Nothing you aren't comfortable with, don't worry." Marcel loops an arm through mine and leads me toward the studio lights. "Trust me," he purrs, and I can hardly do otherwise, when he's dragging me around like this.

But, I realize, I do anyway. Trust him. It's a pleasantly surprising discovery, since I'm not used to trusting my work in the hands of anyone else. Now I've learned how to trust not only Marcel, but Lark, too, with their parts in making my brand a success.

We're halfway through the shoot when a door slams. I glance up to see Sheryl entering, and my eyebrows rise. I hadn't realized she'd be coming today. I raise a hand to wave to her, and she offers me a tight smile and a curt nod before beelining past where I'm stationed at the edge of the stage, without even stopping to say anything.

My stomach tightens. I wonder what's wrong? Because it's clear from her face that something is.

I try to focus on the shoot, but my attention wanders in the direction Sheryl went. I spot Lark standing beside her now, still in his spot backstage. He hasn't tried to approach me all morning, aside from when I went for a coffee, and he handed me one, already prepared the way I like it, with a rueful smile on his face and a "Good morning," that sounded like it cost him more energy to say than it would have to swallow.

I know exactly how he feels. I feel the same way. My whole body is burning for him. Every time we lock eyes, it's a reminder of our conversation last night. Of how devastated he looked by the end of it. Of how much it hurt to walk away after that kiss.

It was the same way I felt, too.

Now, however, as I watch Sheryl and Lark talking—or, more accurately, as I watch Sheryl talking and Lark staring at the floor, his arms crossed, I wonder if maybe some of his mood isn't related to me after all.

Or maybe it is, whispers a nasty voice at the back of my head. The one I can't get to shut up these days. *Maybe Sheryl found out about you two, and she's here to tell him off for sleeping with a client behind her back. Maybe you did all that, finally walked away from him, only to ruin their marriage after all.*

The hard knot in my stomach calcifies into guilt.

"Um, excuse me for a minute?" I whisper, sotto voce, to Marcel.

He nods, barely even noticing me at his shoulder. He gets like this as soon as the cameras click on and the action starts: totally focused on his work.

Or... perhaps not entirely his work, I realize as I notice who's on stage at the moment. The model Marcel kissed earlier.

I stifle a fleeting smile and leave him to it. Then I skirt around the stage the long way, toward the bathrooms. My plan is to hide in there, catch my breath, and hope either Sheryl leaves or her and Lark's conversation calms down in the meantime. Any way I can avoid a confrontation with the pair of them, the better.

But I'm only halfway there when I glance toward the coffee stand to make sure they haven't spotted me, and I freeze. They're not backstage anymore. At least, not anywhere I can see.

I hesitate, torn. This is what I wanted, for them to leave. Or at least to have their fight somewhere I didn't need to witness. Now, though...

My nerves prick at me. Something doesn't seem right. Lark's posture earlier, maybe, or the way Sheryl totally blanked me. If this *is* about me... If this is all my fault... shouldn't I be trying to make it right, if I can?

Maybe I can talk to Sheryl. Tell her I came onto Lark,

that I pursued him, and it was a temporary thing, it's over now. I won't stand between them anymore.

I pace behind the stage, eyes and ears peeled for any signs of the couple. It doesn't take long before I hear the rumble of raised voices, muffled by a door. I trail the sound until I find an office with Marcel's name on it, the door shut tight. But the lights are on inside, and the door is made of a foggy, tinted glass. Through it, I can see the outline of two figures, standing close by.

I pause just on the other side of the door, my breath held.

I shouldn't do this. I should leave them alone. Or else knock and walk in there to announce my presence. But the raised voice is feminine—it's Sheryl, *yelling,* in a way I've never heard before, and so I pause outside the door, my hand on the knob, torn.

"—*get your act together,*" Sheryl's shouting, now that I'm close enough to hear through the glass panel. "Between the red eyes and the whiskey-sweat stench, you could pass for a homeless addict right now."

My eyebrows shoot up my forehead. My stomach clenches. I've never heard her talk like that before, to anyone, let alone Lark. Maybe she's really angry about something—potentially about me—but still...

Also, it hits me. Why *is* he bleary eyed... and does he really smell like alcohol? I didn't notice it earlier when I said good morning to him—and I always notice how Lark smells. Maybe Sheryl's just guessing, because he looks like he didn't sleep last night.

Why didn't he sleep last night? Was he thinking of me, tossing and turning, the same way I was the whole rest of this week?

My guilt feels like a compound, snaky thing, constantly

twisting and finding new soft places where it can bite me, take out chunks, eat away at me.

Lark says something back to Sheryl, too quietly for me to hear more than the comforting rumble of his baritone. I wish I could hear what he's saying. I wish I knew what was going on here.

"We had an agreement." Sheryl's voice drops lower, furious now, and I'm forced to lean closer to the door to hear the rest, which only sets my heartbeat rabbiting in my eardrums. If they catch me out here, it will be obvious what I'm doing. I have no excuse for this. "And this... whatever the hell this is?" Through the glass, I watch the shorter shadow gesture a hand at the taller one. Sheryl, waving off Lark as if he's nothing. "This is not part of our agreement. So I want you to stop moping about whatever sleazy whore you're moaning over—*yes, don't act like I'm an idiot, Lark, I've known you for years*—and get your shit together. Is that clear?"

Another soft reply from him. I still can't hear it, can't hear what he's saying at all, but through the glass, his shadow straightens, shoulders back, arms stiff at his sides. It looks like he's standing up for himself, or at the very least, not cowing before her.

Then the smaller figure pulls back an arm, and I hear a sharp cracking sound.

I don't register what just happened until I see the taller figure's head snap to one side, and a hand raise slowly to cup its cheek.

She just *slapped* him.

My stomach sinks all the way through the ground. Oh, God. She does know there's another woman—but from the sounds of it, she doesn't know it's me yet. *Hitting him,* though?

I'm still standing there, frozen with shock, when she

does it again. Backhand this time. Another sharp crack that makes me wince reflexively.

I know he hurt her, but…

All too late, I realize Sheryl's shadow is now storming toward the door. Reflexively, I leap for the nearest large object—a stage curtain hanging nearby—and wrap it around myself. Just in time, too. The click clack of a familiar pair of heels storms out of Marcel's office, as Sheryl strides back through the studio.

I hold my breath until a distant slam far off in the distance—followed by Marcel's curse, probably as her opening the exit door ruined his lighting. Only then do I dare to exhale, to start to breathe again, my chest aching from the held breath.

I realize I haven't heard Lark walk past. Being careful not to move too quickly or draw attention to myself, I fold a narrow slit in the stage curtains to peer through.

Sure enough, there's Lark, standing only five feet away from me, his brow furrowed as he glares out in the direction Sheryl just left. His fists are balled, and there's a hand-shaped angry red mark on his cheek. My first instinct is to go to him. Offer him ice, tell him it will be okay, offer to cover up the mark with some foundation before anyone else in the studio sees, in case he doesn't want to answer any awkward questions.

But I don't move. Because I'm aware that I was just eaves-dropping on a very private fight—a fight I most likely caused. My heart drops into my gut. This is exactly what I didn't want to happen.

I pull the curtain closed again and squeeze my eyes shut, waiting until Lark leaves too. Like Sheryl, he beelines straight across the main studio floor. When I peer out again, he's paused beside the stage, glancing around, like he's looking for somebody. Failing that, he shakes his head, murmurs something to Marcel, and then heads out of the studio.

A minute later, just as I've summoned the courage to come out from behind the curtain and approach the stage again, my phone buzzes. It's a new text, from Lark.

Sorry I missed you. Had to run. Urgent business matter. You're doing amazing today, though. Just wanted to tell you that. I'm so proud of how far you've come.

He signs it with a simple *x*. I have to close my eyes, pressing my phone against my chest, in order to keep from breaking down.

All I want to do is chase after him, out into the parking lot. To pull him into my arms and kiss his bruise better.

Instead, I square my shoulders and return to the stage. There, I find Marcel, no longer ogling his model beau, but gazing past me out the studio doors, in the direction of the parking lot.

One look at my face, and he guesses. "You saw the state Lark was in?"

I nod, careful.

His mouth flattens in disapproval. But he doesn't offer anything else. He just goes back to watching the photoshoot, this time with his arms folded across his chest.

After a moment, I clear my throat, and venture, "Um... Is that... usual?"

Marcel lets out a long, slow sigh, his mouth pursed in a way that tells me exactly what he's thinking. "No, Cassidy. I don't care who you are, or what your relationship, former or otherwise, is to someone else. That's not usual, girl."

Staring out across the stage at all the pretty models posing and beaming for the cameras... I can't help but agree.

18

CASSIDY

My first check comes in the mail two days later. I call Becky to scream with her about it, because frankly, it's more digits than I've ever seen written on a single slip of paper in my entire life.

Yes, a huge chunk of my profits go to Sheryl and Lark's investment firm off the top first, since they bought such a big investment share in my company. But still. This is so much more money than I ever would have been able to make myself, in a lifetime.

"Spa day," I tell Becky, once we're both done screaming at the top of our lungs at the universal *celebrating girls* pitch. "My treat."

"Cass, you don't have to do that," she protests, but I speak right over her.

"Please. I *want* to. Besides, I haven't seen you in ages, between work and..." I trail off, biting my lower lip. I'm curled on my couch right now—my extremely expensive, beautiful couch, which Lark bought me after ruining my old ratty one. And across the room, I eye my purse, and my cheeks burn thinking about the tie still sitting inside.

I keep telling myself that I just left it there so I could remember to give it back to him the next time we're both going to be at some kind of business thing, either a photo-shoot or an interview or what have you. But really, I think I'm just giving myself a subconscious excuse to hang onto it for just a little while longer.

This is totally different from what I did with Norman's crap, I tell myself. *It's just one stupid tie. And I'm not holding onto it really. I'm saving it for him.*

Even I don't believe me, though.

"Between work and your boy toy treating you like used dog shit?" Becky interrupts my thought cycle.

"He's not *that* bad," I start, but now it's her turn to speak over me.

"What did we agree after Norman?" She clicks her tongue, disapproving.

"No defending guys while I'm in the throes of a breakup," I mumble.

"Right, because you always get into a bad habit of putting *their* needs before *yours*, and that's bullshit." I hear gum pop on the other end of the line. "So, okay. Spa day. If it'll help take your mind off things, I'm in."

I force myself to smile, even though it's harder now that Becky brought up Lark. I'd been hoping for a day of not thinking about him. But she's right. Spa day is just what I need. I tell her the address of my favorite spa in town, a cute one that has hot and cold plunge baths, steam rooms, facials and massages, the works.

Not that I can usually *afford* the works. I'm more of the, wait until there's a 50% coupon day, then go and enjoy the bare minimum activities there, type girl.

Today, though... I grin at my check one more time, planning to swing by the bank on my way to the spa to deposit it. Today, I'm going all out. Fuck it. I deserve the pampering.

I meet Becky in the parking lot, and she pulls me into the tightest hug. I don't realize how much I needed that until I squeeze her back tightly, and we both let go with matching eager grins.

"Okay, time to act like the most spoiled rich bitches there are," she announces, and I snort under my breath, following her inside.

The minute we buy our tickets—all-inclusive packages, thank you very much—the attendant's expression changes, in a way it never has when I've been here before, barely scraping enough together for the discount tickets. She ushers us into a private changing room big enough to fit half my bedroom, then wraps us both in fluffy towel-like bath towels before leaving us alone to change.

Once we're ready, we're taken to a whole different pool area from the one I'm used to. This one is on the rooftop, complete with...

"Oh hell yes," Becky calls over her shoulder. "Swim-up bar!"

Sure enough, the jacuzzi—if you can call a pool this big a jacuzzi, although it certainly feels like one when I wade into it—has its own bar attached. Although, I notice all the cocktails are mostly juice, with a hint of diet alcohol splashed in. Oh well, guess a health spa can only serve so much alcohol before it doesn't count as healthy anymore, right?

We share a green juice cocktail that somehow tastes fortifying, delicious and decadent at once. Then we drift around the hot pool—ignoring the cold plunge pool entirely, because frankly, I came here to get spoiled, not subject myself to borderline torture—waiting for our scheduled massage times.

As we drift, Becky eyes me. I can practically feel her next words coming, and I brace myself. "How are you holding up?"

"Fine," I reply, a little too quick and loudly. I clear my throat and sip more of my tasty cocktail. "I mean, you know... it's not like anybody died. It's just a breakup. And it wasn't that long of a..." I shake my head, laughing, mostly at myself. "God, it wasn't even a *relationship*, really. We just hooked up for a few weeks, that's all."

My stomach tightens at the lie. It wasn't *all*. Not for me.

"You really liked him, though," Becky says, proving once again that the girl notices more than I usually give her credit for. She leans back against the wall, head tipped onto the side, watching me from the corner of her eye as she lets her body float. "It's still hard, even if it was just a short thing."

"Yeah." I sigh, and prop myself up against the wall next to her, setting my cocktail aside for the moment. "It is."

"So, you really are officially done? I mean, you went over to his place and gave him back his tie and everything."

I grimace. I forgot I told Becky about that part.

She notices, and sets her own cocktail down, her expression shifting into another one I'm all too familiar with: stern mother mode. "Cassidy."

"I forgot about the tie, okay?" I bury my face in my hands. "But I did go there and talk to him. I told him I didn't want to pursue things anymore because it's too complicated, and he said he respects that and he'll back off."

Becky crosses her arms. "He'd better. I mean, he was the *married one* leading you on this whole time. What an asshole."

I hesitate, thinking back to the brief snippets I overheard

in Marcel's office. The argument. *We had an agreement,* Sheryl yelled. What did *that* mean? It certainly wasn't how I'd imagine a woman would talk to her happily married spouse, though. Maybe they were in an open relationship?

But then why was she so mad at him for sleeping around?

She clearly was. Her other words, *whatever sleazy whore you're moaning over*, have been playing on guilty repeat in my mind ever since I overheard that conversation a couple days ago. Part of me wants to speak up, defend myself. I'm not a whore.

But can I really argue that, in this position? I didn't know Lark was married at first. Yet after I found out... Our last full night together flashes through my mind. It feels so long ago now. The way he chased me into the dark parking lot after my TV interview, protecting me even while I was too stubborn to let him. And then the way he caught me in his arms and pinned me against his car, our lips colliding...

That whole night afterward. My last night in his bed, my clothing strewn all over his apartment...

It was weak of me. Beyond weak. And then, to top all that off, the other night when I went over to his apartment to end things once and for all, what did I end up doing? I kissed him. Again. Yes, sure, I broke things off after that, but still.

Maybe I am a whore, I think, and my stomach tightens, the healthy cocktail drink suddenly not sitting right in my gut at the thought.

"Hello? Earth to Cassidy Marks." Becky's waving her hand in front of my face now. I zone back in and realize I have no idea what she just asked me.

She takes one look at my face and deduces the same thing. "Cass..." Her voice softens. She squeezes my arm.

"You'll find a better guy, okay? A non-married one. One who respects you."

She's right. I should just nod. Agree. But... "I'm not so sure that's the full story," I murmur.

Becky arches an eyebrow. "What do you mean?"

"I mean..." *We had an agreement.* "I don't know. I overheard this weird thing between him and Sheryl at work the other day. And then she *hit* him."

Becky winces. "Damn. Not cool. But maybe she just found out about... You know?" She glances at me pointedly. "Still not okay to hurt someone physically, but..."

"I know." I grimace. "But, it's more than that. I don't know. I mean, I'm not even completely sure he *is* still married. I just assumed so, after I saw them coming out of couples' counseling and all—"

"Uh, yeah," Becky replies, drawing out all her vowels. "Divorced people generally don't pay for therapy to try to repair their relationship."

"But, they're business partners too, so maybe..." I shake my head. "I don't know." I chew on my lower lip. "Maybe there's another explanation."

"Well, did you ask him about it?" Becky arches both eyebrows now.

"Um..." The green drink churns even worse in my gut now.

My best friend lets out a long exhale that turns into a groan. "Okay, well no use doing it now, since you've finally extricated yourself from the mess." Then she sets her jaw in what I know as Becky's game face. "Let's look at facts. Even *if* he's not married, he didn't exactly disclose whatever the hell his weird current thing with his ex-wife is. And he expected you to just roll with it, all while being in a business relationship with not just him, but *both* of them. You ask me, Cass, married or not, this situation has hot mess written all over it. Find another guy. One who's upfront with you." She squeezes my wrist. "One who doesn't make you feel like you're on an emotional roller coaster all the damn time. Someone steady."

My head bobs of its own accord. "You're right." I know she is. It's just getting harder and harder to keep convincing myself of that.

19

CASSIDY

The spa day didn't relax me as much as I'd hoped it would. Maybe it's because I couldn't stop thinking about my conversation with Becky the whole time I was in my massage.

Did you ask him about it?

Maybe I should have. Maybe that would have been the smart thing to do right off the bat. But I tried to talk to him about his past with Sheryl multiple times, and he always freaked out. I can't imagine it would have turned out any differently if I'd just point-blank asked whether they were still married.

I tried demanding the full story once and he practically ran away.

"It's not as simple as that," I mutter to myself on my long drive home, alone in my car with nothing but the blasting radio for company.

As to the rest of what Becky said... it's true. I should move on. It's what I've been trying to do this whole time. Not to mention, I promised my shrink I would.

But every time I decide to, I'm reminded of the way he looked at me that last time, in his apartment. The desperation with which he kissed me. It was so palpable, I swear I could taste it. A combination of tears and sweat, heartbreak and yearning.

I still need to stop thinking about him.

I pull onto my street, only to notice an expensive-looking car parked in my usual spot, the top rolled down, which is unusual considering it looks like rain. There's no one inside, but I curse at the car anyway, rolling past it and hunting for a different spot. It takes me fifteen minutes to find one, and by the time I do, it's started to drizzle. Wrapping my arms over my head, for lack of a better option since I only have my thin jacket on, I jog for the cover of my front doorstep.

I make it to the door, keys jangling in my hand, shivering from head to toe, and jam my keys into the lock. That's when the back of my neck starts to tingle, some sixth sense alerting me. It feels like somebody's watching me.

I turn around, and sure enough, there's a hazy figure making its way up the steps, no umbrella either. For a moment, I can't see through the haze. Then the figure reaches me, just steps from my door, and I blink, frozen in place.

It's Lark. His hair is soaked and sticking to his head, and his eyes look even redder than they did in the studio a couple days ago, when I saw Sheryl slap him. "Cassidy," he says, and to my surprise, his voice sounds steady. Even. It's completely at odds with the fire in his eyes, the war he's clearly struggling to keep from showing on his face.

"Lark." I glance past him, and realize the expensive car I saw earlier must be his, although it's not the same car he's picked me up in before. I wouldn't put it past him to own several expensive cars though, just for the fun of it. The top is still down. I nod toward it. "Your car's getting wet."

He shrugs. "I'll have it cleaned."

Now I really stare at him. I know he's wealthy, but he's never struck me as the wasteful type before. He's always been so careful with his possessions, so exact about having everything the way he likes it—in his apartment, at work... *in love.*

I force that thought away. I have no idea what Lark is like *in love.* I only know what he's like in lust, and in lust, he's complicated enough. "What are you doing here?" I ask. I'm proud that my voice holds even, too. Two can play at his game. The pretend we don't care game. Pretend it isn't killing both of us to be standing this close to one another, and yet to remain apart.

There's a long pause. I hold my breath, afraid of what's coming next. Afraid he'll make an offer I don't have the strength to refuse. But then he says, "My tie. I left it here a few weeks ago."

"Oh, I..." It's in my purse right now. I haven't taken it out. Not since the day I went over to his house to return it. But my hands freeze. I don't want to admit I've been carrying it around. That makes me seem like some kind of desperate weirdo.

Even if I *am* a desperate weirdo, I don't want him to know it.

"It's inside," I say, jingling my keys. "I'll get it for you."

He nods, and makes no move to follow me as I push open the door. But the sight of him standing on my doorstep, his hair still dripping, his feet leaving puddles on the mat, is too sad to ignore.

"You can come in," I tell him.

He's careful to keep his distance from me, only stepping far enough across the threshold so that he can ease the door closed behind himself. He doesn't come any closer to me.

I wonder if he's battling the same worries. The fear that

if we get any nearer to one another, we'll combust. Or at the very least, do something we regret.

"It's in the bedroom," I say, unable to drag my gaze from his. "I'll just..." I gesture over my shoulder with a thumb, and then beeline into the bedroom, easing the door closed just far enough so that he won't be able to tell I'm rooting through the very purse I had over my shoulder for it.

Once I fish the tie out, looking a little wrinkled for its wear, tied up in a knot at the bottom of my messy bag, I smoothe it out as best I can, square my shoulders, and glance at myself in the mirror. Crap. I look like a mess—my hair is frizzing all over the place from the rain, and my skin is red from the facial I got at the spa.

Any sense of calm I might have found there has definitely evaporated by now.

Still, I square my shoulders. Remind myself of what Becky said. I deserve someone who treats me better than this. Someone who doesn't drive me insane or leave me second-guessing my own sanity all the time.

"This one, right?" I ask him, inanely, as if I have dozens of guys over here potentially leaving ties around my apartment. He arches an eyebrow, and I flush. "I found it the other day. I was planning to bring it back to you, but..." I swallow hard.

He just watches me, his expression unreadable.

Did you ask him about it? Becky's voice whispers in my ear, an annoying bug I can't get out of my head. Because deep down, I know she's right. I should have just had a straightforward conversation with Lark about this, long before now.

I move closer to him. Close enough to catch that infuriating scent. Close enough to see the rise and fall of his chest, the jump along the side of his neck where his pulse beats. I wonder if his heartbeat feels as erratic as mine right now.

I hold out the tie. He reaches for it, but before he can grab it, I draw it back an inch, just out of his reach. I keep my gaze on his when I ask it. "Are you still married?" I ask him.

There. I did it. Point-blank. Straightforward. No way to dodge it.

At least, so I think. Lark's expression darkens, his brow lowering and the set of his jaw turning hard. "Who have you been talking to?" he asks, his tone low and dangerous.

That's when it happens. That's when my heart finally and completely cracks in half. Because that reply is *not* the sort of answer you get from an unmarried man, when confronted with that question. My stomach sinks. "I can't believe you," I say.

He scowls. "Cassidy, it's not what you think."

"All this time. I can't believe it. You told me; you *told* me you were divorced."

Lark holds up both hands and takes a step toward me, placating. "I never said *divorced*, exactly. I said things were over between me and Sheryl, which is true—"

"You're still *married to her*, though. That's kind of a huge thing to hide from somebody you're fucking." The moment the words leave my mouth, I watch him flinch. But I don't care. I'm past feeling sorry for him now. I'm just angry. "You lied to me, Lark."

"I never *lied*, Cassidy."

I shake my head. "A lie by omission is still a lie. You knew what you were implying to me when you told me things were over. I thought that meant they were really over, not that you two were still seeing marriage counselors and the lot."

I don't realize what I just admitted until the words slip past my defenses.

Lark's eyebrows shoot upward. "What did..." His brow lowers. "How did you know about that?"

"Because I saw you there, okay?" I blink hard, embarrassed to realize there are tears stinging at the backs of my eyes. I fight with all my might to hold them in, because the last thing I want to do is break down in front of this liar right now. "I was going for a consultation with my new therapist, and I got lost on the wrong floor, and I saw the two of you coming out of a counselor's office. It said *couples' counseling* right there on the door."

"When was this?" Lark asks, with long slow spaces between the words, as if he's piecing something together in his head.

"Right before I told you I had to call things off," I say. "Because I don't do that. I don't do the whole *being the other woman* thing. I don't want to be some homewrecker."

"That home had been wrecked long before I even met you," Lark replies, his voice hardening. "So *that's* why you broke things off with me out of the blue? God, Cassidy, I thought I'd done something horrible, hurt you somehow, or—"

"Lying to me *did* hurt me," I snap.

"So your plan was just to never even speak to me about it?" He crosses his arms, his eyebrows lifting. "Why didn't you ask me about what you saw? You didn't even give me a chance to explain."

My stomach knots. It sounds far too similar to what Becky asked me at the spa earlier today for comfort. "Because that's not the sort of thing you *can* explain," I reply, trying to hold onto my own fury. I'm the one being done wrong here. "Maybe, *maybe* if you had been upfront about your situation with Sheryl in the first place, I could have trusted you—"

"That's the problem," Lark interrupts me. "That's always been the problem, Cassidy. You don't trust me. You never have. And I doubt it's just me." He takes a step closer, the air between us heating. Or maybe that's just me, my whole body flushing at his proximity. "When was the last time you really let anybody in, huh? When was the last time you had a real conversation with someone you were with?"

"I..." My tongue sticks to the roof of my mouth. *It's just because I'm mad right now,* I tell myself. That's the only reason I can't think of anybody.

But the only face coming to mind right now is Norman's. And he was the *last* person on this planet I could ever have an honest conversation with, let alone trust.

"This isn't about me," I reply, hardening my expression. Tightening my fists where they're wrapped around my own elbows.

"Look, should I have been more upfront with you about Sheryl? Yes, I see that now." He uncrosses his arms. Spreads them at his sides, like an act of surrender. Like he's opening himself up to let me strike him if I want. "I didn't tell you more details because frankly, I was afraid it would scare you away. We'd only just started seeing each other, but I..." His voice hitches. Lowers. "I already knew I really liked you, Cassidy. I was developing feelings for you, and... it was self-ish, but I didn't want to say anything that would jeopardize that."

"So you lied." I tighten my jaw.

He nods slowly, gaze fixed on mine. "So I lied, yes. But..." He runs a hand through his hair and lets out a frustrated groan. "The thing with Sheryl. Our marriage. It's been over for so long, that to me, I just thought... does it really matter what some legal piece of paper says? She and I both know where things stand."

"Are you sure about that?" I can't help but think about her expression whenever she talks about Lark. Not to mention the way she went at him in Marcel's office the other day. Slapping him, to boot. That's not the behavior of a woman who's over things with her ex.

"Yes," he replies, firmly. "Trust me."

But I can't. Not after all of this. I bite the inside of my cheek to keep the tears from spilling over, and then I reach out one more time, the tie in my fist. This time, I have to force it into his hand. "I'm sorry, Lark."

He closes his eyes for a long moment. I can see his jaw working, the muscles of his face tense as he fights with his own emotions. I watch his throat bob with a tight swallow. And then, finally, he nods. "Goodbye, Cassidy," he says, and there's a finality to it this time. A hollow ring that kills me, even as I watch him let himself out my front door.

I wait until I hear his car start on the street outside before I shut myself into my bedroom, plant myself face down on the bed, and finally let myself cry.

20

CASSIDY

"This is a vicious cycle, Cassidy. You see that, don't you?" My therapist keeps her voice carefully neutral.

I stare up at her ceiling, blinking hard through the tears. "I guess."

"You're doing the same thing with Lark that you did after your breakup with Norman. You're letting him set all the rules, letting him dictate your boundaries. You owe it to both of you—yes, both you and him," she clarifies when I look over at her, startled, "to let this go."

I inhale sharply. It comes out a long, pathetic sniffle. "I know," I say. My voice comes out quieter now. Still heartbroken.

My therapist smiles kindly. "It will take time," she tells me. "But the nice thing about time is that it comes whether we want it to or not. This feeling will pass, Cassidy. I promise you that."

Easy for her to say. She's not the one who woke up drenched in sweat again this morning—the same way I have every morning this week—with Lark's name on her lips. During the day, I've gotten decent about fending off the emotions. But at night, when my subconscious takes over, they return with a vengeance.

Like last night. In my dream, I was back at Lark's apartment. Only we weren't in his bed. He had walked me over to the huge floor to ceiling windows that wrapped around his living room, with a stunning, mesmerizing view out over the city. It looked like we had the whole world spread out beneath our feet.

"You're the one I want," Lark whispered against the nape of my neck, his breath so hot I swear I could feel it. He kissed me right there, tongue trailing along the upper vertebrae of my spine. "Trust me, Cassidy."

In the dream, at least, I could. I tilted my face to the side, looked for him, and he caught my mouth in a slow, searing kiss that felt so real I tasted him. Then his hands slid down to my hips, my thighs. He nudged my feet apart with his, until I was standing spread out against the glass, the city below us, close enough to give me vertigo almost, except the adrenaline only added to the moment, made my heart beat faster with desire for him.

I can't remember what I was wearing. Some sort of skimpy lingerie thing. It didn't matter. Lark had soon torn it off anyway, tossed it aside like so much refuse. Then his hands were back on me, searing, strong and in control. He reached over the arch of my hips and trailed his fingertips over the smooth plain of my belly, holding me pressed tight against him so I could feel the hard press of his cock against the small of my back, already rock hard, wanting me.

His fingers slid over my mound, cupped my pussy and gently wrapped around it, the heel of his hand pressed lightly against my clit, his fingertips spreading my lips stroking slowly along the length of my slit. The glass pressed against my front was cold, but Lark's warm, naked body crushed against my back was searing hot, and oh God, he felt so good I almost lost control right there.

I let my head fall back against his shoulder, my lips parted as I gasped with pleasure, as he pressed a finger inside me, gently swirling it around, testing me.

"God I love feeling you shudder against me," he murmurs, his breath hot again, tickling the back of the shell of my ear. He licked along the very edge of that shell, making me shiver from head to toe, and chuckled faintly, as though he were enjoying himself.

He liked it whenever I lost control. I knew that much by now.

And even in my damn dream, he certainly made me do that. He spread my legs wider, pressed the thick shaft of his cock between my thighs, and then—

"*Cassidy.*" My therapist's usual calm manner can't hide a faint tinge of concern now.

I wonder how many times she had to say my name before she got my attention. I flush and straighten in the chair. "Sorry, I...my mind wandered off."

Her eyes soften. "I want you to try to get some sleep tonight, all right?" she says. "Decent sleep. If you're still struggling to in a few days, let's talk and see what we can figure out, okay?"

I nod, trying to focus on her, on the bright office. On anything but the damn dream that woke me this morning, hours before my alarm went off. A dream that made me afraid to fall back asleep, worried I'd only start to dwell in the past even more profoundly than I already am.

She asks me about schedules for next week, and I pencil in my new time, then rise on unsteady legs to shake hands and show myself out of the office.

It's not until I step out into the hallway that I turn my

phone back on. It's one of her policies. No phones in the room, because they might ring or buzz with a text and interrupt the flow of our conversation.

When my cell reboots, it chirps with a new text. I tap it open, frowning at the sender. It's a local area code, but otherwise the number is unfamiliar, and not attached to anybody in my contacts. When I read it, my lips part, my stomach sinking.

All it says is, *There's something you need to know about Lark.*

21

LARK

I stare at the ceiling of my bedroom. The bedroom I had custom-designed to my order, because I was finally, *finally* going to start doing things my way. I was going to pursue what I wanted, live the life I wanted.

Instead, it's all been stolen from me. Again. In the exact same way that it is always stolen, because I failed, yet again, to anticipate the consequences of my own actions. I have no one to blame for the way I feel right now. No one but myself.

I shut my eyes, my hands clenched in tight fists. But that's no respite. Because behind my eyelids, waiting for me, the same way she always is, every time I close my eyes and lay my head down on this pillow at night, is Cassidy Marks.

I can still picture the last glimpse I caught of her, before she shut her apartment door in my face. The pained expression on her face. The hollow look in her pretty brown eyes. I did that. I put that there. And no matter what excuses I gave her, no matter how I tried to talk my way around the full story, she's right.

I never told her the full truth. And because of that, her trust in me is broken. Because of that, I lost my first real chance at happiness in I can't remember how long. Maybe ever.

Behind my eyelids, the Cassidy in my head shifts. Her smile turns sly, inviting. It reminds me of the first time I brought her here, to this apartment. The first time I pinned her against the door before it had even fully shut behind us, and kissed her full lips, her long, lean neck. The way her muscles shifted against my lips when she swallowed, barely able to contain herself. And the expression in her eyes, when I'd drawn back just far enough to take her in...

Fuck. A look like that could drive a man to insanity.

Which is exactly what she's done over the course of the intervening weeks. Driven me mad. It's the only explanation for why I can't get her out of my head, my veins, my *cock*.

Jesus. I'm already hard again and I haven't even pictured her naked yet. I grit out a tight groan, and then I roll over to check the clock at my bedside table. Three in the morning. But it's useless. I'm not going to get any more sleep until I relieve at least some of the pressure building inside me.

I shove the covers off. My cock is already hardening, getting stiffer with each breath I take, each memory that swims to the surface.

Cassidy in this very bedroom, naked and spread eagled. The taste of her navel when I dipped my tongue into it, running my hands along her soft, luscious curves. Digging my fingertips in just tightly enough to feel her wriggle beneath me, those glorious hips of hers rising off the bed to meet me, so soft it made me want to bite her.

The feeling of my teeth nipping at the ridge of her hipbone, when I gave into that urge and *did* bite her.

I wrap a fist around the hard length of my shaft, my eyes shut tight, so that I can remain more fully in that memory. Fantasy. Whatever you want to call it. I picture the way

Cassidy's chest heaves when she catches her breath. The way her nipple hardens when I roll my tongue across it, then suck it between my lips, teasing at her breast, toying with her.

I remember the deep, animal instinct that rose up in her when I kissed her, hard, her body pinned beneath mine on this bed. She kissed back every bit as hard as I gave her. And she rose up off the bed to meet me, hands fisted in my hair, when I pressed her down against the satin.

And, God, the sensation when she spread those soft, smooth thighs to let me slide between them...

If I concentrate, I can taste the soft folds of her pussy as she moaned and twisted against my sheets. I can feel the wet smoothness of her on my fingertips, when I slid them inside her, one at a time, until I had three knuckle deep in her tight, hot pussy. I curled them, stroked along her walls to draw those sounds I love out of her. The throaty, breathy sounds she makes when she's utterly lost to the world.

And the feeling when I finally positioned my cock at her entrance, pushed into her an inch at a time, savoring the way she folded around me, her pussy tight and clenching with want, but so wet I glided in easily anyway. Being inside her had felt like coming back to a home I hadn't even known existed.

Like finding peace again, after going through the hellish war my life has become these days.

I grit my teeth, move my fist harder, tighten my fingers in a cheap imitation of her pussy clenching around my cock. It's not the same, of course. Nowhere near it. But for a brief instant, spread out on my bed, slicked with sweat despite the cool air and my naked body... It's enough to drive the rest of it out of my head. The stress and the worry. The uncertainty of what comes next, where we go from here. How the fuck I'm going to fix this.

Because I have to. I have to fix this somehow, have to get her back. Win back her trust, if it's the last thing I do. Even if she wants nothing to do with me again romantically—and she might not, I warn myself, *you fucking idiot, you might have ruined it for good*—I need to show her the truth. She deserves that much, at the very least.

She deserved it from the start, but I was too broken and blind to notice it. I was so focused on what I wanted, I didn't stop to consider what she *needed* from me.

The orgasm, when it hits me, isn't nearly as satisfying as I'd hoped. A groan, a tightening behind my solar plexus, and a soft, wet fall across my fist. I reach for tissues on my bedside table, clean myself up. Then I give up and pad all the way to the shower. If I thought this would help me sleep, I was wrong. I'm more awake than ever now.

More focused on exactly what I've lost.

But standing under the pouring water of the shower—set on the coldest temperature I can possibly stand at this hour in the morning—I make my mind up. One way or another, I'm telling Cassidy the truth. There will be consequences, I know. But it's nothing I haven't already been through before. If telling her pushes me right back into the hell I only just managed to climb out of, well then...

I gaze around the bathroom, with its simple, minimalist design. A design Sheryl would have hated. The exact style she always seethed about. Even though I had this apartment designed with one goal in mind: starting over fresh, starting over as my own person—there are still vestiges of her in it. Touches I added only because I knew they'd piss her off.

That's not healthy. That's not a complete break, not truly.

But what I have with Cassidy? That can be. So I owe it to Cass to walk back into that furnace one more time and claim my freedom once and for all. Even if it means losing this apartment, my livelihood. Everything I've worked for. She's worth the risk.

Where we go after that will be her decision. Our future, if we have one, is up to her. But this? This is the step that's up to me. And for once, I'm going to rise to the occasion.

22

CASSIDY

I take a deep breath. Then another. It doesn't completely clear the lump in my throat or chase the tears from my eyes, but it definitely helps.

Beside me, perched on her plush chair set next to the couch where I'm currently folded over my knees, my therapist watches me with a half-smile. "It's normal to feel like this, Cassidy. Even though you've made your decision and are on the path to change, it's completely normal to still have emotions about what you've chosen. To mourn the direction you decided not to take."

I nod, because my throat feels too tight to speak again. I just got through talking about Lark. The breakup, the way I can't stop checking my phone for messages from him, even though I told him I didn't want him to contact me, so he's only respecting my wishes. Some twisted part of me still wishes he'd ignore my rules. Push through the boundaries I set to chase me anyway, even though it's exactly what I need to not be encouraging right now.

Beside me, my therapist shifts in her seat. "I'd like to talk about something a little different today, if that's all right with you?"

I take a deep breath and nod again. Different would be good. A distraction from Lark would be good.

"Last time you were here, we talked about recurring patterns in your life. For example, your difficulties in setting boundaries with Lark, and before him with Norman. Sometimes—not all the time, mind you—but sometimes these sorts of difficulties stem from childhood relationships. From the relationships you saw modeled between your parents growing up, or the way that your parents treated you. Does that sound like it might relate to you?"

My stomach sinks. Of course she's hit directly on the only possible subject that could be worse to discuss than my tragedy of a love life. My parents.

More specifically, my mom.

"Um... Well, my dad wasn't around. He left before I was born. I know his name, but..." I shrug. "I never wanted to meet him. I never really understood that urge. He abandoned me from the start, so why should I chase him?"

"I see." My therapist makes a quick note, and I fight the urge to ask her what she's writing. "And what about your mother?"

"Um... We don't talk much anymore," I admit, as I reach over to pluck another tissue from the box at my elbow and use it to daub at my eyes. At least my new waterproof mascara, which we're launching widely next week, seems to be doing its job. There's not a smudge out of place, despite my tearing up this whole session. I smile at the tissue for a moment, before I realize the therapist has asked another question.

"Why is that?"

"Well." I clear my throat. Where to begin with Mom?

"She can be... pushy. She has a really specific way she wants me to lead my life, and if I don't live it that way..."

"What way is that, exactly?" The therapist nudges her glasses further up her nose.

I squint past her at the clock. Fifteen minutes left. I can get through this. I let out a sigh. This is what Becky meant, when she told me she was proud of me for doing the work. Confronting these emotions. Actually talking everything through.

It's called work for a reason, Becky told me this morning on the phone, when I called her on my drive over here, anxious about yet another session of getting my head poked around in.

"For one thing, she never had a job. Or at least, not one that lasted more than a month or two. She tended to live off of the guys she was dating. First my dad, and then when he split, there was a whole string of them... Most only lasted a couple years at a time, until Rick. They were actually married for five years. He was pretty well-off, so the divorce gave her a chunk of change to support herself for a bit until she met the next guy. She was always pushing me to date guys with money, telling me that working for yourself was a sucker's game."

"I see." My therapist finally stops writing in her notebook to look at me. "So the relationship pattern you saw the most when you were growing up wasn't perhaps the healthiest, would you say that's accurate?"

I laugh. "That's putting it lightly." I chew on my lower lip for a moment. "I never wanted to be like her. As soon as I graduated, I started working on my business ideas, so I could support myself. It's why, when I first met Norman, I didn't want anything to do with him. I was convinced if I dated some rich guy, then... well, I'd wind up like Mom. She never seemed like she was *dating* these guys. It was more like she was... taking care of them. Doing everything for them, in exchange for access to their bank accounts. You know?"

"And you didn't want that for yourself."

"No." I shake my head hard. "I wanted something real. But Norman..." I shrug. "He met Mom a couple times, and I think after that was when he got convinced that I was doing the same thing. Trying to use him. I tried to show him I wasn't. I tried to show him how much I really cared, but we always wound up fighting about money anyway, about how my business wasn't doing well, and without him I'd be out on the street, and shouldn't I be more grateful and just give up that work and take care of him instead..." I squeeze my eyes shut.

"So, in trying to avoid the patterns you saw your mother falling into, you actually recreated them?" My therapist keeps her voice neutral, but I hear judgment in it anyway.

Or maybe that's just me judging myself and projecting. "Yeah. I guess."

"Does your mother ever act this way with you, or is it only with the men in her life?"

I press my lips together to stifle another laugh. "Oh, yeah. As soon as she realized Norman and I were together, suddenly she started calling me all the time, talking about how broke she was, how she couldn't pay her rent, she was going to be evicted. I fell for that once or twice when I was fresh out of school, begged Norman to help me help her out. Until I visited and found out she wasn't behind on rent at all; she'd just wanted extra cash to splurge on some designer shoes. And of course, when *he* found out, he blamed me for being soft and an easy target..."

"How long has it been since you last spoke to your mother?" My therapist peers at me over her glasses.

I shrug. "A couple of months." My stomach tightens. "Actually, she tried to call me last week." Right after my TV interview segment went life. It might be a coincidence, of course. Or it might mean she's realized I'm finally starting to get successful in my own right, and she's looking for an easy influx of cash again.

"And you avoided her call?"

"Is that bad?" I meet my therapist's gaze, feeling guilty.

But she just smiles, reassuring. "It's not about whether it's good or bad, Cassidy. You have every right to set boundaries with other people, even—and perhaps *especially*—with relatives. If talking to your mother isn't something you want to do right now, you don't have to."

"But..." My stomach knots even worse. "I mean, *shouldn't* I? Isn't that something you're supposed to tell me to do as my therapist, to like face my fears and stand up for myself or something?"

She chuckles under her breath. "Is that what you *want* me to tell you to do, Cassidy? Is there something you've been wanting to say to your mother that you've held back?"

"Well... I mean." I shift on the couch. "I guess I want to tell her about my company. I want her to be happy for me. I just don't also want her to start begging me for money all the time again."

"Could you tell her that upfront, so that you both have the same expectations going into a conversation?"

"What, 'Oh hi, Mom, I'm not giving you any money, but I made some finally'?" I laugh. "You can't just *say* that to your parent."

"Why not?" The therapist arches an eyebrow.

I blink, thrown. "I mean..." To be honest, I've never thought about being that straightforward with my mother. Or with anyone, honestly. When I was a kid, anytime I was too honest about what I really thought with Mom, it tended to get me in trouble. If I didn't like her current boyfriend, she'd tell me I had to suck it up and learn to like him because he was paying our bills. Hell, even if she asked for my opinion on a dress she was wearing, if I didn't say it looked amazing, she'd accuse me of thinking she was fat and I was trying to make her feel insecure.

Talking to my mother has always been like navigating a field of landmines. So, after a while, I just stopped trying to cross the field.

"I guess I just figured she'd get too upset if I said that," I reply, after a long pause.

"It's understandable to want to avoid a situation that would upset both of you," my therapist replies.

"So I *shouldn't* call her back," I say.

She laughs. "I can't tell you the right answer, Cassidy, because there isn't one. It's a decision you'll need to make for yourself, whether or not you want to open that door. But either way, you should know that you have every right to set boundaries with your mother. Boundaries that make you comfortable." She glances over her shoulder, and then leans forward in her seat. "I'm afraid that's all the time we have for today, but I think we made progress, don't you?"

I smile and nod. But this session has left me feeling even more confused than ever. Could she be right? *Do* my relationships with guys stem from how I watched my mother behave as I was growing up?

If so, maybe I *should* call her. Just to try to untangle these messy feelings. After all, she only lives a couple hours away now. Opening the door a little bit isn't going to be like before. She can't barge in and take over my life again the way she has in the past.

My brow furrows as I trudge out of the office. My

stomach is already in knots, but I've made my decision. By the time I reach the ground floor of the elevator, I'm at peace with it. I pull out my phone and scroll until I find my mother's name on my missed calls.

She tried again last weekend, but she didn't bother to leave a message. It seems she's learned by now that I don't usually listen to them. They're always not-so-subtle requests for money, anyway.

I take a deep breath and square my shoulders. Then I hit dial.

Mom answers on the third ring. "Cass, honey! I've been trying to reach you for ages," she coos, in a tone that tells me she's already had at least one drink today.

I check the time on my phone just to be sure, but yep, it's barely after 2pm on a Tuesday. I wince. "Hey, Mom. Sorry I haven't called in a while. Things have been pretty busy here."

"I'll say!" she exclaims. "I was calling to tell you I saw that interview you did on TV. You were amazing, honey! I'm so proud of you."

"Thanks, Mom." I keep my tone level, cautious. Although I'll admit, it does feel good to hear her say that.

"And let me guess," Her voice turns a little teasing, "you haven't even properly celebrated yet, have you?"

"Sure I have!" I retort. But then I think about it. Have I, really? I went to the spa with Becky the one day, and promptly made myself nervous again about five seconds later. Aside from that, I've spent all my time working. At least, all my time that I've not spent in therapy or trying my best to forget about Lark. "Kind of," I add, and on the other end of the line, my mother lets out a knowing sigh.

"Tell you what. Why don't I come by? We can go out for a nice meal, maybe see a movie or something. My treat!"

My eyebrows shoot skyward. Whatever I'd expected to hear from my mom after that TV interview, it wasn't this. Guilt settles heavily into my stomach. Maybe I've been unfair. Maybe *I'm* the one who's been stuck in the past, remembering how my mother used to treat me when I was younger. Who knows, maybe she's changing too. Turning over a new leaf, the same way that I'm trying to.

A smile drifts onto my face as I cross the parking lot toward my car, the phone tucked against my shoulder. "Yeah," I say slowly. "I'd like that, Mom."

"Great! Tonight work?"

I laugh. "You really want to drive all the way here tonight?" It's at least two hours, if she manages to leave before rush hour, which I'm pretty sure at this rate, she'll get stuck in.

"Of course! It's been too long since we've had mother-daughter time. I'm on the way now, honey."

"Okay. If you're sure. Then let's do it." We talk for a few more minutes, making plans for where to meet in a few hours' time. By the time I hang up, I have a genuine smile on my face. After a moment's consideration, I shut my phone off. I'm feeling good right now, and I don't want that bubble to burst if I get more work emails or something else flooding in.

Tonight, it's all about me and Mom. And that's all I need for right now. Something simple and good.

23

LARK

Her phone goes straight to voicemail. Again. I stare at it for a moment, wait all the way until the beep before I finally disconnect. What I have to tell Cassidy can't be done over a goddamn answering machine.

I need to speak to her, face-to-face. I need to *see her.* I've waited to do this for long enough. Left her hanging in uncertainty for too long already.

I grit my teeth, staring at my useless phone for a solid minute before I come to a decision. If I can't reach Cassidy right now, that's all right. There's still one more confrontation I need to get out of the way before I really lay everything bare to Cassidy anyway. And it's a fight I should have finished a long time ago now, if I'm honest. Cassidy is just the push in the right direction that I've needed all along. A reason—the ultimate reason—to tie up my loose ends once and for all.

Unlike Cassidy, Sheryl answers on the first ring. "Darling," she says, her voice a low purr, the same way she always says that, even though I've been asking her to stop it for months now.

My jaw tightens reflexively. I can't believe I used to find that endearing. Her tone sounds so fake to me now, so transparent. "We need to talk," I say.

"About what?" Still that lighthearted, innocent tone. As if she doesn't know exactly what I'm about to say.

"I want to finalize it."

There's a long, weighty pause on the other end of the line. At least she doesn't ask me what I mean. Part of me expected her to stay in denial right up until the bitter end. "We've talked about this, Lark." When Sheryl speaks again, her cutesy tone is gone. She's all business now. "It's not in either of our best interests."

"Actually, I think it would be in both of our best interests. Don't you want to start fresh, Sheryl? Find someone who can actually give you what you're looking for?" I glare at myself in the reflective glass of my apartment building.

"The last thing I want is to *start over* at my age, Lark," she snaps. "And I can't believe you're still talking about doing this, after all the work we've done in therapy."

"You know the only reason I signed up for those sessions," I bite out, my voice dropping. "I'm done doing this. I'm done pretending. Sign the goddamn papers."

She laughs. Actually laughs. "Fat chance. I know what you want, darling. And unless you're okay with giving it up, then face it. I'm going to get what I want eventually."

"What you're asking is unfair," I reply, trying to keep my voice as even as possible. Calm and collected. Even though my pulse is beating hard, and I swear a vein at my temple is about to pop.

"Not according to our pre-nup, it isn't," she says in a singsong voice.

I clench my fist around my phone. "This isn't the situation we were anticipating at all, and you know it."

"Too bad. It's the situation we've wound up in, darling. So if you want to end it, fine by me. You already know my price. Otherwise? Well, just think about it. What I'm asking for isn't so bad, darling. We've been there before. We made it work, once."

"That was before I knew who you really were," I reply, unable to help rising to her bait.

All it earns me is another long, low laugh. "Please. You liked my ambition when we first started dating, Lark. You should have known this is what it entailed. You should have known I wouldn't give up on us without a hell of a fight."

"There is no *us* anymore, Sheryl. There hasn't been for a long, long time."

There's a pause on the other end. A faint intake of breath. I think maybe I've finally hit a nerve. But then her voice drops again, dangerously low. "It's that new investment isn't it? The Marks bitch. She's exactly your type. Doe-eyed and dumb."

"Don't talk about her like that." I scowl at my own reflection.

"Not denying it, are you? Interesting. I wonder what she'd say if I told her the truth about us."

"You've done enough damage already, believe me." I shut my eyes. I need to stop giving her a rise. I need to stop letting her get under my skin so easily. "Just sign the goddamn papers Sheryl. I'll have the lawyer bring them by your office tomorrow."

"Then I'll see you in court the day after tomorrow," she retorts. And I know exactly what she'll be gunning for.

"You know what?" I'm at the end of my tether. "Fine. Let's play this out. But you leave Cassidy out of this, or believe me, I will make it a thousand times worse on you."

"As if you have the guts," she hisses, just before I disconnect the call.

It doesn't matter. Sheryl doesn't matter anymore. She's my past. Even if it ruins me to claw my way free from her, I'm going to do it. Because I can't pretend anymore. I can't dance on her leash. Not now that I've met Cassidy, now that I've tasted what true happiness could be like.

Whatever happens now, whether she accepts me or not, I'm choosing Cassidy. If I wind up alone and heartbroken, at least I can say I gave it my all.

I shove my phone into my back pocket and stride across the apartment, grabbing my coat along the way. It's time to make this right, once and for all.

24

CASSIDY

I stare across my wine glass at my mother, on the opposite end of the restaurant table. Behind her, the lights of the city glimmer. We're on a rooftop, one of the slightly bougie ones in midtown that I've never actually been to before but always wanted to try.

Between us on the table are two finished plates of steak. The portions were, naturally, ridiculously small. But the food was delicious. And at least the sides had a bit more meat to them—metaphorically speaking, anyway—so I'm decently full. And it feels nice. It feels *good*, to reconnect.

We've spent the whole meal catching up. Mom told me some hilarious stories about a guy she was dating for a few months, a firefighter in her town who sounds like he was more entertaining than an actual prospect. But at least he's got a real, regular job. He's not like her usual types. It sounded like she actually had fun with him, even if it was only for a little while.

It also sounds like she wasn't actually using him for cash.

"So, what are you doing these days?" I ask her, because

she just ordered us another bottle of one of the mid-range wines to split, and I can't help it. Even though she told me on the phone it would be her treat tonight, I can't shake the sneaking suspicion that there's something else she wants. That this is some kind of setup.

How terrible of a daughter am I? whispers a voice in the back of my head. That I'm suspecting my own mother of setting me up, just because she invited me out to a nice meal.

God, maybe my head really is messed up. Maybe I don't have any idea how to trust anyone, anymore.

"Oh, you know." Mom waves a hand, grinning at me over the rim of her wine glass. I really don't, actually. "This and that, trying things out, seeing what I enjoy."

I run my tongue along the inside of my cheek, resisting my gut instinct, which is to keep pressing her until she admits she's unemployed, yet again. *Maybe you're leaping to conclusions, Cassidy.* Before I can actually reply, though, Mom leans forward, setting her glass back down.

"You know, Cassidy." She stretches her hands across the table, palms up. After a moment's hesitation, I place my hands in hers, and bite back a wince when she squeezes my fingers too tightly. "I'm really proud of you. I don't tell you that enough, and I'm sorry for that. But it's so exciting what you've been building for yourself. Your whole little makeup empire." She winks and squeezes my fingers one last time before releasing me. "You must be so happy. It's everything you've always wanted, no?"

"Yeah," I reply, a smile stretching across my face. "It is."

"And now that you've finally got those career goals out of your system, I'm sure the right man will come along soon too." Mom's grin widens. "After all, men love a successful woman these days, don't they?"

My cheeks flush, and my gaze drops before I can help myself. "I guess." When I look back up again, Mom's frowning this time.

"What's wrong?" She tilts her head, narrowing her gaze. "Is there someone you haven't mentioned?" She straightens in her seat, her eyes brightening. "Did Norman come back into the picture?"

My stomach knots at the sudden, unexpected mention of his name. "No," I snap, a little too loudly and harshly. A couple at the neighboring table glance over, and Mom raises a disapproving eyebrow.

"I always liked him, that's all," she's saying.

I lean forward in my seat. "It's not Norman," I tell her. I ignore the part about her liking him. That's my fault, really. I never told her how bad things got with him. Because part of me suspected she wouldn't understand. Or she'd tell me to suck it up and deal with his flaws, because at least he had money, and money kept people safe.

Never mind that he was making me *unsafe*, monetary support aside. I felt caged with him, resented and controlled at once.

But I never explained all of that to Mom, so how could she know?

"But there is *some*one," she replies, her voice dropping to a purr. "I know that look, Cassidy. You get the same doe-eyed expression whenever you're smitten; you've been doing it since preschool."

I groan and roll my eyes. But I nod, too. "There's some-one. Or, there *was*. He turned out to... not be such a good idea."

She frowns, suddenly all sympathy. "Unemployed? Bad prospects?"

I grimace. "*No.* Not that that should be a reason to break up with someone," I add.

"Well, I'm not saying you should break up with someone who just lost a great job. But if it's someone with no ambition, no drive, would you really be happy dating them anyway? I mean, we were just talking about all your career goals... You need someone who's as driven as you are."

Or someone with tons of money I can mooch, don't you mean? I resist the retort. "He wasn't a good fit," I tell her. "Because he lied to me. He told me he was divorced, and he wasn't." At least, not officially.

"Oh." Mom sits back in her seat and waves a hand. "Well, relationships can be complicated, sweetie. Sometimes one starts before the previous relationship has quite finished fizzling."

"Are you seriously telling me you support cheating right now?" I raise an eyebrow. "That's pretty bad even for you, Mom."

Her eyebrows draw together in a tight line. "What does that mean? *Even for me?*"

"I..." *Damn.* I'd been trying to behave, to be nice to her for once. But the words just slipped out. "I just mean, with your track record."

"What *track record* is that, exactly?" Her voice rises.

"You know." I gesture vaguely in her general direction. "You tend to... well... go through guys a lot. And it seems like you normally only like what they can do for you, rather than who the guys themselves are."

"I can't help it if I'm attracted to successful men. Would you rather I pick a bum off the street to date, is that it? Or just say yes to anyone who offers?"

"That's not what I mean, Mom. But, come on. You seriously think I should date a guy who's *married*?"

She crosses her arms on the table and leans toward me. "All I'm saying, Cassidy, is that you can be a bit naive about these things. There's married and then there's *married*, you know?"

I shake my head. I really don't know.

Mom just shrugs, though, and tugs her napkin off her lap to daub at the corners of her mouth before she folds it on her plate. "Sweetie, I'll admit, I came here with an ulterior motive."

My stomach knots all over again. Great. Here it comes. Time for a speech about hard times, about how she's trying but just can't find the right situation... And then she'll ask for money. Like always.

Mom meets my gaze, her own expression deadly serious. "I'm worried about you," she says.

Whatever I expected, it wasn't that. I blink, thrown. "About *me*?"

"What I said earlier—I *am* proud of you. I'm proud of your career, of your hard work. But, well... it's not like you've been at this for very long. You're seeing some success now, but what about your future? Have you started saving any money for retirement yet? And have you considered looking into purchasing property instead of renting? If you're going to continue on through life the way you've been going, these are things you'll need to think about."

"What do you mean *the way I've been going*?" I protest.

"You know." She gestures at me, as if that should make it obvious. "If you plan to live your whole adult life a single woman."

My jaw drops. "So, just because I said I didn't want to date a married guy, you assume I'm going to, what, grow old alone and die a spinster?"

"Sweetie, at a certain point, you just need to be realistic about where you're headed."

"I'm going to date!" I exclaim. "Once I find the right guy."

"Well, if you wait too long, Mr. Right will already be married and the father of several children by then. You need to start looking *now*, sweetie, while your prospects are still good. I could set you up if you like; a few of my friends have some very cute sons living nearby. Well, within an hour's drive, but that's not *too* far, for a serious relationship."

"What is this obsession with getting me a boyfriend?" I protest.

"I'm not getting any younger," Mom replies. "And neither are you. Then there's the matter of children to consider, and, well... I just don't want you to wind up like me." She sighs then, wistfully. "I've just never been able to make it work long-term. I put so much time and effort into the men I date, and none of them stick around to help me or offer me a sense of security. I'm all alone, with no one to turn to for support now."

"You know that's not true," I say, even as my instincts kick in yet again.

She smiles at me. A little too broadly. "Oh, I know I can always count on you in a real emergency. I just don't want to have to ask you for more money, again. You've got enough on your plate without worrying about your poor old mother."

Old. As if she's some wizened crone, instead of a pretty lively 49. "Mom..."

"I just want better for you. I want you to find a man who will stay by you, through thick and thin. Someone who can take care of you, the way you deserve." Her voice drops an octave, and she looks away. "Lord knows I never got what I deserved."

I frown. "Is there something you need help with?" I can't help it. I hate seeing her like this. Dejected and down on herself. Even if part of me knows it's all an act.

But her gaze jumps to mine almost at once. "Of course not, Cassidy. What did I just say? I can't ask you to help me again." She laughs, a little too high pitched. "A mother can't *always* rely on her daughter for support. Even her very successful daughter, whose business is taking off so well..."

And there it is. The real reason she came here today, I'm sure of it. "Spit it out, Mom," I say, my voice dropping into a sarcastic register.

Her jaw drops. So does mine, honestly. I've never actually called her out before. Part of me feels guilty—what if I'm wrong, what if I'm misreading this situation?

But another part of me, a bigger part, thinks that my therapist would be proud if she could see me right now.

"What on earth do you mean?" my mother replies, flustered, her cheeks turning pink.

"How much do you want this time?" I fire back. "It's obvious why you asked me here. You need money again. So, how much are you in debt for?"

"Well. I... you... what." Her face, if possible, reddens even more. "Of all the ungrateful—"

"Mom, please. We've done this dance enough times for me to recognize the opening lines." I lift an eyebrow at her.

"Can't a mother want to spend quality time with the daughter she hasn't seen in months? A daughter who, I might add, is *terrible* at returning my calls. I can't miss you without having some ulterior motive?"

"That's what I thought." I spread my hands on the table. "But then you start bringing up money, again, and, well, this is too familiar for my liking."

"It's not my fault you're making more than me right now,

Cassidy." My mother's lips purse. "If I were in your shoes, with all that business investment money and my face all over the television, I would help *you* out."

I snort into my wine glass. "Would you, though? Because in the past, it's always been, 'you need to learn how to support yourself, Cassidy,' and 'I spent all my money raising you when you were a child, Cassidy.'"

"I *did*. You have no idea how expensive it is to raise a child, especially as a single mother." Mom scowls.

I just laugh. "Good thing you had all those boyfriends to help us along the way, then." I raise my hand, and gesture for the waiter. "Tell you what, Mom." I lean forward, smiling, and take a slow, pointed glance around the nice restaurant. "I'll pick up the check for this. Least I can do, since you're right, we haven't spent any *quality time* together in so long. But after this? I'm done helping you out monetarily. It's time for you to learn how to support yourself," I tell her, mimicking a phrase she's used since I was fresh out of college, and one that's always set my nerves on edge.

To judge by her souring expression, Mom doesn't like hearing her own words any more than I ever did.

"I love you," I add. "But I'm done being used. By you or by anyone else in my life."

The waiter drops the check, and I slip enough cash to cover the bill, along with a healthy tip, inside. Then I rise and gather up my coat, smiling. My mother continues to glare at me, muttering words under her breath. But for once, her words just roll right off my back. Because I know, without a doubt, I'm doing the right thing.

I'm setting boundaries. Creating a new pattern for myself. Just like I promised myself in therapy.

For once, I leave a meal with my mother actually smiling.

25

CASSIDY

The smile lasts until I make it home from our lunch. It falters, however, the second I pull into the parking lot outside my apartment complex, and I register the shape leaning against my front door frame. Even with his back turned, even though I only glimpse him briefly as I'm stepping out of my car, I know at once who it is. I'd recognize him anywhere. Not just his face, but his height, his lanky body, his way of standing and his posture and even his gait when he walks, shoulders thrown back and chin high with confidence.

He doesn't look so confident today, though. He's slumped against my door, and his hair is a tousled mess. Even before he turns to face me, I already guess his face will look gaunt, drawn with stress.

Lark.

It's only been a few days since I last saw him, yet it had already started to feel like a lifetime. As if my time with him were a dream, pleasant and all-consuming when I was in the middle of it, but painful as hell to wake up from. It made the real world stark and gray by contrast.

As I start up my steps toward him, a welcome counter-emotion floods in. Anger. He has no right to keep showing up like this. We made it clear the last time we spoke. Things were over between us. I thought he was finally respecting me, giving me the space I needed to get over him. But now...

The anger, however, is short-lived. It falters the moment he hears my foot on the steps behind him and turns to look at me.

God. I knew he looked dejected, but seeing his face... His eyes are red, lined in deep purple bruises, like he hasn't slept since I saw him last. He's still handsome, of course. Handsome enough that I want to shove him for it, back up against the door he's leaning against, and then grab his lapels and pull his face down to—*No.* I stop myself right there.

Handsome or not, sad or not, he still lied to me.

"What are you doing here?" I ask. My voice comes out harder than I intended, but I don't apologize for it. He's over the line right now.

"I'm sorry," he says, immediately. "I know I shouldn't be here. But I tried calling. I didn't get an answer."

I think about my phone, shut off for the duration of my lunch with Mom. I didn't turn it back on afterward. I was still buzzing from finally standing up to her. That, and I didn't want to see if she called me afterward, to leave me guilt-tripping voicemails about how I'd just acted.

"You can't just show up like this," I say, shaking my head. "We talked about this. About how I need space now."

"I know, but." He takes a step toward me, hands outstretched, and for a moment, I catch his scent, the familiar, heady musk that always makes me want to close my eyes and sink into his arms. To let myself go, to feel safe in his embrace—even if that safety's a lie. "I can't stop thinking about you, Cassidy," he says.

My stomach tightens. *That makes two of us.*

"I just... I know I messed up. I should have told you everything, from the beginning, and let you decide whether you wanted to get mixed up in my damn drama. I realize that now. Keeping this from you was wrong. Which is why..." His throat bobs with a tight swallow. But he holds my gaze. The whole time he's saying this, those green eyes of his never leave mine. "I want to tell you everything now. The full truth."

I bite my lower lip. Glance away, toward my front door, hesitant. This is pretty much the opposite of what I promised to do in therapy—to set boundaries and hold them firm. I told him we were over. To let him in now would be...

As if reading my mind, Lark lifts both hands, palms extended toward me. They hover in the air between us. Even his hands seem nervous, trembling a little, the nails bitten down to the quick. "No strings attached," he says. "You don't have to take me back or give me another chance or anything. But even if we never see each other again, you deserve to know the truth."

That, at least, I can agree with. I press my lips together, still internally debating. But searching his gaze, curiosity rises inside me, overwhelming the part of me that says it would be safer to tell him to leave. "Fine," I say, eventually, and his shoulders sag, relief blooming across his face. I hold up one finger, though, to stop it. "But you're right. No strings are attached. This doesn't mean I'm giving you a second chance or anything. You do owe me the truth, though."

He nods, all too eager to agree. "Whatever you want, Cassidy."

What I want is to go back in time, I think bitterly. What I want is for him to have opened up to me from the start. But since I don't have a time machine, I step around him to unlock my front door.

Inside, I take a seat on the couch. I don't offer him a drink, or even water. He doesn't seem to expect it, at least. And unlike last time, when he sat so close to me that I could hardly breathe, he takes a seat at the far end of the couch, perched on the edge of it, his whole body still tense, like he's ready to jump up and leave any moment that I order him to.

"First of all, I just want to apologize, again," he starts. "It... I know my life is a mess. And I don't blame you for not wanting to get involved in it. Honestly, that's the smart reaction." He squeezes his eyes shut for a breath.

I hold mine. I'm not giving him anything. No sympathy. Because he's right. It is smarter of me to stay detached.

When he opens his eyes again, they find mine. Lock on. "Sheryl and I *are* getting a divorce. We filed for it a year ago. Well, actually, I filed for it. She contested... it's been a whole back and forth."

I press my lips together, waiting. I knew this much, at least.

"But... well. Due to some bad decisions on my part, the contract of our company, Anderson Investments, it's..." He clears his throat. "We set the whole thing up in Sheryl's name when we first founded it. She talked me into it; I wanted to make us 50/50 partners, but she convinced me it would be simpler to keep it all under her. She was the finance person, after all; I was the one who worked with our clients face-to-face, and more on the marketing and business-building side. I don't..." He bites his lower lip. "My only explanation is that I trusted her, back then. I mean, she was my wife. I thought..." He shakes his head.

My chest tightens. I take another breath, unaware I'd been holding mine.

"Anyway, long story short, she has complete control over what happens to the company. And we've spent years working on it, I... I poured everything I had into this business. When things between us soured, when I started feeling unfulfilled and unhappy in my marriage, I dealt with it by working harder, putting all my hopes and dreams into the company. It's my baby, really." He laughs, a little bit bitterly. "And now, well... That's her leverage, I guess." He blows out a long sigh. "Sheryl knows how deeply I'm invested. She couldn't care less about how the business does, whether it thrives or not—as long as she can skim her usual cut off the top of the profits and sustain her lifestyle."

I wince, and glance across the room, at where my stacks of makeup supplies sit. I know how that feels. To pour your heart and soul into a company. One that may or may not succeed. I spent so much time struggling on my own company, after all. And it was only with Lark's help that I was able to break out.

"I like helping people," Lark says, as if reading my mind. "I like being that angel investor who can swoop in and make dreams come true for people like you. Smart people with great business ideas who just need that first leg up to make it in the world." He smiles, for the first time since he stepped inside.

Too late, I realize I'm smiling too. My mouth answering his without my permission. With effort, I wipe the smile off my face and stare at him, waiting for him to go on.

"Anyway, at first, Sheryl said she'd change the company structure. She'd let me buy out her shares and take over the company as the sole investor. She'd have enough money to start something new, and I'd have what I want: the whole company to myself, to run how I want. But her stipulation was a year of marriage counseling first. She told me, she *promised* that if I went to counseling for one year, she'd change the business structure, even if I still wanted a divorce afterward. I guess she thought we could work things out, I don't know... But counseling only made it clearer than ever that we don't belong together. She spends every session beating me up, and even when the counselor asks her to confront her own issues, to look at places where she may have contributed to our relationship breaking down, she refuses. Just twists everything back on me."

I sigh, thinking about my mother earlier. And about Norman. I know how that feels. "So that's why you're still married," I murmur. "To try to save your business." The realization washes over me slowly. All this time, I thought I was the one being taken advantage of—that I was just some side fling for Lark, while he worked on his marriage in therapy. When really, he's been trapped. The same way I was once trapped with Norman. Being manipulated, made to feel like I could never get free, never survive on my own...

He leans toward me, eyes bright. "Yes. That's the *only* reason, Cassidy. But I realized something, when you and I split up, and when Sheryl started in on me..." He bites his lower lip for a moment, keeping his gaze fixed on mine. "She's never going to give it up. She's just going to keep moving the goal posts, to keep me attached to her by any means necessary."

"That's terrible," I murmur. I know what it feels like to be controlled like that. To have someone dangle your wants and needs over your head to make you dance on their strings.

"Yes." And then, to my confusion, Lark smiles. I blink, thrown, but he shuffles closer to me across the couch, his expression more intense than ever. I couldn't look away if I wanted to. "But then *you* came along, Cassidy, and you made me see..." His eyes jump back and forth, searching mine. "You made me realize, I don't need the company. I don't need the security I built. I created that once; I can do it again. The way you did with your makeup—you didn't have the funding you needed, you didn't have the security when you set out to do what you loved, but you made it anyway. So can I."

I swallow hard. "What... what do you mean?"

He catches my hands, and I let him. His hands are warm and solid around mine, and when he folds them against his chest, my heart jumps at the same rhythm as his. Erratic and jagged. "I'm going to tell Sheryl to keep the company," he says. "You inspired me."

My lips part. "But..." I can't ask him to walk away from his dream. Not for me. It would make me just as bad as Sheryl. "But you can't do that for me," I start. "No one should give up on what they love for someone else, even someone they care about—"

He shakes his head, cutting me off. "It's not *for* you, Cassidy. Although you're the one who made me realize I could do it." He squeezes my hands again, tight enough to hurt, but I don't mind. I realize I'm squeezing his back, too. "It's for me. I can't let Sheryl control me anymore. I need to be free of her, so if the only way to do that now is to walk away from Anderson Investments, then that's what I'll do."

"Are you sure?" I breathe. I don't know when he moved, but he's closer to me than ever now. Sitting just inches apart on this couch—the couch he bought me, what feels like a lifetime ago now. His leg brushes mine, and it sends sparks through my whole body. I remember the last time we sat like this, side by side. The way he pulled me onto his lap, spilling makeup everywhere.

Heat surges through me. I want him to do it again. Even though I promised myself I wouldn't.

But I didn't know the full story then. I didn't realize he was in the same position I used to be in myself. And I know what it feels like—the fear, the uncertainty, the *how can I do this on my own* dread.

Lark reaches up to tuck a long strand of my hair behind my ear. His fingertips brush the curve of my ear, making me shiver. "I've never been surer of anything in my life," he murmurs. And suddenly, I don't think he just means his marriage or his business.

My eyes jump back and forth between his. It feels like the air between us is filled with sparks, heavy and electric. I tilt toward him, slowly, all too aware that he's doing the same thing, mirroring me.

"Lark, I..."

He stops at the sound of my voice. Takes a deep breath, like he's trying to remember his place. His promise to leave me alone. He starts to pull away, but I reach up to catch his shirt in one fist, stopping him. He freezes in place, his eyes going wide.

"Thank you," I say. "For telling me."

His throat bobs with a tight swallow. "Like I said," he replies softly, "you deserved the truth."

I nod slowly. "And so do you." I lean back a little, releasing his shirt. Just far enough to get some air. Although neither of us shift apart on the couch, our legs still pressed together, as I look away. "I know how you feel," I tell him, my gaze focused on my living room table now. "I've... been in a similar situation, before. It's hard to get free from that, when you've been manipulated by someone you loved and trusted."

Lark's hand comes to rest on my thigh, searing heat through my jeans. "I'm sorry, Cassidy. I didn't know that you..."

"My ex." I shut my eyes, which are suddenly stinging. Then I laugh, a little bitterly. "Well. Not just him. My mother did it too, before him." When I open my eyes again, I feel hot all over. Fierce, suddenly. "But you're right. I made it on my own. And you can, too, Lark. We can get free together."

I spin around to face him, and before I can think about what I'm doing, I swing one leg over his. Shift until I'm kneeling over his lap, my hands cradling his face between them, gazing down into those familiar, deep green eyes.

"You can do this," I tell him, and I'm talking to him, but also to myself. To the past me who fought her way free from Norman. To the me who just told my mother off earlier today. And then, I lean down and press my lips to his.

26

LARK

For a moment, all I can see, hear, smell, *think about* is Cassidy. Her soft lips against mine, which part in a sigh as I pull her further down over me, my hands tight around her soft curves, sliding up her back to trace her shoulders, then back down, down, until they land of their own accord on her firm ass.

She moans a little, a soft breathy sound, the one that always drives me over the edge when we're in bed together. I love hearing her make those noises, knowing I'm the reason she can't help herself. That I'm making her forget about everything but the heat between us.

I part her lips with my tongue, and she inhales sharply. I pull her body flush to mine, her soft curves practically melting into my pecs, my abs. I kiss her harder, claim that perfect, pert little mouth of hers, and revel in the feel of her wriggling against me. She arcs her hips, presses them down over mine, and now it's my turn to groan, faintly, in the back of my throat, because *fuck*. She's wearing jeans, but even through them, the feel of her hipbones hitting mine, her mound pressing down right over my rock hard shaft, drives me wild.

All I want to do is flip her over right here and tear off every layer of clothing she's wearing.

But I hold myself back. Take my time. Because another part of me, a stronger part, wants to savor this. I finally have Cassidy where I want her; where I've been dreaming about having her for weeks. Hell, ever since the first night I touched her, if I'm being honest. She's a drug, and I don't give a damn what I have to do to get more of her, I will.

She draws back from our kiss, just far enough to gasp for breath. I take advantage and trail my lips along her jaw, down the side of her neck. She lets out another of her faint little sounds, almost a mewl this time, and I grin against her pulse point, tracing my tongue over her soft, smooth skin for a moment. "You like that?" I whisper, knowing my breath will feel hot where I just licked her.

"Mm, can't you tell?" she replies, and of course I can, because she's already breathless, and with my arms around her and her body pressed to mine, I can feel every twitch and tremble in her limbs, every inhale she takes and every shiver that passes through her.

I bend to nip at her neck, gently, right where my lips had been a moment ago. There's that shiver again, more violent this time, her arms tightening their grip around my neck. "I had some idea you might, yes," I reply, grinning, and she laughs.

"Damn it, Lark."

When I look up again, she's gazing at me with new emotion in her big brown eyes. "What is it?" I reach up to tuck a stray strand of hair, newly fallen across her face, behind her ear. She shivers again. But whereas before, she'd normally pull away from me now, put up a wall between us, now... She stays.

"I thought the right thing to do would be to stay away from you," she finally admits, her voice low with feeling. "I thought I needed to learn how to... to be on my own, and to walk away from messy situations. But now..."

I raise an eyebrow. "You're elbow-deep in my mess, is that what you're saying?"

She laughs again. "That's not exactly how I'd phrase it." She leans in to kiss my cheek. I can feel the graze of those soft lips against the 5'o-clock shadow that's on my cheeks. Then she shifts. Kisses my lips, feather-light. It's too quick for me to catch her and deepen it. She's there and then gone, sitting back to look into my eyes again, and I want to have this conversation, I do, but *God, fuck* she's still sitting with those hips against mine and her thighs draped around mine, and another part of me just wants to reach down and push those stupid jeans of hers off.

Her cheeks turn a delicate shade of pink, as if she guesses what I'm thinking. But she doesn't move, either. "I just mean... I'm sorry."

I blink, taken aback. "What for? You didn't do anything wrong."

"Well. Maybe." She shakes her head. Worries at her lower lip, in a way that makes me jealous. *I* want to be the one biting her lip right now, damn it. "I could've heard you out sooner, though. Demanded the full story."

"You did," I point out. "I wasn't ready to tell it yet."

"Yeah, but..." She sighs. "I just, this could have been easier if we'd both opened up to one another fully from the start."

"True." I tilt my head. Slide one hand up her back to brace against her spine, right between her shoulder blades. I can feel the steady pulse of her heartbeat against my finger-tips, like a drum. Steadying me. Fortifying us both. "But we're doing that now," I say. "We might have gone through some difficult things, but... it's so worth it. To have you here now, to be totally open with each other."

Her smile widens. "I'm glad I let you inside," she says.

I let out a faint laugh of my own. "Me too." I can't imagine how I must have looked standing on her doorstep. Pathetic, probably. Or like a man in love.

Because...

Fuck. I think I am. In love with this woman, truly.

Then I lose that train of thought, because she kisses me again, and this time, I can't hold myself back any longer. I grip her waist tightly and flip her around, sitting up in the same motion, and following her back down, all while she squeals against my lips, until we've rolled over completely and she's pinned beneath me on the couch.

"Now," I say, grinning down at her. I kiss her again, slower. The heat pools between us when I break away once more. "Let's talk about getting rid of some of these damn clothes." I reach for the top button on her shirt.

She arches her chest up to meet my fingers, lets me undo the top button, and then the next. One glimpse of her lacy bra underneath, and I groan, bending to kiss her chest, my tongue tracing her collarbone. I give up on the buttons and pull, hard. Her shirt flies open, buttons flying around the room.

She lets out a startled yelp, and then a laugh. "Shit, Lark."

"I can't wait any longer," I tell her. "I've needed to get my hands on you for weeks now. You have no idea what it's been like..." I dip to trail my tongue along the arch of her cleav-age. Dip it between her breasts, even as I drop one hand beneath her back to undo the bra. "I've dreamt of you every night. I couldn't stop feeling your body beneath mine, hearing your gasps."

She twists beneath me, and her bra comes free. I throw it aside, already consumed by the sight of her, half-naked beneath me, her nipples hardening in the cool air of her living room. I bend to trace one with my tongue, lapping at the tip, with a smile as she shivers.

And then...

Her fucking phone starts to ring.

It's a jarring sound. Who uses ringtones anymore? And it's one of the loud, alarm-sounding ones too. "Shit." Cassidy twists again, this time away from me. I lean back, and she scrambles off the couch, diving for her purse where it's discarded by the front door. "I'm so sorry," she mumbles as she goes, shooting me an apologetic glance. "I forgot to turn it on silent, but this is..." Her face pales as she looks at the screen. "This is... only for emergencies. One second. I have to take this."

Before I can say another word—before I can offer to help with whatever's wrong—she darts into the bedroom and slams the door shut behind her. I sit on the couch, staring at her bra discarded beside it, and her shirt crumpled nearby. Then I let out a sigh and lean back against the couch. I did a good job choosing it at least, if I'm allowed to say that. It's comfortable.

But it's hard to get comfortable anywhere with the raging goddamn hardon in my pants. I stare down at it, straining against the zipper of my jeans, and I know I'm going to lose my damn mind if I can't take care of this soon. I wasn't lying when I told Cassidy she's all I could think about for weeks. All I've wanted since the minute I laid eyes on her.

I glance toward the bedroom door again. A low murmuring sound comes from behind it. Cassidy's individual words are impossible to make out from here, but she sounds agitated. There are a few more long pauses and yelped responses from her, and then finally, she reemerges from the bedroom once more...

With a new shirt on.

I stare at the crop top she's put on, confused. I get even more confused when she crosses to the door and starts to pull on boots.

"I'm so sorry," Cassidy's saying, her back to me. "Something's come up. It's a family emergency, I just... I have to go and handle this. I hope that's okay."

"Of course." My chest tightens. I rise from the couch and shoot a glare downward. My cock, of course, ignores me. "Do you need help?" I ask. "I can drive if you need me too; my car is right outside."

"No," she replies, quickly. Too quickly. Then she glances back over her shoulder at me, biting her lip guiltily. "I'm sorry. It's just, it's something I have to handle on my own. I'll explain later, I promise." Then she glances down, and I realize she's staring at my erection. Her cheeks flush. "Oh *God*, I'm so sorry to leave you hanging right now, Lark."

I laugh. "It's all right, Cassidy. If it's important, you should go."

But she doesn't. Not yet. She crosses the room first, and loops her arms around my neck. I bend to kiss her, a searing hot, slow kiss. I grab her hips for good measure, hoist her against me until my cock presses against her belly, just for a moment. Okay, so maybe I want a *little* revenge for her leaving me in this state.

When we part, she groans, and I know at least I'm not

the only one feeling deprived. "Can I make it up to you?" she asks. Then she actually bites her lower lip.

It's adorable. Almost adorable enough to make me forget about how she evaded my question, and how guilty she's looking now, as she glances from me to her purse, with her phone inside it, and back again. "Any idea how long your emergency will take?" I ask, forcing a smile to my face.

She shrugs. "Not sure. Maybe the night." She winces once more.

Before she can apologize again, I hold up a hand. "Then why don't we do tomorrow. It's supposed to be a nice day; maybe we can hit the beach or a rooftop pool."

Her smile brightens, and her shoulders sag a little with relief. "I'd love that. Thank you for understanding, Lark." She rises up on her toes one more time, and I kiss her again, slower.

"Of course," I tell her, gazing directly into those deep brown eyes as I do. But at the same time, a small, ugly part of me can't help itself. My traitor brain looks at this beautiful girl, the one I just opened myself up to, spilled all my secrets before... And I can't help wondering. What secrets is Cassidy hiding from me?

27

LARK

I have to admit, when I suggested a rooftop pool, I was not thinking ahead to what Cassidy would look like in a bikini. Now, I'm wondering if this was a bad idea—because there are at least a dozen other people lounging nearby around the poolside bar, and all I want to do is tear the sexy, bright red two-piece she's wearing off her luscious curves.

"You're staring," Cassidy points out, peering at me over the top of her sunglasses in a way that nearly sets me over the edge.

This woman drove me wild enough yesterday, leaving just as things had finally rekindled between us. Memories of her body sinking into mine on the couch kept me up half the night.

And now this.

"You're torturing me," I reply, and I'm rewarded with a flash of a smile, before she turns away to gaze out across the sunny rooftop and the crystalline water of the pool.

"This was *your* idea," she reminds me.

"And it was a terrible one," I amend. "Let's call it a day

and get back to my place. Or, hell, the car has tinted windows, it's downstairs..."

She laughs and fires a grin in my direction. "Now who's torturing who?" She arches an eyebrow. "Is this revenge for when I left you hanging yesterday?"

"Oh, absolutely. But I don't think this is quite enough payback." I slide around on my lounge chair so I'm positioned closer to her, my knees grazing her arm where it's draped over the side of her seat. She shivers, and I watch goosebumps rise along her arms, stifling a self-satisfied smile. "Do you know what I would do to you if we didn't have company up here?" I ask her, my voice pitched low.

Her gaze flits toward the bar again. It's midday, but we're at one of the hotels in town, so there are a handful of tourists enjoying their "it's 5'o-clock somewhere" cocktails. One of the guys, I've noticed, keeps glancing in Cassidy's direction, his eyes lingering for far too long on her long legs, crossed along the lounge chair and soaking up the noon sun.

It makes me want to stride over there and confront him. Or better yet, throw Cassidy over my shoulder and whisk her out of here, away from anyone else's leering gaze. Somewhere only *I* can leer at her like that.

I shake my head and focus on her again. She's looking at me with her brown eyes wide behind her oversized sunglasses.

"What would you do?" she asks, in a voice that trembles slightly, as if she's nervous to find out. Or excited. Maybe both.

I smirk, and bend closer, until my lips graze the shell of her ear. "First, I'd tear off that ridiculous top." My fingertip slides up her waist, along the edge of her curves, drawing a delicious shiver out of her, before I slip one fingertip beneath the edge of her bikini top. Not far enough to draw any attention.

Yet.

She sucks in a breath, her eyes going hooded and intent. "Like you tore off my shirt last night?"

"Exactly." I lift on eyebrow. "But this time, I'd make sure to take the bottoms, too." My gaze drips down the soft planes of her stomach to the bikini bottoms she's wearing. They're high-waisted, but they hike up far enough to reveal the arches of her hipbones beneath them. "Seeing you stripped bare in the sunlight up here would begin to make up for yesterday..."

She laughs, but it sounds breathier than it did before. I can tell I'm getting to her. I glance up at the bar—creeper man isn't looking at us anymore—and then I slide my hand fully beneath her bikini top.

She gasps and tenses. But when she looks over, she notices that no one is watching us, too. Still. "Lark," she hisses, a hint of admonishment in her tone.

"I'm afraid there's only so much resisting you can expect a man to do around a woman like you, Cassidy." As I speak, I trace her nipple with my thumb. Trail my nail over that delicate, sensitive skin lightly, and then press down with the pad of my thumb, swirling gently until I feel her nipple beginning to harden under my touch.

She bites her lower lip, hard. "So that's all you would do?" she whispers, after a pause. "Just strip me naked and leave me here?"

"Oh, no." My smile widens. "But I would take my time with you..." I dip my head to lick her earlobe, and savor the shiver I feel. "I would make sure to taste every inch of your glorious body." I kiss the sensitive spot just beneath her ear now, at the edge of her jaw. "Kiss, and..." I trail my tongue along her jawline. "Lick, and..." I pause at her mouth. She arches up toward me, expecting a kiss. I suck her lower lip into my mouth instead, and bite down gently. "Bite every inch of you," I murmur when I pull back.

She groans. Probably because I'm fully massaging her hard nipple now. And my free hand is wandering down her waist toward her hips. "Okay, I get it. This is definitely payback."

"Nonsense." I arch an eyebrow at her. "Payback would be if I left right now on some mysterious errand I refused to tell you about."

Her face flushes. "Lark, I—"

"It's okay." I shake my head. "Keep your secrets." Then I kiss her again, softer this time, to accentuate my point. "I don't mind, as long as I get to keep toying with you in between." I pinch her breast, not hard, just enough to make her gasp and jump a little. Then I withdraw my hand and slide back over to my chair, reclining on it casually.

When I peek over again, she's glaring at me. I can't help but laugh.

"You are the worst," she grumbles. But she's smiling, too.

"Still against my car option?" I reply, smirking right back.

Her cheeks flush. But she darts a glance toward the bathroom—the single stall, handicap style bathroom, and I can already read where her mind is going.

"Interesting idea, Ms. Marks," I murmur.

Her cheeks, if possible, turn even redder. "I didn't mean—"

"Oh, but I do." I grin. "Go on. Head to the bathroom. I'll be right behind you in a minute."

She hesitates, like she's still not sure. So I dip close to

her ear again. "Did I mention where my tongue would end up, after all of that kissing?"

That apparently decides it for her. She levers herself off her seat and fires a flustered look at the people by the bar again. Lord help this girl, she would *not* survive as a spy. Her embarrassment is written all over her face. But it only makes me want her more.

This girl who's willing to step out of her comfort zone for me. Who's as desperate to be with me again as I am to make her come screaming my name.

Well. Maybe not screaming, if we're trying to be stealthy.

Then again, I wouldn't mind if the pool-drinking crowd caught us. It would wipe the leer off the creeper's face, at any rate. Let everyone on this rooftop know that the most beautiful, vivacious, whip-smart woman around is here with *me*.

I force myself to lie still and count to ten after the bathroom door closes behind Cassidy. Somewhere around eight, I decide I can't wait anymore, and I push upright, wrapping a towel around my waist before I pad over to the stall. I knock once, twice, and wait.

Cassidy unlocks the door and opens it a crack, glaring. "I thought you were going to wait a couple minutes," she protests.

I ignore her and pry the handle from her hands, pushing the door inward to step inside. It's a tight space, but not cramped, plenty room for enough for two. And surprisingly clean for a poolside bathroom. I'm guessing that's because it's still early in the day, and the drinking crowd hasn't needed it quite yet.

"I couldn't wait any longer," I tell her, and to judge by the answering flash of heat in her gaze, she knows what I mean.

I wrap my hands around her waist and hoist her onto the edge of the sink easily. At the same time, I dip my head to kiss those full, luscious lips. Cassidy sighs against me, and the whole world narrows down to this. To the heat between our bodies, the sweet, almost floral scent of her consuming my senses.

I peel her bikini top off and drop it onto the floor. Both of her nipples are hard by now, and I dip my face down to suck on one, my hands toying with the other, as she leans back against the mirror over the sink, her lips parting.

"Fuck, Lark. I couldn't... I can't get you out of my head. Ever."

I draw back just far enough to read the sincerity in her eyes. The force of emotion behind her words. "Neither can I," I tell her, suddenly serious. "Even when I thought you wanted nothing to do with me, I couldn't stop thinking about you. You drive me fucking wild, Cassidy Marks." I hook one thumb under her bikini bottoms.

She arches up against me, giving me enough room to tug them off. While I'm doing that, she gets one of her hands under the hem of my boxers and starts to work pushing them down my tanned thighs. "I know the feeling," she replies. Her throat works tightly with a swallow.

She has to unhook her legs from around my thighs in order for me to finish peeling her bottoms off. When I do, they land on the ground with a wet sound, even though neither of us has been in the pool yet.

I smirk at her. "Clearly," I say.

Her cheeks are still that sun-kissed, flushed pink. It would be adorable if it wasn't so fucking sexy. I bend to kiss her again, stepping back between her thighs, and she hooks her ankles behind my lower back.

My swim trunks hit the ground, next, and I don't need to look down to know that my cock is already rock hard. I can feel the blood rushing to it, every muscle in my body tightening with the need to fuck this woman. To relieve myself of the ache I've been feeling since yesterday—no, since I met her.

If I believed in magic, I'd be pretty sure Cassidy is a sorceress, the way she has me obsessing. I've never needed a woman this much; so much I couldn't get her out of my mind even when I wanted to.

I pin her back against the sink and kiss those sun-kissed lips of hers. When we draw back, I grin down at her. "Think you can stay quiet enough not to get us caught?" I ask.

Her eyes flare with heat. "If that's a challenge, I accept."

I take a step closer to her, until the shaft of my cock touches her bare stomach. She breathes in again, sharp, and I trail my fingertips up her inner thighs, tracing her soft skin until I reach the spot where her hips meet her thighs. I trace those ridges, dancing around her mound, not quite touching her yet.

She squirms, just a little.

"What about now?" I reply, my smile widening. At the same time, I part her slit with two fingers and delve a third into the soft folds of her pussy, tracing her slit, not quite entering her yet.

She bites her lower lip. "It's a good start," she murmurs.

I laugh, and dip to kiss her jawline. Her neck. All the while, my fingertip strokes back and forth along her, collecting the juices pooled there. "You're so wet for me, Cassidy."

Another shiver. But she reaches up between us, and folds both hands around the hard length of my shaft. "I'm not the only one excited."

"Mmm..." I chuckle against her throat, trailing my tongue along the edge. "You have no idea." I press my finger into her entrance. Savor the feeling of that wet, warm pussy tightening around my fingertip.

She inhales sharply. Twists against her perch on the sink, while I slide another finger inside her.

Then I curl them, gently dragging my fingertips down her walls.

A low moan catches in the back of her throat, and I grin. "There we go."

She meets my gaze, stubborn. "I'm... fine."

"Really?" I lift one eyebrow. Then I add a third finger. She gasps, and I start to stroke in and out of her, gently, my fingers moving with slick ease. On my next thrust in, I graze the edge of her clit with my thumb, and she cries out faintly.

Not quite loud enough to get us caught. Yet. But I'm getting there.

She must read my self-satisfaction on my face, because she twists against me, her pussy pressing up closer into my palm as her hips rise off the sink a little. "Is that all you've got?" She arches an eyebrow, and I laugh again, enjoying the sight of her like this. Enthralled, and yet still stubbornly trying to resist me.

"No, it certainly isn't," I murmur. I slide my fingers out of her with a slick sound. Then I raise them to my lips, and suck them clean, one finger at a time, my gaze on hers the whole time. The taste of her nearly sends me wild. As heady and almost as sweet as I remember.

I position myself between her thighs again, and grip the base of my cock. "Let's see how you deal with my cock instead," I tell her, and her eyes flash with desire.

She spreads her legs, the pink folds of her pussy so damn inviting. "Fuck me, Lark," she breathes.

I don't need any more invitation than that. I press the tip of my cock against her entrance, and slowly, slow enough to drive us both wild, I push myself inside her. One inch at a time, maddeningly slow.

Another moan escapes her throat, longer and lower this time.

Finally, I push fully inside her. I wrap my hands around her hipbones for purchase, and she keeps those soft, lush thighs of hers wrapped around my waist, her ankles hooked behind me.

I pull out and thrust into her again, as her head falls back, her hair cascading over her bare shoulder. "Fuck," she whispers.

"God, you have the most perfect fucking pussy," I murmur, thrusting into her again. Again. Her muscles tighten around my shaft, the hot, wet heat enveloping me, going straight to my head.

"It's yours," Cassidy whispers, which sends a pulse of white hot heat straight to my cock. "I'm yours."

I slide my arms up to cradle her waist, slowing to a gentle thrust now. Drawing out and pushing back inside her over and over. "And I'm yours, Cassidy Marks. For good."

I can feel her body relax in my arms, even as she angles her hips up toward me. Surrendering. Letting me take her the way I want to.

I keep the motion slow for as long as I can stand. But there's only so long I can resist this woman. In the end, I tighten my grip on her and fuck her faster, harder, savoring every breathy gasp until the pressure builds up in her, too much for her to contain.

She lets out a sharp cry as she comes, and I keep my gaze focused on her, drinking in her wild abandon.

I finish moments later, crushing her body tight against

mine as I do. We're both breathing hard, slicked with sweat by the time we part, and when our lips collide, I want to keep her right here forever. With me, in our little bubble away from the world.

By the time we slip back out onto the pool deck, there's a line for the bathroom. A middle-aged woman glares at us, and a younger guy whoops when we exit. Cassidy's face heats up bright red. I ignore them all, though. Because I have eyes only for her.

We cross back over the pool deck to our chairs. But the moment we sit down, Cassidy checks her phone, and her face pales.

"What's wrong?" I ask.

She hesitates, worrying her lower lip in a way I'm coming to be familiar with. Her nervous expression.

"You can tell me," I reassure her.

She lets out a soft sigh, and slumps back against her chair. "I... It's kind of awkward. It's about business."

"All the more reason to talk to me," I say, imitating her to lounge on my own seat. "We're business partners, after all. You're one of our biggest investments. Your problems are mine, too."

She glances at her phone again for a long, quiet moment. Then she squares her shoulders, as if deciding. "Speaking of investments. I need another one."

I blink at her for a long moment, not following. "But, I've been watching the budgets. You haven't spent nearly what we gave you yet."

"I know, it's... It's some old stuff. Debts that I didn't realize I'd need to pay off already. I'm sorry, I know it's last minute and weird of me to ask right now—"

I sit upright. "Wait a minute. How much more money are we talking?"

"I-I don't know. A few thousand? Maybe more?"

"What are these debts? Why didn't I hear anything about this in our initial pitch meeting?" I stare at her.

She turns her face away, unable to meet my gaze. "I was embarrassed. I thought I could get out of this hole on my own; but the money that's come in so far hasn't been able to cover it."

"Hang on." I glance from her to the bathroom and back. "Did you... wait until we'd just had sex to ask me for money?" I can't help it. Memories claw at me.

That was always Sheryl's favorite tactic. Any time I didn't agree with a financial decision she made, she'd ply me with sex. Wait until I was half-asleep afterward and then ambush me with the least sexy pillow talk imaginable.

I don't want to believe Cassidy would do the same, but...

Beside me, she sits bolt upright in her chair and whips around to face me, her jaw dropping. "Is *that* what you think of me?"

"Well, did you?" I raise an eyebrow. "We've been in contact about finances for weeks. Why not ask me about this sooner?"

"I can't believe you think I'd try to get *money* from you in exchange for sex." Cassidy shoves to her feet now. "Do you think I'm some kind of gold-digger?"

"I didn't..." I grit my teeth and shut my eyes. "Cassidy, wait. I'm sorry I leapt to a conclusion. But this is all really strange, you have to admit that."

But she's already shaking her head. "I thought I could trust you. I thought we could be honest with each other. But I guess we can't." With that, she grabs her purse and storms toward the exit from the rooftop.

I leap up to follow her, but she's moving too fast. Already halfway across the roof before I even find my shoes.

Watching her walk into the women's changing room, without a backward glance, I give up. I sink back onto the edge of my chair and rest my forehead in my hands.

Is she just using me? Or did I just shatter the tentative peace between us for nothing?

28

CASSIDY

This is just like Norman. How could I have thought things would be any different? I stare at my reflection in the mirror of the changing room. Tears streak down my cheeks, and my eyes are red and puffy from crying. I don't know how long I've been standing in here, afraid that if I go back out, Lark will have followed me, or be looking for me by the elevators.

I wrap my arms around my waist, shivering. *How could he think I'm a gold digger?*

But then... I did ask him for money. Out of the blue. Without explaining myself. *Fuck.* I lean my forehead against the mirror for support, shivering.

On my phone are a string of texts from my mother. *Need to go to the hospital,* read the first one. A long series below it. *I don't have health insurance. I don't know what I'll do if this operation costs more than I can afford. Did you know hospital overnight stays alone can costs tens of thousands of dollars??*

I exhale and watch my breath fog the mirror. I don't *want* to doubt my mother's words. This would be an insane thing to make up, even for her. But I can't shake my own doubts. I can't stop remembering all the other times she's lied to me to get money for other stuff. Frivolous spending, or gambling in Vegas, or weekends away with boy toys drinking herself blind.

If she's in the hospital, I want to be there for her. Help her. I don't want her to worry about money. But what if she's lying again? And what if I just ruined everything I could have had with Lark by believing her?

He still shouldn't have accused me like that.

I shouldn't be allocating company funds to a private issue, either. I chew on my lower lip. Shit. Am I the one in the wrong here?

And then I ran away from him when he asked me to talk about it. *Again.* No wonder he thinks I'm just using him. If I can't even open up enough to have a real conversation about something serious...

I think about Norman again. I tried to open up to him in the beginning, but he just always shut me down. I learned to keep my feelings to myself. I learned that anything upsetting, anything he might not like, should be hidden, not discussed.

Am I going to let Norman steal Lark from me to? Am I going to let the past define my future?

I wipe at my cheeks, then bend to splash some water on my face. He's probably long gone already. But on the off chance that he's not...

I grab a towel from the hooks near the lockers and sprint outside, not even caring that I'm barefoot. I race to the pool deck first, but the chairs where I left Lark have been taken over by a couple skinny brunettes, sunbathing. And Lark's shoes and towel are gone.

I scan the bar. No sign of him. I hurry to the men's bathroom, tap on the door. Open it a crack. "Lark?" I call.

A pause. "No Lark here," some guy calls back. "But I can entertain you if you're looking."

"Gross," I mutter and let the door slam again.

Downstairs. He could still be in the lobby. I press the elevator button so many times I'm surprised it doesn't break. Then I wait for the elevator to ding open and sprint into it, leaving puddles on the clean floor. I hit the ground floor, hold my breath the whole way down. The elevator stops twice to let other people on, all of whom eye me sideways, but I ignore them, and just pull my towel tighter.

At the ground floor, I sprint out of the doors before anyone else can move.

"Hey!" someone shouts. A hotel bellman, maybe. "You need to wear shoes down here!"

I ignore him and sprint toward the exit. Lark used the valet parking. Maybe it will take them a while to fetch his car. Maybe...

Outside, a wave of heat hits me. My feet sting on the pavement, both hot and filled with pebbles. I scan the row of people waiting for their valet cars. No Lark. But then...

There. His car, just about to turn out of the driveway into the hotel. He's waiting for a row of cars in the street to move first.

I run as fast as I can, not caring about how much my feet hurt. I reach the back window first and pound on it, hard enough to make Lark startle in the driver's seat and turn around. When he spots me his eyes go wide.

I hold my breath, shivering despite the heat, the towel clutched tight around me. If he drives away now, I don't know how I'll ever explain this. How I can possibly apologize.

But after a long, agonizing pause, he puts the car in park, and opens his door.

29

LARK

"What the hell are you doing?" I ask as I climb out of the car. Somewhere behind me, I hear wolf whistles, and some guy shouting something obscene and honking as he passes.

In her towel, Cassidy does look nearly naked. Still, I flip the traffic off in general, and take a step toward her.

"Are you insane?" I murmur. "Did you run through the hotel like this?"

Her cheeks flush red. "I needed to catch you before you left." She ducks her head. "I wanted to apologize."

I watch her closely now. "For what, exactly?"

She raises her chin to meet my gaze once more. There's such deep, pained sorrow in her gaze, it tugs at my chest in spite of myself. "You were right," she says, and the words hit me like a punch to the gut. "I was trying to use you."

Whatever I expected her to say, it wasn't that. I take a step back toward my open driver's side door, but she stops me, reaching out to grab my arm.

"I just..." Tears start to slide down her cheeks. "It's my mom. She's in the hospital; I need money to pay her bills.

But it's so complicated, she's lied to me before, and I don't know if she's doing it again now, and I should never have asked you for money like that, but I didn't know where else I could get it or who else to turn to and—" She breaks off, hiccupping, and before I can think better of it, I step forward and wrap both arms around her tightly.

"Hey, hey." I squeeze, hard. "Cassidy." Warmth floods through me. Not just at having her in my arms again. But at finally understanding where all of this is coming from. "Look at me, Cass."

She sniffles, but she tilts her chin back to obey, meeting my eyes again.

"I just wanted to help her," Cassidy whispers. "I'm so sorry."

The pain in her voice breaks my heart. Even worse is the realization of how I reacted when Cassidy asked me for help. I assumed she'd be just like Sheryl. That she'd want to wring as much money from me as she could for no other reason than to have it herself.

"I'm sorry too," I murmur. "I should never have jumped to conclusions. My ex..." I grit my teeth. "She left me more fucked up than I realized, I think. I shouldn't have judged you by her actions."

A car honk sounds, longer than the rest. I raise my middle finger again, but it's coming from behind us this time. I turn to realize there are a line of cars waiting to get out of the hotel parking lot. All while I'm parked at the exit, holding a nearly naked woman in my arms.

"Come on," I tell her, taking her hand and tugging her toward the car. "Get in. Let's go back home and we can talk about this."

"Really?" Cassidy gazes up at me, wiping at a fresh tear. "You mean, you don't hate me?"

I laugh. "Cassidy. I could *never* hate you."

Her lower lip quivers. But then, slowly, she nods. "Okay," she murmurs. "Let's go home."

30

LARK

Somehow, Cassidy looks even more attractive when she's dressed in my clothes. She's curled up at the far end of my couch in a pair of my sweatpants and a baggy T-shirt. It should not make me want her, and yet, every time she glances in my direction, catching my gaze over the rim of the mug of steaming tea I made her, all I want to do is pull her off this couch and strip her back down.

But that's not what we're doing here. Yet.

"So," I say, my voice quiet and yet still somehow startling in the silence.

"So," she agrees. Her hands tighten around her tea mug. "Um. Thanks for the clothes." She gestures at herself with a shrug. "And... the... tea."

I stare.

She swallows hard. "I'm not getting out of this, am I?"

"We said we were going to talk, Cassidy," I point out. "I think it's well past time that we do."

She nods, her gaze dropping back to the tea cradled in her lap once more. She takes a few breaths, and I think she's going to go quiet on me again, but after a moment, she clears her throat. "My mom has spent her whole life living off of other people. At first it was the guys she dated. And I never wanted—I *swore* to myself, I would never be like that. I wanted to make my own way in life. But after I graduated, in between breakups, she started coming to me for money too. And... I mean, it's my *mom*. What can you do? She's family. So I supported her when she needed it. I pretended to believe all the lies she told me, about various debts that weren't her fault, or overdue loans that didn't exist... I guess I humored her." Cassidy worries at her lower lip.

It makes me want to lean over and kiss her until she stops biting her own skin. But I resist. Because I need to hear this.

"And, look, I know I should be talking to my therapist about all this—and don't worry, I have been. But you deserve to hear it too. My mom just... she made me never want to rely on anyone else. Or even ask anyone else for help. Because I look at her, and I just... never want to be that desperate. And then, when I was dating my ex..."

Heat flares in my gut. I restrain myself, because this is Cassidy's past. It shouldn't affect our present. It *doesn't*.

"He was so controlling." Cassidy's voice drops lower. "He made more money than I did, so he wanted control over my whole bank account, everything I did... He said it was to help me, to ensure I didn't wind up like my mother. But for him, it was just another way to control me, to ensure I could never leave him, even if I wanted to. Which I didn't for way too long, because I had no idea how to recognize emotional abuse. I didn't understand what a healthy relationship should look like." Cassidy squeezes her eyes shut. "Until you."

I breathe out slowly. "Cassidy..."

"No, I know. That's pathetic. And I know it wasn't

healthy how I asked you for money earlier, but my mom really scared me this time. I don't know if she's lying again, if this whole hospital thing is another scam, but on the off chance that it's not—"

I reach over to catch her hand, which silences her almost immediately. "If your mother needs help, then we'll help her," I say. And it makes my chest ache, the way relief and shock flare in her eyes at the same time.

It makes me realize that Cassidy has never been treated like this before. With simple, basic respect. I want to go back in time and throttle her ex. Fight everyone who ever made her believe that she's less than worthy of all the love in the world.

"I don't want to make you feel like I'm using you, or—"

"Cassidy." I squeeze her hand. "You don't. Look, I was projecting some of my shit with Sheryl onto you. And I get that you have a complicated past. I understand—so do I, obviously. But it's understandable to want to help your mother through a difficult time. And it's equally under-standable to be cautious about that, if you're not sure about your mother's motivations yet. That's all normal."

Her breath hitches. "It's definitely not normal," she starts.

She breaks off when I lean in to kiss her, hard. "Fuck normal, then," I whisper. "I don't care about normal. I care about you. About what's best for you, Cassidy Marks."

Her pupils dilate as her gaze meets mine. "I care about you, too, Lark. So much." Another bite at her lower lip, again. "Which is why, I can't ask you to give up your busi-ness for me. You love this. You started this company; you're the reason it's gotten to where it is today. I can't imagine you would have the customers you do without your support. Sheryl's just grasping at straws trying to hang on to her share. It's obvious to anyone on my end of the investments that she doesn't really care. Not the way you do."

My heart leaps at that. Not just at her saying that I'm the heart of this company—which, to be honest, I already knew. But she said she cares about me. The same way I care about her. "If losing the company is the only way I can really be with you, Cassidy, then I don't care. I can start another company. Build up from scratch again. I don't care. But I can't build another you."

Her cheeks flush bright red. Still, she shakes her head. "I can't let you do that. Not for me." She leans in to brush her lips against my cheek, so lightly that it sets me on fire. I want to grab her, toss her down on this couch, and...

I reign myself in with difficulty. The harder point is disguising the way my cock is stiffening against the seam of my jeans, impossible to control. "I want to," I tell her, firmly.

She shakes her head. "I don't care if some piece of paper says you're married, Lark. I know your heart belongs to me. Just like mine belongs to you. That's what really matters. Not the law. So if you want to keep your business, just stay married to Sheryl, I don't mind. Really."

Your heart belongs to me. Her words thunder through my body, like an electric current. I've never felt this awake and alive. Or this sure of what I needed to do.

I reach out to wrap my hands around her shoulders, drawing her back in close to me. "Cassidy... I don't care about the business. What really matters is what's right here in front of me. *You.*"

"What are you saying?" Her eyes widen ever so slightly. Between that and her flushed cheeks, her trembling lower lip, it's almost impossible to keep my hands off of her.

But I manage, for now. Because there's something left I

need to confess. One last thing I need to tell her. "I love you, Cassidy."

Her breath catches audibly. I know the feeling. I'm holding my breath too, waiting for her reply. Wishing that it will be what I want. Bracing myself, in case it's not. After what feels like the longest pause in the world, though, Cassidy leans forward, until her forehead is resting against mine. "I love you, Lark," she breathes.

And there we have it.

I bend forward to cover her mouth with mine, catching her in a slow, deep kiss. The rest of the world fades out.

31

CASSIDY

One moment Lark's lips are on mine, covering mine. The next thing I know, one of his arms is around my waist and the other is sliding behind my knees. He scoops me up off the couch like I weigh nothing at all—a move that, I have to admit, is seriously hot. I wrap both arms around his neck and kiss my way down his jawline to the spot where his neck meets just below his ear. I bite him there, lightly, and my reward is a low growl in the back of his throat.

"I've waited far too long to have you back in my bed," he says, and the words send a thrum of desire through me, pulsing out from my stomach all the way to the tips of my toes where they curl in Lark's borrowed socks.

But the words don't turn me on nearly as much as what he said before this.

"I love you," I whisper again, testing. Repeating. It's the first time I've ever said those words to a man and truly meant it. It unlocks something new inside me, a depth of feeling I never knew existed before.

"I love you, Cassidy," he replies, and I was wrong before.

This is more emotion than I've ever felt at once, a torrent rushing through my whole body.

Because he feels the same way I do.

When we reach the bed, I expect him to toss me onto it. Instead, he lowers me gently, like I'm precious. Breakable. When my back hits the mattress he kisses me again, slow and forceful. Then he moves, his mouth trailing kisses down my jawline to my neck, my shoulder. He undoes my shirt with steady hands and peels it off, pausing only long enough for me to shift beneath him so he can unclasp my bra too.

He takes his time tonight. He kisses every inch of me, his lips moving over my shoulders, down my arms, until he sucks my fingers into his mouth one by one, teasing and smirking at me the whole time.

"I haven't been able to get you out of my mind since the first night we met," Lark murmurs, still kissing his way across my body, my curves now, my belly, the slope between my breasts. He cups one breast in his palm, soft yet firm, and his fingertips brush over my nipple lightly. Even that is enough to make me shiver, from the crown of my head all the way through to my toes.

"Neither have I," I admit in a low whisper, and he leans back, eyes hooded with a mixture of desire and feeling.

"Show me what you do when you're thinking about me, Cassidy," he murmurs, and a warm flush creeps up my throat to my cheeks.

But there's a low thrum of command in his voice, something I can't ignore. And the way he's watching me, as if he can't get enough, just turns me on more. I reach up to trace my hands down my curves, feeling the heat of all the places where his hands were on me a moment ago.

While I do, he sits back, those intense eyes fixed on mine.

"You mean like this?" I ask, smiling just a little, as my hands slide over the flat plane of my stomach.

He grins. "A good start."

My hands reach waistband of my borrowed sweatpants. I hesitate for a moment. I've never undressed myself in front of a guy. Normally I let them handle that, since they're eager to get their hands all over me anyway. But Lark is different. Patient. And the wait makes the payoff all the hotter.

I slowly inch the sweatpants down my thighs. His gaze traces over my body, and I swear my skin heats up beneath his gaze almost as much as I flushed from his touch, his tongue.

"God, you're so beautiful," he breathes once I kick the pants aside, and I'm lying before him naked from the waist down.

My fingers trace the familiar lines of my mound. Down to my pussy, where I part the lips slowly, wetting the tip of my finger. Tracing it back and forth, I flush. I'm already so fucking wet. Lark always has that effect on me.

He leans closer, so his breath dusts my cheeks, before he kisses my jawline. The edge of my mouth. "I want to watch," he says, voice low and heated. It sends a thrill through me, all the way to the tips of my toes.

"Spread your legs," he murmurs.

My breath hitches, but I do it. I spread my legs wide, and his gaze drops to watch as I push my finger inside myself, curling it, stroking slowly and steadily. There's a wet sound when I draw it out to brush my clit, and he grins.

"Tell me, Cassidy. Do you always get this wet when you think about me?"

"Always," I breathe, and he laughs softly, before he leans

in to kiss my lips. "My turn." Then, before I can react, he slides down my body, and gently nudges my hand aside. I let it fall to the comforter, and he presses his tongue where my fingertip was a moment earlier, sliding it between my pussy lips.

He trails his tongue along my slit, slow and steady. Savoring. Then, with a low animal growl, he presses it inside me, and I arch up off the bed with a gasp. He feels so good. Hot and wet, his tongue strong inside me.

He curls it, lapping at my pussy as if he could swallow me entirely. It feels incredible. But it's not what I need right now. When he pulls back for a breath, I grab his hair in both fists and pull him toward me. "I want you inside me," I gasp, not able to wait any longer. Too on fire for that.

He grins and pushes his jeans off, kicking them aside.

When he draws his cock out of his boxers, I can tell I have the same effect on him that he has on me. He's already rock hard, standing at attention, a small bead of precum gathered at his tip.

I lean down to lick it off, and his eyes flare, white hot.

He does push me back onto the bed now, leaning over me, bending to kiss my mouth. He still tastes like me, and him, all mingled together in a flavor that only makes me hotter. More desperate. "You want me to fuck you now, Cassidy?" he breathes into the crook of my neck, his breath nearly as hot as his cock feels against my inner thigh.

"Fuck yes," I gasp.

He laughs softly. "So impatient."

"I need you, Lark." The words escape before I can stop them.

He leans back to meet my gaze. In his, I see my own emotion reflected. The sheer depth of it takes my breath away. "Cassidy..." When he guides himself to my entrance, the tip of his cock poised there, it doesn't feel like the other times we've been together. I feel more open now, somehow. More naked than I've ever been, completely exposed.

And yet, I don't mind. In fact, I want to stay in this moment forever. Two hearts completely bared to one another.

He pushes inside me so, so slowly. I wrap my legs around his waist as he does, arch up against him so I can feel every inch of his lean, muscular body against my soft curves. "Lark," I moan as his cock pushes fully inside me, straining my walls, making me feel deliciously full.

"I love you," he murmurs, like someone who's testing the words, savoring the way they feel. He kisses me again, slower, heated. And he draws out, then thrusts back in, our mouths still pressed together.

I slide my tongue between his lips. Taste myself more fully on his tongue, as ours entwine. He laughs against my mouth as I reach down to grip his ass, hard, and he draws back just far enough to meet my gaze.

"Have I mentioned how fucking hot you are, Ms. Marks?" He kisses my jaw. My neck. "You're like a drug. I can't get enough."

The words add to the heat building in my belly. I wrap my free arm around his neck, hold on as he starts to move faster, thrusting harder. "I... never want... this to end," I manage to say, as it gets harder to speak, the faster my heart beats, the harder and faster he begins to thrust.

Lark meets my gaze, a knowing smile on his mouth. "It doesn't have to," he says. And I realize, as the orgasm starts to build deep within me... he's right.

We can have this for the rest of our lives, if we want.

32

CASSIDY

A distant pounding sound wakes me far too early. I groan and try to roll over, only to find my movement restricted. There's a strong, familiar arm wrapped around my waist, pinning me back against a lean body. I turn to peer over my shoulder at Lark. His eyes are still shut, his lids twitching faintly in a dream.

It must be a good dream. I can feel the hard press of his cock against my ass.

Grinning to myself, I wriggle against him, and savor the way he moans, low in the back of his throat. He doesn't wake though, not yet.

Last night floods through me in a pleasant rush. *I love you.* He meant it when he said it. So did I. And he's right, together we can figure all of this out. We can help my mom with whatever she needs, hospital bill-wise, and then I can put my foot down and explain to her that I'll only help for emergencies like this. Not for every tiny thing that crops up.

As for his ex, well... We'll figure that out too.

Lark shifts beside me, and an idea comes to mind. I'm

about to slip under the covers and execute it when I hear the pounding again. Louder this time.

What the hell *is* that?

With a groan, I disentangle myself from Lark—the man sleeps like the dead after sex, I swear—and pad across the bedroom.

There's a small door beside the elevator shaft. I stare at it in confusion, and it bangs again. I realize it's the back entrance to the apartment, in case of emergencies when the elevator's out of order.

And someone is knocking on it.

Strange.

I slip back into the bedroom and grab the first things I see. Lark's baggy tee draped over a chair. It hangs low enough to reach mid-thigh on me, so it at least covers the necessities.

Then I pad back out into the living room, rubbing sleep from my eyes. "One second," I call blearily. It takes me a moment to figure out how to undo the bolt lock on this mysterious side door. Then I wrench it open, and my jaw drops.

So does the person's on the other side.

Sheryl stares at me like an apparition. As if I'm all her nightmares come true. She glances from me to the apartment over my shoulder and then back to me, and the shirt I'm wearing. Lark's shirt. I can practically see the wheels clicking in her head.

"I can't believe this," she says, when she finds her voice.

"Sheryl, hi." My heart hammers in my throat. "Um, if you're looking for Lark, he's still asleep, but I can go grab him—"

"You fucking *homewrecker*," Sheryl yells, and I'm pretty sure I won't need to wake up Lark anymore. Hell, the neighbors can probably hear this, even through all the advanced soundproofing of Lark's penthouse. "I can't believe I *trusted* you, and all this time you've been fucking my husband behind my back."

She looks more furious than I've ever seen her, her entire face twisted in anger.

I take a step backward, startled, and she uses it to her advantage, barging into the apartment.

"How *dare* you." She's still fuming.

Finally, I find my voice. "He's not your husband anymore," I say.

"Tell that to our lawyers." Sheryl laughs, actually laughs. "So *this* is why he suddenly started talking about divorce again. We were fine, we were working this out, and then *you* came along and wrecked it all."

"Oh please." I cross my arms over my chest, all too aware that I'm braless right now. "Lark told me all about why you haven't signed the papers yet. You're basically blackmailing him with his own company."

"Till death do us part," Sheryl shouts. "That's what he and I promised each other. It's not *blackmail*, I'm just trying to save my marriage." Something in her voice cracks, and for a moment, I glimpse behind the angry façade. I see the sad, desperate woman behind it, and she looks way too familiar.

I reach for her arm. "Sheryl, listen. I went through a bad breakup too, and I hung on for way too long to something that wasn't working because I was afraid of being alone—"

She jerks away from me. "Don't you dare try to talk to me about *relationship advice,* you whore."

I reel backward as though struck. My whole face has gone beet red. "I'm sorry we didn't tell you, but—"

"Don't you dare call her that." Lark's voice breaks through the room, low and rough with sleep and fury combined. He's in nothing but boxers, yet he still manages to look more put together than Sheryl in her neatly pressed business attire. He crosses the room to my side and wraps one arm around my shoulders, protective. Bracing. "Your issue is with me, Sheryl, not Cassidy. Don't drag her into this mess."

"You're the one who invited a third party into our marriage," Sheryl snaps.

"Our marriage has been over for years," Lark replies coolly. "You know it. I've told you a million times. Cassidy's right, Sheryl. You need to accept this. Move on."

She laughs, high pitched and mean. "You already know my terms, Lark. If you want to call it quits, the company's mine. End of story. Otherwise, I'll see you at counseling tomorrow."

With that, she whirls on her heel and storms out of the apartment, back down the staircase. Only now does it hit me that she must have climbed all twenty flights up here just to do this. Yell at Lark in his own house.

He's realizing the same thing, glaring as he crosses over to shut the door behind her and bolt it. "I told the doorman not to let her up anymore. Guess she still has a key to the service door though." He sighs. "I'll talk to building management about switching it." Then he runs a hand through his hair, his expression sour. "I'm sorry you had to see that, Cass."

"Don't be." I walk toward him, opening my arms. He wraps his around me and buries his face in my neck. "Your problems are my problems now, Lark. We're in this together."

He laughs softly, face still pressed against my neck.

"What?" I ask.

He turns to meet my eyes, smiling. "It's just... nobody's

ever stood up for me like that before. Especially not to Sheryl. She even scares my own family."

I laugh, too. "After today I can see why." We both glance at the service door. Lark's expression sobers. "Hey." I nudge his side. "Don't worry. We'll figure something out. Some way to work around her. And if you have to keep going to counseling for a while to keep the business, I don't mind. It's a weird situation, but it's fixable. Everything is."

"With you on my team?" Lark leans down to kiss my temple. "I don't doubt it." Then he sighs and straightens, glancing toward the kitchen. "Right. Drama this early in the morning calls for a reward. I'm thinking waffles?"

I grin and let him tug me toward the kitchen. "Sounds good to me, chef." But worry still nags at me, even after Lark seems to brush Sheryl off. I watch him whisk eggs and sift flour, and then pour the batter inti the waffle maker, the most delicious smell emanating through the kitchen. All the while he hums along to the radio and tells me about his plans for the day. And watching him, a heavy weight sinks into my stomach.

Is he going to have to choose between his dream company and me? And if so... how can I possibly ask him to make that sacrifice?

33

LARK

For once in my life, I'm early to my counseling appointment. I wanted to get here before Sheryl, because I wanted to see the look on her face when she walked in and saw me on the couch, my back ramrod straight, my hands fists on my knees.

She's tried calling me half a dozen times all last night and today. Probably to find out whether I'd show today, or whether she should start calling our lawyers about drafting the contract that will fuck me over the hardest.

I'm making the right decision. It was easy, actually. After Cassidy and I really talked, after I found out how she feels about me... There's no other decision I can make, now.

The counselor opens the door to let herself and Sheryl in. As expected, Sheryl's jaw drops when she spots me inside the room already. I rise from the couch, offering the counselor my hand. "This is going to be our last session," I tell her, before anyone else has a chance to speak.

"All right," the counselor replies, her eyes jumping between me and my ex-wife carefully. She takes her seat across from us. Sheryl sits down too, on the couch where I'd been a moment before, way too close for comfort.

I perch on the arm of it instead, to avoid any contact. "This situation—this marriage," I amend, "is untenable for me. I've realized Sheryl is not going to change, and neither will I. We just aren't compatible, Sheryl." I look at her, now, and behind her fury, I notice genuine tears forming in her eyes.

"This will be better for both of us," I tell Sheryl. "We need to go our separate ways. You need to let me go."

"I've told you," Sheryl starts, and I raise a hand to stop her.

"I know your terms," I explain. I glance at the therapist. Back at my ex. "You can keep the company. If that's what you need to get back on your feet and to feel like you have closure, it's all yours."

Now her jaw drops for an entirely different reason. "But..."

"Do I think it's fair? No." I laugh under my breath. "But I don't care anymore, Sheryl. I built that company from scratch once, and I can do it again. So, you win."

She takes a shaky breath.

Across from us, the counselor claps her hands. "Well. This does seem like a breakthrough. Sheryl, how are you feeling?"

I resist the urge to groan.

"How am I *feeling*?" Sheryl clenches her fists. "This is insane. You're only doing this because that whore you've been cheating on me with suggested it. The Lark I knew would never—"

"The Lark you knew didn't exist," I interrupt. "You never knew me, Sheryl. You just projected what you wanted to see. And for the last time, don't you dare insult Cassidy."

Sheryl's smile turns ugly and bitter. "If you cared about that girl at all, you wouldn't do this. Do you really think her little startup is going to survive without my investment?"

"Cassidy has already surpassed our wildest expectations," I reply coolly. "And with my help on the business side, she'll continue to."

Sheryl barks out a laugh and leans back on the couch. "Oh, so *that's* your plan. You're going to live off of... what, the profits from her little *makeup* outfit for the rest of your lives? You can kiss that penthouse goodbye, Lark."

"I'll be happier in a tiny ramshackle flat with Cassidy for the rest of my life than I ever would've been in some mansion with you," I reply, my voice steady. Sheryl can't get to me anymore. Her words have no effect. Thanks to Cassidy, I'm finally free.

I reach into my bag and pull out a folder. Then I set it on the table between us, in full view of the counselor. "Divorce papers," I say. "I've already signed. They give you full control of the company. The only stipulation is that you release your shares of Cassidy's business to me." I've done the math. It's a drop in the bucket compared to our other investments. Don't get me wrong, Cassidy's star is on the rise, but some of our clients we've had for years, and their big-name businesses rake in millions.

Sheryl would have to be an idiot not to take this deal. And my ex might be many things, but she's not stupid.

Her eyes narrow. "What's the catch, Lark?"

"No catch." I spread my hands wide. Glance at the therapist as a witness. "This is what you wanted. So I'm offering it. That's all."

The counselor watches us both. "It does seem like this arrangement would cover the stipulations and concerns you've raised in here before," she says after a moment, looking at Sheryl.

"But..." Sheryl splutters. Then bites her lower lip, clearly fuming. "I'll have to have my lawyers look it over," she says a moment later, more calmly, once she has her frustration under control.

"That sounds sensible," the counselor speaks up. "Lark, would you agree to that?"

"Of course." I push off the couch. "But I'll need an answer by the end of the week, Sheryl. Otherwise, I'm taking this to court. And I don't think either of us want this to get any messier than it's already been."

With that, I stride out of the office, leaving the two of them to talk this over behind me. I have a feeling Sheryl's going to need the counselor's help far more than I will.

I'm not sure how I expected this to feel. Scary, or maybe gut-wrenching. I loved that business. It was the one thing we built during our marriage that I really cared for and was proud of.

But I've been mourning the possibility of losing it for a year already. To my surprise, as I walk out of the building, all I feel is relief. As if the papers I left up there in the office were a thousand pound weight around my neck, one I didn't even realize I was lugging around. Not until I finally threw it off.

Feeling better than I have in years, I reach for my phone and dial Cassidy.

34

CASSIDY

My phone buzzes. I glance at it, grateful for the interruption. When I asked my mother if I should come and meet her at the hospital, or if she needed a ride to the doctors, or what all the operation entailed, I expected details. Instead, she invited me out to lunch in town again, over near me. Meaning she's well enough to drive, at least.

It should be a relief. But it only makes me worry more. Worry that this time, my mother has crossed a bigger line than I'll be able to forgive.

Before I can reach for the phone, my mother's voice interrupts.

"I can't believe you're going to answer a call while we're at the lunch table," she says, her tone snippish.

Which is rich, considering why she's here. I lean back in my chair and cross my arms. "So, did the hospital release you early?" I ask.

"What are you—" My mother cuts off abruptly, her whole face flushing as she remembers what she said to me. "I mean. Yes, of course. Obviously, or I wouldn't be here."

I scoff. "Unbelievable." We're in a small restaurant this

time—no more overly expensive places since I know full well that I'll be footing the bill. But this is still one of my favorite spots, an unpretentious, cute little restaurant with an owner who always sneaks me extra portions at dessert.

Across from me, Mom is pushing her food around her plate, her nose wrinkled, like she can't possibly bring herself to eat this swill. It's the same thing I order here every week, and it's perfectly good. It's just not the bougie, overpriced meals she's used to indulging in, I guess, when she's got a sugar daddy on the go.

Now, I'm assuming she doesn't. Judging by how far she's going to con her own daughter.

"What do you mean, unbelievable?" Mom eyes me with that expression of perfect innocence that I've fallen for one too many times with her.

"I'm used to you making stuff up, but a *hospital visit*? You had me scared shitless. Are you really that desperate for cash?"

Her face flushes a bright, angry red. "I didn't *make it up*, Cassidy. There's a very important procedure I need done, and it's expensive."

I stare, unmoved, my jaw set hard. The old, usual guilt I feel whenever I face down my mother is nowhere to be felt today. I'm standing my ground, for once. "You scared the hell out of me, you know. I thought you were having a heart attack or something. Now you're acting like you don't even remember telling me there was an issue. At least try to keep your own lies straight, for God's sake."

"I never said it was an *emergency*," Mom replies, lips pursed. "It's hardly my fault you leapt to that conclusion— you're always so dramatic."

"Like that wasn't exactly what you wanted me to do," I

burst out. "Panic and give you all the money I've worked so hard to earn without asking any questions."

"Daughters should want to help their mothers," she coos, her voice lowering now. "If I'm going to find a new husband, I can't go back out on the dating market looking my age," she says.

My stomach churns as it hits me. "Oh, my God. You want money for *plastic surgery*?"

"Just a chin tuck and an eye lift," she protests. "And a little work on my breasts—those are your fault, I might add, they were perky as anything before I had you. It's the least you can do. Your company has money coming in aplenty, and I know that boy you've been seeing is rich. Surely he'll grant you one little favor."

That does it. I ball my fists under the table and sit ramrod straight in the chair. "I am *not* begging Lark for money."

Mom's expression shifts into a scowl. "Honey, haven't I taught you better than this by now? You can't be with a man who you can't depend on. If he's not willing to help you and your family, how can you trust that he's got your best interests at heart?"

"That's not love, Mom. That's not a healthy relationship, and deep down, you know it."

"So you're saying I'm unhealthy." My mother sniffs and straightens in her own chair, too.

I groan. "Kind of! You keep living off other people, expecting them to do everything for you. First it was men, now your own daughter?"

"And *you* never ask for help, or take what you're owed from anyone," my mother retorts. "This is history repeating itself all over again. First you date that Norman, perfectly fine young man with plenty of money, but you let him run roughshod all over you. You never asked him for anything, and so he never felt a responsibility toward you; he never took *care* of you. But you have a chance to do it right this time."

"Mom, Norman was an abusive piece of shit," I reply, before I can stop myself. The moment the words leave my mouth, my mother's eyes fly wide open. So do mine, honestly.

I've never said that out loud before.

It feels good. It feels freeing. And moreover, it's the truth.

"I never told you because I didn't want you to worry about me. But it got really bad by the end." I stare into her eyes, and watch as the anger melts from her expression, replaced by worry. I force myself to keep talking. "I'm okay now, though. Really. I've been seeing a therapist I really like, and she's helped me reframe a lot of the unhealthy ways I look at the world. The bad patterns I seek out in relationships. Because, well... kids tend to mirror what they see growing up. And I had a lot to mirror with you."

Then I slide my hand across the table, palm up. My mother stares as if it's a snake that might bite her. But, after a moment, to my utter shock, she takes it.

Mom opens her mouth to say something, but I cut her off. "You don't need plastic surgery, Mom. You're as beautiful now as you've always been, if you just let yourself see it. And you don't need other people's money to live, either. You are strong enough to make it on your own. And so am I."

I squeeze her hand tightly.

There's a long pause, during which my heart rises into my throat. But then, finally, she squeezes back.

I set a card on the table. "This is my therapist's number. She's got appointments free, if you want to go. I think it could be good for you." Then I fold my arms on the table and lift a hand, waving for the check. "But Mom... this meal is the last payment you're ever going to be able to guilt out of me. Understood? I'm on a new path now, I'm healing, and I'm learning how to set boundaries and take care of myself. I hope you can do that too. But I'm not going to enable you anymore."

"Cassidy..." Her voice sounds tight. Scratchy. Like she's holding back tears.

So am I. But I won't let her sorrow move me. Maybe someday, if she goes to therapy too and works through her own issues, my mother and I can work on rebuilding our fractured relationship. I hope so. But until then, I meant what I just said. I won't let her use me anymore.

My mother's gaze drifts to the card and back to my face. "I was trying to teach you how to survive in a world that's cruel to women. A world where we need to take every advantage we can get our hands on."

"I understand that. But it's not healthy. And it's not the way we should be surviving."

The waiter finally approaches with the bill. I slip payment into it, leaving a hefty tip like I always do. Mom would disapprove, but then, I'm breaking free of her restraints now. I'm learning to live my life the way I want to. Not the way I was taught.

I take my coat and rise, scooping my phone off the table. There's a message from Lark. Probably telling me how the meeting with the counselor went. He told me this morning, before he left, what he planned to do. I only hope that it works out, somehow. Maybe there will be a miracle and Sheryl will realize she's being a complete asshole. Do an about-face and let Lark keep his share of the company he built.

Somehow, I doubt it. But hey, a girl can hope.

"Goodbye, Mom." I lean down to kiss her cheek. She doesn't kiss me back.

But she does, I notice, pocket the therapist's card, just before I turn to leave. It's a small action. A tiny step. I only hope that for once, my mother will choose to walk the hard road in the right direction.

35

CASSIDY

"Can we afford this?" I ask, laughing, as Lark leads me by the hand out onto the rooftop of one of the newest restaurants in town. There's a panoramic view of the whole city glittering at our feet, and hardly anyone else up here.

In fact, now that I'm looking around more closely... There's *no one* else here, except for a team of waiters, all eying us like we're a king and queen who just waltzed in. My suspicions rise even further.

"Lark..." I say.

He nudges me. "Relax, Cassidy. I called in a favor with an old friend, that's all."

It's been a few months since our big showdown with both Sheryl and my mother. It took some more arguing on Lark's part, but Sheryl did finally sign the divorce papers. He's out a company, and we're both starting over. We spent a last long fun weekend in his gorgeous penthouse, and then we moved his stuff into my place for the time being.

He turned a healthy profit selling the penthouse, but he didn't want to buy another place just yet. "This is my investment money now," he told me the night the sale went through. "And I already know the business I want to pour it into."

My cheeks flushed when I realized what he meant. "Lark, I've told you a million times, the last thing I want is your money—"

"I know," he cut me off. "And I'm not giving it to you, Cass. I'm investing in your future. You're the business genius now." He'd ruffled my hair, and my chest swelled with a mixture of pride and pleasure.

With that money, we've been able to continue to keep up with the increased demand my little startup makeup company was already seeing. More and more orders have been flooding in every day, and we even expanded to a workshop in town. I hired a couple employees—really fun, upbeat people who are eager to make their mark on this industry too.

Judging by the way our profits are soaring, we'll be back on our feet again soon enough. I've already caught Lark eying sweet little townhouses in the neighborhood near where we set up shop. I can tell he wants to keep it a surprise, though, so I've pretended not to notice him browsing real estate listings late at night, while I'm getting ready for bed.

It's funny. I thought success would be what makes me so happy. But it's not. It's knowing that I can do this on my own. I can make my own way in the world and survive just fine. I don't need to rely on anybody else.

But it is nice to have a teammate in this fight. I reach over to catch Lark's hand and squeeze lightly. "You didn't have to do all this," I tell him, grinning. I know he still has friends in high places around the city, from when he used to be one of their best customers.

But I'm not sure why he decided to call in a favor

tonight, of all nights. When we were just going out for what I thought would be a quiet dinner, the two of us, to unwind after a long week of working at the shop.

He grins and leans in to kiss me, his lips lingering for a moment, stealing my breath the way they always do. Then he crosses to the table and draws out my chair, whipping the napkin like he's a professional. "Oh, but I did," he replies. "Don't you know what tonight is?"

I laugh, and take my seat, letting him fold the napkin over my lap before he takes his own chair. "It's... a Friday?" I guess.

He shakes his head, tsking. "Am I the only sentimental one?" he says. Then he lifts a hand, and one of the waiters approaches with a bottle of champagne whose label I recognize. It's expensive. But Lark winks, and I know he's got it under control. If my man knows anything, it's when to budget... and when to splurge on spoiling me.

He reaches over the tablecloth and catches my hand, his thumb tracing now-familiar circles over the back of my palm. "Today marks exactly six months since we first met. Did you realize that?"

I lift my eyebrows. "You were keeping track since the *day* we met?"

"Of course, Cassidy." He leans forward, and I mirror him, our gazes locked over the candlelit table. "That first night we met, I knew we had something special. I just didn't realize yet *how* special."

"You're so sappy," I tease, but I'm grinning like an idiot too.

"You love it," he retorts, and I nod, cheeks flush.

"Definitely." Then I'm the one to lean in and kiss him, slow, savoring this moment.

When we break apart, he's smiling like a kid on

Christmas morning. "But that's not all we're celebrating," he says. "I got some... news, today."

"Oh?" Both my eyebrows lift. He raises my hand, still grasped in his, to his lips and kisses the back of it.

"The divorce has been finalized."

My jaw drops, and my heart soars. "Already?"

"We were able to fast-track it, since we both agreed to the terms. My lawyer told me I was being an idiot; he thinks I should have taken Sheryl to court, that I could've gotten more out of her. But I just wanted it done and over with, you know? There are more important things to me than money, these days."

I squeeze his hand tightly, knowing exactly what he means. "I'm sorry," I say. "About the company."

He shakes his head. "Don't be. I got the better deal out of this." He winks at me. "I got you."

A happy rush trickles through me. Lark is free of his past now. We both are.

As for me, my mother did start seeing a therapist, finally. It took a few months before she caved in. But she seems happier now. We even managed to eat an entire meal together without fighting—and at the end of it, she footed the bill, without so much as a single snarky comment. It's slow progress. But we're getting there. And more importantly, I've learned how to hold fast to my boundaries. How to show myself as much respect as the other people in my life.

"Look at us," I murmur, smiling. "We've come so far in just half a year."

"We really have." Lark tilts his head to look out over the side of the rooftop. "I'm proud of us."

"Me, too," I whisper. Then I follow his gaze, going quiet. We take a moment to gaze out over the city at our feet, like we're the only ones in our own private world right now. I feel... comfortable. It's an unfamiliar feeling. I didn't realize before, how much of my life I spent yearning and struggling. Not until I finally found a comfortable balance with Lark.

Now, I understand balance. I understand how to work hard, but also how to give myself a break, and balance that hard work out with self-care, days off, time with the ones I love.

"Thank you, Cassidy," Lark murmurs, startling me out of my reverie.

I turn back to him, smiling. "For what? I'm the one who forgot our six month anniversary," I joke. "I should be the one thanking you."

But he shakes his head, his expression suddenly much more serious than it has been since we walked out here. "I mean it. Before I met you... I was willing to just settle for mediocre. I thought it was better to be secure financially but miserable in every other way. I thought..." He pauses, a rush of emotion coming over his expression. "I thought I'd never really know what love was. Not the kind other people talk about, where you'd do anything for your partner, where you put their happiness before your own and vice versa. But then I met you."

I couldn't break my gaze away from Lark's now if I wanted to. Those deep, handsome green eyes pull me in like gravity.

"You made me see that I could be happy again—really happy, not just getting by." A smile touches the corners of his lips, ever so slightly. "And you taught me that I can start over if I really need to. That I've still got what it takes to build something from the ground up."

Now it's my turn to hesitate, if only because my throat has gone tight. "Lark..."

"I'm so glad I met you, Cassidy." He doesn't blink. Doesn't break my gaze. He extends his other hand too, the one I'm not already holding, and I reach out to let him take both of my hands now. His palms feel warm and familiar against mine. Reassuringly strong. I always feel safe when he holds me like this. "I can't imagine the rest of my life without you," Lark says softly.

I let out a little laugh, now, my chest clenched with emotion. "You sound like you're proposing," I say, if only to break the tension, because if I try to say anything else, I'll start to cry, I just know it.

Lark lifts one eyebrow, and nods at my wine glass.

Frowning, I look down at it. I hadn't even noticed the waiter pouring the champagne earlier. I'd been so focused on Lark, on being here with him.

At the bottom of my glass, something's glittering. Bubbles drift around it, obscuring it. But... it looks circular, maybe. With a different shape on one end.

When I look up again, Lark is kneeling next to my chair. On one knee. Holding only my left hand, now.

My stomach leaps up into my throat. I let out a strangled sound, half cry, half laugh, and my free hand flutters up to cover my mouth. "What..." I manage to say, but Lark shushes me, a little half-smile he can't quite suppress on his face.

"Cassidy Marks. You've been the best thing to happen to me in my entire life. For all the reasons I just listed, and about a million more. You are the reason I believe in love again. And, if you'll have me, I want to be yours. I want you to be mine. For the rest of our lives." He lifts one eyebrow, the sly, knowing expression that I first fell in love with crossing his features. "Will you marry me?"

A huge, stupid smile breaks out across my face. "Of course." The words have barely left my mouth before he tugs me to my feet. We meet standing, and our mouths collide with force, my hands burying themselves in his hair before I even realize I've moved. He winds his arms around my waist, pulling me up and against him, bending to deepen the kiss.

Dimly, on the edge of my perception, I'm aware of someone playing music.

When we finally break apart, both of us breathless, a quartet has started playing on the far side of the rooftop. The waiters are all clapping and cheering, and a blush heats my face.

While I'm still standing there trying to surreptitiously pinch my arm and make sure this is real, Lark reaches for my flute and uses a fork to fish the ring out. "I wondered how long it was going to take you to notice this on your own," he teases, and I let out a shaky, breathless laugh.

The ring... oh, my God. The ring is beautiful. A single princess cut diamond that glitters in the low lights of the rooftop. He slips it onto my finger, and it fits perfectly, the rock so big that...

"Tell me you didn't dip into savings," I tell him, one eyebrow lifted.

He laughs and shakes his head, bending to kiss me again. "It's my grandmother's ring," he says. "Family heirloom. I never used it before, because..." he stops and bites his lower lip. "Well. Maybe a part of me always knew my first marriage wasn't right. But I want you to have this. I want you to be a part of our family now."

My heart races. I rest my hand on his chest, and the diamond glitters brightly. Then I lean my head on his shoulder, and Lark draws me into a slow dance, swaying across the rooftop. "You're perfect, you know that?" I murmur, head still pressed to his chest.

He laughs. "Far from it." Then he brushes a fingertip beneath my chin and tilts my head back so I meet his gaze. "But *we* are perfect, Cassidy," he whispers. "Together."

* * *

Thank you so much for reading my books. If you liked this one, or even if you didn't, it means the world to me if you let me know! Reviews are so important to authors. You can leave one right on Amazon where you bought/borrowed it from. Sending you major hugs and kisses!

-- Penny

xoxoxo